Port and Proposals

A tale of love, regret and second chances

Mark Brownlow

Lost Opinions e.U.

Port and Proposals
© 2020 Mark Brownlow
All rights reserved

ISBN: 978-3-903230-07-1 (print)
ISBN: 978-3-903230-06-4 (ebook)

Author: Mark Brownlow
Cover design: Aimee Coveney of Bookollective
Editing: Sarah Pesce, Lopt & Cropt Editing Services
Formatting: Polgarus Studio

Publisher: Lost Opinions e.U.
Paschinggasse 8/28
1170 Vienna
Austria

For more Austenesque creations, see:

Web: lostopinions.com
Twitter: @markbrownlow
Facebook: facebook.com/lostopinions/

Books by Mark Brownlow

Mr Bennet's Memoirs
Cake and Courtship
Port and Proposals

Charlotte Collins Mysteries
The Lovesick Maid
The Darcy Ring

Short stories
A Third Proposal

For Renate

A Departure

"Accept the invitation, Papa. It will do you good to leave Longbourn for a few days." Lizzy left her hand in mine, even as she settled into the carriage. "What objection can you have to such a trip? I thought John a good friend, one whose company you enjoy?"

"I am very fond of him, as you well know, but I cannot abandon your mother and sisters." We both looked back to where my wife waved a handkerchief without enthusiasm. Kitty and Lydia had already returned inside, but Mary—silent and unmoving—still stood on the steps below the front door.

Lizzy's fingers tightened around mine. "Why not take them all with you?"

"I said I was fond of John."

"Be serious, Papa."

"I always am, Lizzy. Now, remember me to your uncle and aunt in London, will you? Send my love to Jane, too. And give my particular regards to Mr Collins when you finally reach Hunsford. Say we hope he might visit us again. Though only tell him this if you are certain he will not do so." I withdrew my hand from my daughter's grip and closed the carriage door. "Be off now. Last night's rain will make the journey difficult enough. You know how the March roads can be, especially around Hatfield." My nod to the driver saw the horses take up their burden, drawing creaks of protest from wood, leather, and metal.

Lizzy leaned out of the carriage. "You will not explain your refusal? Why will you not visit the Bartons, Papa?"

"Write often," I shouted, as the vehicle moved out into the drive. "I may even be persuaded to write back."

My daughter's head remained visible through a hedge reluctant to throw off winter's grasp, though the rattle of the wheels and sharp clop of hooves hid any reply she might have made. I turned to see Mary walk back inside, but her mother waited for me beneath the old clematis that struggled its way around the entrance to our house.

"To think she might have travelled to Kent as Mr Collins's bride." My wife pressed her handkerchief against her cheek.

"Be of good heart, my dear. Perhaps Mrs Collins will arrange for Lizzy to meet a gentleman of wealth and distinction during her stay. After all, a rector's wife cannot help but make connections among local society."

Mrs Bennet bristled at my words, her tears seemingly forgotten in the face of such crass ignorance. "No gentleman of means would be seen in Hunsford, husband. There is little of note there beyond a blacksmith and an inn. No officers. Not even a draper. Lizzy will find no suitor in *that* village."

"An inn, no draper, and a marked absence of officers? The more I learn of Hunsford, the more it endears itself to me."

"Oh, Mr Bennet!"

I proffered my arm. "Shall we go in?"

~ ~ ~

It was Pope who wrote "hope springs eternal in the human breast," a concept only a single man could ever express with such conviction. Our diminutive poet drifted close to the truth, though, with his choice of words; it was spring that always filled *my* breast with something like hope. She had already cast a shimmer of green over the trees, and grubs and beetles would soon wake to her whispered promise of more temperate days. I found it hard to remain cynical in the optimism of the season, despite my many years of dedicated practice.

Nets and jars already called to me from the dark shelves that filled the study, though I chose to ignore their cries. The words of Mrs Barton, spoken a few months earlier in London, had shackled my enthusiasm for collecting butterflies.

They are wonderful creatures. So delicate. It is a shame some gentlemen seek to pin them down in boxes, don't you think?

My gaze drifted to a wall adorned with row after row of glistening teal, rich crimson, and pale lemon, each pair of wings pierced by a shaft of cold metal.

"At least I may still enjoy the chase," I grumbled, plucking a long wooden stem from a stand and resting it on my desk. While examining the attached muslin for any holes that might offer its captives an escape, my attention fell on the paper trapped underneath; the decorative curls around the capital B of Bennet stood out even through the white material. Ever the artist, John Barton did not so much write an address as paint it. I put the net back in its place with a sigh and picked up my friend's letter once again.

Since my wedding, I find myself a figure of interest in Gloucestershire. We have received numerous visitors, few of them truly welcome; you know neither I nor Anne enjoy such society. Please say you will visit Rudford soon and offer us the relief of true companionship. We often speak of Longbourn and your family, particularly when Anne's mother visits. Both ladies grew much attached to Miss Elizabeth during your Bath stay. Indeed, Mrs Hayter talks of our time together in that city with uncommon regularity whenever she joins us.

My eyes returned to the last name mentioned, the sight of it drawing out memories of our trip to Bath in January—the murmur of teashop gossip and the chink of cups; my continuing wonder at how Abigail had changed so little; her fingertips reaching toward mine across the table, almost touching.

Almost.

Lizzy would not understand my fears, and I had no inclination to explain myself to her.

"Papa?"

I thrust the letter behind my back.

Mary stood in the doorway, her face expressionless. "Cook has baked macaroons, and I have saved you two. Will you join us?"

"Macaroons and the company of my daughters? Who could refuse such an offer?"

After Mary turned to leave, I tucked John's missive into a pocket. Then I followed my daughter like a small child trailing behind his disappointed governess.

"Now that Lizzy and Jane are both away, we shall have so much fun." Lydia's shrill voice carried to us as we crossed the hall. "No one will tell us what we may or may not do."

"Except your parents, of course." I gave my voice a little extra timbre on entering the drawing room, where the scent of almonds hinted at the promised biscuits.

"Do not be silly, Papa," said Lydia. "Mama understands that young ladies must enjoy themselves." She and Kitty lay sprawled across their chairs among the debris of abandoned embroidery.

"And what of your father?" I eased myself into an armchair. "Has he no say concerning the means of pursuing all this enjoyment?"

Lydia and Kitty exchanged looks before falling into laughter.

"Well," I said. "At least I am still valued enough to warrant a macaroon." A perusal of the room, however, revealed no more than a few crumbs on an empty plate.

"Oh." Kitty lifted a hand to her mouth. "Were they for you?"

"Let me pour you some tea, Papa." Mary rose from her seat, frowning at her sisters.

"Thank you, but no," I said. "In the face of such crushing disappointment, something stronger is called for. A glass of wine, perhaps? If you would be so kind as to fetch one?"

The armchair drew me deeper into its cushioned embrace; nothing disturbed the room's silence, except for a gentle snuffle from Mrs Bennet. She lay on a sofa with her arms folded across her front, her eyes closed, and her skirts spilling over the side to brush against the carpet. Lydia and Kitty continued to languish in their chairs as if posing for a study in ennui by Caravaggio.

Mary soon reappeared, armed with a glass of Weintraub's best red. I nodded my thanks as she placed the vessel on the table next to me, the dark wine seeming to glow on the oaken surface. Perhaps it recalled happier times in a wooden cask.

Returning to her seat, Mary took up a small book. She sat pillar-like, holding the leather-bound tome like a piece of porcelain and giving all her attention to its pages of supposed wisdom.

The book's title proved illegible from a distance, though I could make out a large capital M at the start. The word "morals" or "merits" likely followed, no doubt penned by an author with little of either—perhaps some self-righteous individual possessed of the certainty of the ignorant. Or a clergyman, though the two are often one and the same.

The room would have been as still as a painting, were it not for the stuttering rise and fall of Kitty's needle; my second-youngest daughter had summoned the energy to return to her frame and thread. Now and then, she would pause after an upward thrust and sigh like some sailor's wife awaiting the return of her loved one.

One sofa stood empty, two dips in its surface betraying the absence of Jane and Lizzy, the laughter and conversation of my eldest daughters no longer there to chase away dull spirits. On the other sofa, an arm slipped from Mrs Bennet's chest to hang at her side.

"And what work of art do you have there, Kitty?" I leaned forward to get a better view of her stitching.

My daughter answered with one of those indistinct sounds the young believe pass for language. Across the room, Mrs Bennet mumbled something in her sleep.

"Well, if this is what now passes for entertainment, then I shall require more wine." I drained my glass swiftly and got to my feet. "Should anyone need me—unlikely though that event might be—you will find me in my study. Or in the library. Or, perhaps, in Africa. I have a mind to visit the Gold Coast and end my days smuggling precious artefacts to Russian merchants in St. Petersburg. If that meets with your approval?" Nobody looked up, and the whispered response was merely a page turning in Mary's book.

John's letter seemed to grow heavier in my pocket.

Butterflies and Biscuits

"Good Lord, Bennet, if ever there was a man in need of a drink, it is you." Fielding pushed a glass toward me. "Spring is here, and a world of animals awaits our attention. There is no call to look so downcast. You can have no justification for ill temper at such a time. Is that not so, gentlemen?"

"Indeed," said Elliston and Stanhope, almost in unison, while Jackson simply waved a slice of cake.

As always, Mr Tincton had given us one of the Flighted Duck's private rooms for our meeting. The five-man committee of the Meryton Natural History Society met regularly to manage the accounts, plan activities, and discuss the various delights brought forth by God, nature, and Mrs Tincton's kitchen.

The morning rain had left its calling card, so the window revealed little more than vague shapes and colours: the drab browns of tradesmen and labourers, splashes of red marking soldiers, and occasional brighter hues that suggested a lady or two out shopping. The colours would come together, then separate, creating a swirl of society across the muddied window as the folk of Meryton went about their business.

"Trouble at home, Bennet?" said Elliston.

"Of sorts. But nothing of significance." A mouthful of port soon eased thoughts of Longbourn and Rudford, and I straightened in my chair. "Now, we have much to discuss. In particular, the venue for our committee's annual excursion. We have talked of the chalk meadows to the south of London." My finger landed on a small dot on the map laid out in front of us. "I propose Dorking. What say you all?"

"Such a long way," said Jackson.

"Nonsense." I waved away my friend's protest. "It is no more than sixty miles. Besides, what is such a distance to a man who once crossed an entire ocean?"

"For the King, Bennet. Not for butterflies. Years ago, too." Jackson's chair groaned alarmingly as he shifted position, and crumbs of cake tumbled from his waistcoat to join a growing number of their brethren on the floor.

"There is good walking in Dorking," said Elliston.

Lines began to form on Jackson's forehead, and he looked around the assembled party with growing alarm. "Not planning physical exertion, are we?"

My friend considered regular exercise an admirable concept, but one best left to others to explore in practice.

Fielding stretched across the table to place a hand on Jackson's arm. "It will be hard to chase butterflies from the comfort of a carriage or inn, my friend. You must submit to at least a little activity. But then the evening meal will be all the more pleasurable for having earned it."

"I suppose. But the travel..." grumbled Jackson.

"What if we were to break the journey?" Stanhope pointed at

a dark spot above Dorking. "In London. Visit a bookshop or two en route."

I beamed at Stanhope from across the table before raising a glass to our bibliophilic companion. The word "bookshop" had a curious magic to it, seeming to always lift our spirits at its every mention. Much like the words "cake," "port," "wine," and "Jenny Stantham," the latter being the name of the maid who always served us the largest portions of apple pie.

"If we must travel so far, then stop at Egham." Jackson's finger rested on a tiny mark to the west of the capital.

"Egham?" I said. "Why there?"

"It is decently halfway." Jackson shuffled in his seat.

"As is London," said Stanhope.

"Plenty of lodgings in Egham." My cake-loving friend's shuffling grew more pronounced.

"London hardly suffers from a dearth of accommodation." I narrowed my eyes. Jackson's moustache put me in mind of a kitchen broom, all dark bristles flecked with the remnants of cinnamon cake and petticoat tails. "Of course," I said. "I should have known."

"Known what?" Jackson's moustache seemed to quiver guiltily as he spoke.

"Would a preference for Egham have something to do with the presence of Swinfield's Teashop and the edible attractions within?" A red tint spread across Jackson's cheeks like spilt wine on a tablecloth.

"No need to look so, Bennet." My plump friend stared down at his plate. "Best biscuits west of Paris," he muttered.

The others all gave a collective sigh of understanding.

"Jackson," said Fielding, "empires may come and go, but some things do not change. And we are grateful for it."

"Then may I propose Dorking for early August with an overnight stay in Egham?" My suggestion met with murmurs of approval.

"Let us drink to our success." Elliston lifted his glass. "To Swinfield's biscuits."

My sip of port burned reassuringly in my throat.

"And to butterflies," added Stanhope.

I only wet my lips at the second toast.

~ ~ ~

"Let us hope, Fielding, that our trip does not prove too much for Jackson. He has become rather fond of soft chairs and sweet dishes." As was our wont, the two of us had stayed behind to enjoy a final drink together. A bottle of port sat before us, the rest of the table a chaos of glasses and plates covered by a veil of stains and leftovers.

"Jackson has earned his pleasures." Fielding rubbed at his left shoulder, where I knew a scar marked our time together in Virginia.

"True," I said. "We all have." In that moment, the dull light through the dirty window reminded me of early evenings and woodland glades, the scrape of ramrods on musket barrels, and the tired smiles of men too tense to laugh at the bawdy tales of their comrades.

"And now perhaps you might tell me why you were so despondent earlier." Fielding's words woke me from my reverie. "You seemed rather unmoved by the prospect of our excursion."

"I have lost a little of my enthusiasm for collecting, that is all." My hands cupped my glass as I stared at the few drops of port left at the bottom. "Though there is also my situation…"

"Ah, your situation, yes." Fielding shook his head sadly, as if contemplating a pupil who had failed Latin grammar for the fifth time. "You know, I had never seen you quite so content as at the Barton wedding. You were reconciled to your circumstances at home, and the groom's happiness had chased away those regrets of yours. Yet here you are, once again, with that look on your face—the one that has been my companion across a great many tables." Fielding reached out for the bottle. "So, let me pour us another drink while you enlighten me anew concerning your 'situation.'"

Unlike Jackson, my closest friend had lost little of his youthful frame, though the lines of silver above his ears and other tell-tale signs marked the many years we had travelled together.

"It is nothing so dramatic," I said over the clink of glass on glass. "Lizzy is in Kent visiting her friend, Mrs Collins."

"And with Miss Bennet still in London, conversation at Longbourn is…?"

"Notable for its absence. Unless you count gossip as conversation. If Mrs Bennet knew the movements of the French troops as accurately as those of Meryton society, the war in the peninsula would be over in a month. I do my best to escape, but a man has to eat. Lizzy has been gone but a week, and already I yearn for a time when I might enjoy breakfast amid talk of anything but muslin, calico, and cambric."

"Well, then," said Fielding. "In such circumstances, travel is called for. Perhaps join Miss Bennet at your brother-in-law's house? You always speak well of the Gardiners. Or why not to

Gloucestershire? The Bartons would be sure to welcome you to their home."

"Jane's welfare is burden enough for the Gardiners, and I despise London, as you know. And regarding Gloucestershire, well, John has invited me. But I do not wish to go."

Fielding frowned. "You surprise me."

"There is simply too much to do at Longbourn." I poured myself some more port, even though my glass was still half full. "I do not have the time."

"Oh, come now, you have a steward for all that. You shall have to offer a better explanation, my old friend."

"Very well." I topped up my companion's glass. "Since you ask, I have no wish to disturb John and Anne so soon after their wedding. It would be presumptuous. An imposition."

"Yet they have asked you to do so. Besides, you need not go immediately. Why not travel in two or three weeks? Give yourself something to look forward to and the Bartons time to adjust to their new situation." My friend leant back in his seat with the smug look of a lawyer convinced of the jury's verdict.

"Really, Fielding." The slap of my hand on the table sent a spoon clattering to the floor. "*Must* you always apply logic and reason to our conversations? It is quite unfair, for I am unused to encountering either."

My companion retrieved the fallen piece of cutlery and placed it back on a plate. "Then I have persuaded you to go?"

I folded my arms. "No, you have not."

"Then I must conclude that you simply do not wish to visit young Mr Barton, even though you regularly praise him and your friendship. How strange." Fielding took a swig of port, rolling the drink around his mouth before swallowing. "Ha!" He jabbed a slender finger in my direction. "It is because of *her*."

"I have no idea what you mean." I turned my face away briefly from my closest friend.

"So, it *is* her. The mysterious Mrs Hayter."

We stared at each other, Fielding's eyebrows slowly rising like two ancient bears awakening from their winter slumber.

"Confound you." I threw my hands in the air. "It is complicated."

Fielding settled back in his chair again, the edge of a smile on his lips. "I have time."

I rose and walked over to the window, which stood in shadow now the sun had slipped behind the clock tower atop the post office opposite. "I *am* content, Fielding. I *have* reconciled myself to my situation. And I *do* take great pleasure in John and Anne's marriage."

"Indeed. You positively glow with joy." My friend shook his head at me once more. "Your problem, Bennet, is that acceptance always follows regret, then regret follows acceptance. You are content, then not. Reconciled, then not. You really ought to make a decision. To accept what you cannot change and change what you cannot accept."

"I know, I know. It is simply that, well…it is just that…" I stared at my fingertips and imagined them touching another's across a marbled table in Bath. "It is simply that, yes, Mrs Hayter—Abigail—might indeed be there."

I returned to the table and slumped down into my seat.

"We did not part on the best of terms in January. Then we barely spoke at John's wedding." I rubbed my forehead. "She implied I was not the man she once knew."

"Did she?" said Fielding. "But, then, who among us has not altered with age?"

"Hopefully, we change for the better. Abigail clearly thought otherwise in my case. But that is not my concern. You see, contentment and reconciliation are all very well, but they can never remove those feelings that burden my conscience and heart; they merely suppress them. I fear seeing her would show me again what I discarded, remind me of my failings as a husband, and perhaps even seduce me into behaving like a young fool. She would tease me, too. In short, it would be extremely discomforting. I can imagine more pleasant ways to pass my time."

"Hmm." Fielding pursed his lips. "And you are sure she would be there? At Mr Barton's estate?"

I shrugged. "It is certainly possible. She often visits her daughter."

"Well," said my friend. "Think on this—if a man falls from his horse and fears the saddle, what advice do we give him?"

"To ride again as soon as possible."

"Precisely. And another question—how many years will you delay visiting your friends, simply to avoid the possibility of meeting a woman you once loved?"

"If I had only loved her once, I would not have this problem."

The Final Straw

Fielding's words followed me into my carriage, through Meryton, and out among the meadows, pastures, and woods that marked my way home. An early swallow joined me on the journey, its fleet form darting above the hedges before landing among the broken eaves of a cottage that marked the halfway point to Longbourn. Though the bird's chirrup proclaimed the coming of warmth and colour to the landscape, its song carried an air of melancholy. Perhaps it knew it sang alone, no mate to heed its call.

A little later, the horses slowed as we entered the Longbourn drive, and not just because of the harsh turn off the road. A black-clad fellow withdrew to one side to let us pass, his back slightly hunched as if he carried more than just the leather satchel that hung from his shoulder.

The carriage halted at my command, though one of the horses stomped and whinnied, as if protesting the delay and eager to reach home.

"Good day, Mr Spigott." I preferred to keep clergymen at a distance, but it does not do to ignore one of God's servants entirely, for you never know when you might need him (or Him).

"Mr Bennet." The curate attempted a smile, but it foundered on the rocks of his traditional anxiety when confronted by a member of the parish.

"It appears you are on your way to my home, unless…have you perhaps lost your way?"

"No, no, I am not lost." Mr Spigott laughed like a courtier uncertain if the King has made a joke. "Though are we all not a little lost? Spiritually, I mean."

"You seek to visit Longbourn, then?" I spoke quickly, eager to forestall any lecture on wayward souls and how they might be returned to the path of righteousness.

"I do." Mr Spigott opened his bag to reveal a sheaf of papers tied with string. "Miss Mary Bennet expressed interest in some interpretations of scripture."

"Did she indeed?" My rap on the carriage roof brought a shudder to the vehicle as harnesses tightened. "We will see you shortly, then."

I should, perhaps, have offered to take Mr Spigott with me. But sometimes it is better to ignore one of God's servants after all, particularly if he carries pamphlets.

～ ～ ～

"Arise all, arise," I shouted on entering the house. "We expect a visitor imminently."

The noises began quickly, reaching their peak in slammed doors and the clatter of eager feet on wooden floors. Lydia found me first, no doubt propelled by curiosity and a wish for first claim on any gentleman who might cross our threshold.

"A visitor, Papa? How exciting. Is it a gentleman? Where is he?" My youngest stopped before the hall mirror, smoothed down her front, then pinched cheeks already flushed by her rapid descent of the stairs.

"It is a gentleman," I said. "And he is on foot right behind me."

Lydia rushed to a window, head craning like a heron seeking a plump fish.

"A visitor!" Mrs Bennet approached from the kitchen waving what looked like a piece of pie. "Who is it? Why was I not informed earlier? Husband?"

"Calm yourself, my dear. It is only Mr Spigott come on some religious undertaking."

"Mr Spigott?" Lydia turned away from the window to frown at me. "How very disappointing."

"A visitor!" Kitty skipped down the stairs, all the while twisting some ornament into place in her hair.

"It is Mr Spigott." Lydia spoke as if announcing a harmless, but embarrassing, skin condition.

"Oh," said Kitty. She turned back upstairs, closely followed by her sister.

"Poor Mr Spigott," I said. "It appears he lacks the approval of our two youngest daughters. Though I might count that in his favour. Will you welcome our guest, my dear? He should be here in a moment, and I would retire to my study; I have endured enough conversation for one day."

As I moved to go, my wife placed her free hand on my arm. "Perhaps he has come to visit Mary?"

"So he said, yes. We spoke at the turning. He has pamphlets."

"Pamphlets?" Mrs Bennet nodded as if the word had a deeper meaning. "Yes, I was certain he smiled at Mary only last week in church."

"A smile? How very bacchanalian. And in a house of God, too."

"It is a sign." My wife pronounced the last word with a distinct capital S.

"You do not think he was merely happy?"

"What has Mr Spigott got to be happy about? No, he was making his affections clear."

"And did she return the smile?"

"Of course not." Mrs Bennet scowled at me. "It would not be proper."

"It would not be Mary," I said with some conviction.

"He is only a curate, but, well, beggars cannot be choosers." Mrs Bennet looked about her before lowering her voice. "As you know, Mr Bennet, all my daughters are my favourites. Yet Mary is my least favourite. We will not easily be rid of her."

"Rid of her?"

"Oh, you know very well what I mean." My wife shook my arm with vigour. "Mr Spigott may be her only opportunity. If we cannot find a husband for Jane with all her beauty, what chance do we have with Mary? I never imagined we would find someone willing to court her. We should put him at ease and welcome him to our home."

"And does Mary have any say in all this?"

A half-hearted knock put an end to our whispered discussion.

Mrs Bennet waved the pie again, which showed great fortitude in refusing to disintegrate. She bid me open my mouth, shoved the food inside, then licked her fingers before opening the door.

"Mr Spigott!" My wife looked the curate up and down like a horse trader viewing a lot at the cheaper end of the auction. "You are most welcome. Do come in. We all so look forward to reading your pamphlets."

"You do, Mrs Bennet?" The curate removed his hat, stooping as he entered. He put me in mind of a young stork—tall, somewhat spindly, and still a little surprised at the world around him.

"I shall be at my desk," I mumbled through pastry, nodding my own welcome to our visitor as I left them.

~ ~ ~

My joy at reaching the study untroubled by company doubled at the sight of a freshly delivered letter resting on the small table by an armchair. Even at a distance, I could recognise the handwriting—strong and neat, yet prone to the occasional rushed consonant that spoke of impatience with the task. I forgot all thoughts of Mr Spigott as I broke the seal quickly, like a child opening a gift.

It seemed as if Hunsford society conspired to torment my dearest daughter. Mrs Collins clearly ensured her husband troubled Lizzy as little as possible, but the rector's wife had scant influence beyond their parsonage.

> ...*we had the pleasure of dinner at Rosings Park, a name you will recall from Mr Collins's constant mention of it. You would approve of the food there, dear Papa, and I*

shall be quite spoilt for my return. The house is almost as impressive as our cousin would have us believe; I am now quite the expert on its fireplaces and chimneys. In conversation, Lady Catherine seeks to display her superiority in all matters, thus confirming its absence in her character. I cannot say if I like her daughter, Miss Anne de Bourgh, having had no conversation with her on which to base an opinion. I suspect she has little opportunity to speak, given Mr Collins and Lady Catherine's love of the spoken word...

A knock at the door silenced my chuckle. I did not recognise the reluctant tap of hand on timber.

"Enter," I said.

The door remained firmly closed.

"I have no wish to disturb, Mr Bennet," came a disembodied voice. "But Mrs Bennet said you were curious about my pamphlets."

"Oh, Gods," I whispered.

Opening the door revealed Mr Spigott, pink of face and clutching his papers to his chest.

"Did she?" I said. "Her kindness towards me knows no bounds. You had better come in, then."

The curate contemplated the threshold like Caesar might once have considered the Rubicon. A bead of sweat meandered its way down his sunken cheek, hesitated briefly at the precipice of his chin, then dropped to the floor. I pointed toward an armchair, a gesture that convinced him to brave the room and fold himself into a seat.

After pouring myself a glass of port, I held up the bottle and gave my guest an enquiring look. The curate shook his head.

"I have many pamphlets," said Mr Spigott. "And papers. Full of…words." His endearing uncertainty suggested a degree of honesty quite unexpected in a man of his profession.

"I do not suppose you have one on insects?" I spoke more in hope than expectation.

"Insects?" Mr Spigott blinked slowly, then began to thumb his way through the pile of documents resting on his lap. A few moments later, he pulled out a dogeared text with faded lettering and a slash or two of some grass-like stain on its front. "Malvern on Exodus 10. Let me see. Ah, yes. 'And the locusts went up over all the land of Egypt, and rested in all the coasts of Egypt: very grievous were they; before them there were no such locusts as they, neither after them shall be such.'"

"Well, yes, that was not precisely what I—"

"'For they covered the face of the whole earth, so that the land was darkened; and they did eat every herb of the land, and all the fruit of the trees which the hail had left: and there remained not any green thing in the trees, or in the herbs of the field, through all the land of Egypt.' Not any green thing, Mr Bennet." Mr Spigott smiled weakly at me.

I reached for the bottle of port.

~ ~ ~

In some trepidation, I put my head around the door to the drawing room. "Has he gone?"

Mary sat perfectly upright on a sofa, reading what looked like one of Mr Spigott's monographs, if not the very same one I had endured some two hours earlier. My wife rested in an armchair, holding a cup and saucer.

"He has left." The teacup rattled as Mrs Bennet spoke. "But I am certain he will visit again very soon. We may have ourselves a summer wedding. In fact, I am quite sure of it. Well, Mary, who would have thought you would be the first?"

"Mama, please." Mary took a tighter hold of her pamphlet. "Mr Spigott and I merely share an interest in moral texts. We neither of us have the inclination for the kind of discourse my sisters indulge in so readily. There is no understanding between us." Her voice showed no sign of emotion, but a hint of red blossomed in her cheeks at her final words.

"Well, there is time for an understanding to grow." My wife shrugged. "I cannot see Mr Spigott marrying anyone else anytime soon."

"There is no suggestion that Mr Spigott has any interest in me beyond that of a fellow student of scripture." Mary turned a page with an exaggerated flourish.

"Excellent," I said. "Then we will be spared much ecclesiastical nonsense. And for that I am grateful, for there is enough in Mr Collins's letters. The clergy should listen to Polonius, so they might grasp that 'brevity is the soul of wit.' Though speaking of Hamlet, 'the lady protests too much.' At least methinks she does."

A frown seemed to do battle with a tenuous smile on Mary's face; the frown had the advantage of fighting on familiar territory.

"Is that one of his pamphlets?" I asked.

Mary looked up at me over her spectacles. "Malvern on Exodus 10." On the page before her, a badly drawn locust bore a disheartened look, as if the poor insect tired of rampaging ceaselessly across the Egyptian landscape.

"Now there is an unpleasant prospect," I said. "Imagine a horde of locusts—grievous or otherwise—ravishing my hollyhocks."

Mary's smile rallied briefly before beating another hasty retreat.

"Of course, if such an understanding were to develop, then May would be a fine month." Mrs Bennet's definition of conversation had no requirement for more than one participant. "Though I do like a June wedding. Or July. My sister married in July."

"Well, you will find me in my study." I withdrew my head, but a raised voice from the bottom of the stairs stopped my progress back up the hall.

"It is mine, I say. Kitty, let go." Lydia appeared ahead with her sister behind her. They held a bonnet at arm's length between them.

"It is not yours," said Kitty. "Lizzy said I might wear it while she was gone."

The two girls lurched ever closer, like two porters carrying a heavy trunk across slippery ground.

"But it suits *me* better," said Lydia. "You know it to be true. All the officers pay me far more attention."

Kitty's eyes widened and her grip tightened.

I retreated into the drawing room. "My dear, I believe you are needed."

"There is much to be said for August, mind." Mrs Bennet frowned. "No, too hot. Mr Spigott sweats enough as it is."

"Mine!" Lydia shuffled into the room, back still turned to me.

"Mine!" said Kitty as the two swung around, ignored by

Mary, who continued to immerse herself in tales of divine punishment.

Then, with the inevitability of rain on a Scottish moor, the bonnet tore apart. Kitty tumbled across Mary, crushing Mr Spigott's pamphlet and dislodging a painting on the wall.

"Kitty!" screamed Mary.

"Enough!" I bellowed.

All three girls froze in position. Kitty lay sprawled over Mary, whose spectacles now hung half off her face. Lydia sat on the floor, holding a piece of the bonnet like the severed head of a vanquished foe. Beneath it, a ribbon flapped forlornly in the draught from the open door.

I walked over to the wooden frame knocked askew by Kitty. The painting—a recent present from John—showed the French army retreating at the Battle of Aspern. In the foreground, a horse struggled to regain its feet, its rider prostrate on the ground; the cavalryman still held the reins in one hand, though his left arm lay trapped beneath the fallen animal. The face of the French soldier spoke of pain but also of determination to get back on his horse. The picture seemed to give form to Fielding's words.

I returned the frame to its original position before facing the room, where all four women stared at me expectantly.

"Right," I said. "If this nonsense is all Longbourn can offer while Lizzy is away, then there is only one thing for it. I am taking us to Gloucestershire. We shall visit the Bartons. Perhaps Rudford will improve both your behaviour and my enjoyment of it."

On Expectations

Fully dressed, I perched on my bed the following morning and reflected on events in the drawing room. My sudden decision to visit John put me in mind of the words of Maria Edgeworth:

> *We cannot judge either of the feelings or of the characters of men with perfect accuracy, from their actions or their appearance in public; it is from their careless conversations, their half-finished sentences, that we may hope with the greatest probability of success to discover their real characters.*

I wondered what my careless outburst the previous day might reveal of *my* character, of desires unknown even to their owner.

The passage came from a novel, a form of book Lizzy often attempted to interest me in, though with little success. She would read to me, sometimes, on winter nights, perhaps hoping the glow from the fire would draw me into new realms of the imagination. I did not discourage her, though my pleasure came not from the words but through her voice and presence.

"It is kind of you, husband, to think of our daughters so."

My wife stood in the open doorway to the bedchamber, her appearance sending motes of dust to play chase among the morning sunbeams.

"How so?" I stood, patting my stomach to calm the growls of hunger induced by the smell of baking from downstairs.

"A visit to the Bartons may throw them into the paths of many a fine gentleman."

"Then I rejoice in your pleasure, dear."

Gloucestershire society had much to offer Mrs Bennet, mostly in the form of an imagined number of bachelors, all desperate to share their considerable incomes with a young lady imported from beyond the county borders. While I shot pigeons with John, my wife would hunt larger prey.

"I thought we might plan how best to present the girls," said my wife.

"Perhaps later." My stomach sent up a further reminder of the time since my last meal. "I am more concerned now with the prospect of food than our trip."

"That is all fine and good, Mr Bennet, but we need to order new gowns as soon as possible. We cannot delay if we want the best material. It will mean additional expense for which I would have your approval."

I stifled a yawn. "And this approval cannot wait until after breakfast?"

"It can. But it would settle my nerves to have it now before you become distracted by your books and what not."

"Well, I suppose." The scent of fresh bread from the kitchen seemed to grow stronger. "But really, dear, have you nothing else to occupy your mind at such an early hour?"

"If I do not address such matters with urgency, Mr Bennet, then who shall?" My wife put both her hands on her hips, which should have alarmed me. "Will *you* do so?"

"Of course not," I said. "I am entirely unsuited to such affairs, which is why I leave them in your capable hands."

My wife wagged an accusing finger at me. "A happy excuse. Yet you were most active on John's behalf. And now he is married. You have done far more for him than for your own daughters."

"You know I had a duty to his father."

"And you have none *as* a father? To Jane? To her sisters? To me? Where were you when I encouraged Mr Collins? Where were you when I encouraged Mr Bingley? And how quickly you scurried away when Mr Spigott called." My wife made a running motion with her fingers.

"Given the outcome of your efforts, my dear, perhaps it is not I who is most unsuited to the task of matchmaker."

Mrs Bennet's eyes narrowed. "I might have achieved more had you helped rather than hindered. Oh, you delight in my troubles when you should share them."

"I do no such thing. Besides, have I not fulfilled my duties to the girls adequately? You all want for nothing."

"We want for nothing but a secure future when you are gone from us." My wife half turned to go when another burst of anger seemed to take her. "There is much you do not give us; there is much more you do not give me. I am long reconciled to it, as you know. But do not chide me for doing what you will not. That I do ask of you, Mr Bennet." She waved her hands as if shooing away a troublesome fly. "And now I shall see to it that breakfast suits your obvious appetite. You go off and enjoy your beetles and butterflies and all that nonsense. I am sure they must keep you remarkably busy indeed."

The door closed behind my wife with enough force to suggest she would be vexed for a good hour. I decided to leave breakfast until a little later and dedicate myself to the self-indulgent resentment every man shelters behind when his wife reveals the truth to him.

~ ~ ~

"Will John hold a ball, do you think?" Kitty tore at her roll as if it held some precious gem within its leavened interior.

"Most certainly." My wife passed Kitty the butter. "John is a gentleman and a man of considerable worth." I assumed she did not mean his character.

"Are there officers in Gloucestershire? Will he invite them to the ball?" Lydia had already finished her breakfast. She rarely dawdled at any table lacking in new rumour or gossip. "Papa, you must write to John and insist he invites officers to his ball."

"I will do no such thing." I sat behind the protective wall of *The Meryton Chronicle*, erected in case I had miscalculated the duration of my wife's vexation. Food and my daughters' enthusiasm seemed to have softened her disposition, though the noise she made as she stabbed at the cold cuts suggested I was not yet entirely forgiven.

"What a merry evening we shall have there," said Lydia. "And how jealous will Jane and Lizzy be when they hear of it."

The chatter continued without further participation on my

part before weaving its way to the anticipated and expensive conclusion.

"You shall need new gowns, girls," said Mrs Bennet. "We cannot have you look anything less than your best. Not when there are officers to impress. Your father will not mind the expense. There is nothing he will not do to secure your futures."

No doubt a suitable glare in my direction accompanied her words. I decided to risk entering the conversational fray and lowered my paper.

"John has never spoken of officers, nor is he particularly fond of their ilk. And yet you have them lining up at his table to court our daughters."

"Every county has its soldiers, husband. John will know his duties as host." My wife lifted herself up, knocking a plate to one side. "Come, girls, let us away to Bracegirdle's. They will need a week or two. We cannot expect much in the way of trimming since we travel so soon, but it will just have to do." She paused as she made to leave, one hand still resting on the table. "Mr Bennet, you might ask John to decorate the estate in yellow for his ball, so we may match the girls' gowns to the colour. Lydia wears primrose particularly well."

"Is there anything else I should include in my note? Should John arrange for a bachelor of some particular income—shall we say two thousand a year—to propose to Lydia while we are there?"

"What an excellent suggestion, husband. I knew you were not so oblivious to our needs as you pretend. But would not five thousand a year be more suitable? If they are to live in Gloucestershire, they will need carriages and a house in Bath."

"I shall suggest ten thousand, my dear, then they might have a house in London, too."

I shook my head before retreating behind the *Chronicle* once more.

"What about me?" said Kitty. "Can John not find a husband for me?"

"Of course," said my wife. "I am certain we shall return from Gloucestershire with more than one offer for you both."

Knowing no words could now breach the battlements of maternal optimism, I remained silent as my wife, Lydia, and Kitty left the room, all of them clucking in joyous abandon like hens around the threshers.

"You have no wish to join them, Mary?" I peered over my paper.

My daughter looked up from her plate, on which a poached egg lay half-eaten, cut around its edges to leave a precise circle of white surrounding a golden heart. "I do not care for balls, Papa, as you well know. Nor for officers."

I put down my paper and rested my hands on my lap, contemplating my daughter for a few moments. There was nothing out of place with Mary, not even a loose hair or thread. Her egg even rested on a pedestal of toast that formed a perfect square.

"What *do* you care for?" I said. "Apart from, it would seem, geometry."

"What do you mean, Papa?"

"I know much of what you claim to dislike: balls, gossip, drink, and more. It is a lengthy list. But what is it you enjoy? What do you wish for in your life?"

My daughter did not answer and took a sip of coffee, face as inscrutable as ever.

"I do not mean to pry," I continued. "You have your books and pamphlets. They likely make more sense than most people of my acquaintance. You are wise to put your faith in printed words, for they, at least, will remain constant." I turned my attention to my food.

"I should not be averse to marriage." Mary spoke quietly.

My mouth fell open like that of a trout fresh from the river, but my daughter continued with her breakfast as if she had merely passed comment on the state of the weather.

"Well," I said. "That is unexpected. Though hardly a rousing endorsement of the state of matrimony."

"We are taught its value in principle, Papa. But…" Mary looked up at me, and I raised an eyebrow. She put down her cutlery. "How are we to judge who makes a good husband?"

"That is quite a question, child. Does scripture not have something to say on the matter? The Bible invariably has an answer, if not always the right one."

My daughter's eyes grew distant for a moment. "It says, 'For husbands, this means love your wives, just as Christ loved the church. He gave up his life for her.' Ephesians."

"You wish a husband willing to give up his life for you?"

"A husband who would…love me." Mary's head and voice dropped as she spoke the last two words. Then she picked up her knife and fork and began cutting vigorously at her egg, which bled yellow before the onslaught.

"We all wish for a partner who will love us." I paused for a moment as I thought back to my earlier conversation with Mrs

Bennet. "But it is denied to many."

Mary stopped cutting and raised her head again. We stared at each other, like two deer emerging from a copse into an unfamiliar field, uncertain of our next step.

"I am not like my sisters." The words came out hesitantly.

I reached out to touch Mary's hand, but she pulled her arm away.

"There is joy in diversity," I said.

"Men do not look at me and see a potential wife. Or even...or even a woman. I am not given to lively conversation. I have some talent at the pianoforte, but I am...plain."

"Come now, Ma—"

"No, Papa." My daughter raised her hand for a moment. "It is but the truth, and we are urged to honour the truth. I have my qualities, but they are not easily recognised. I am nobody's favourite. Not Mama's. Not..." She turned her head away from me.

My stomach tightened. "You are cherished by your mother. And by myself."

"Am I?" Mary's voice was barely a whisper now. "Lizzy has her intelligence, Jane her beauty, and Lydia her confidence. Kitty has Lydia. What do I have? Who pays notice to me?"

Mary trembled a little, and for a moment I saw past the stiff back and assured morals that had previously left me in little doubt of her character. "Mary, I—"

We both jumped at the clatter of the door.

"My, how serious you look," said Lydia. "You will never find a husband if you will not smile, Mary. Come along, Mama is waiting."

I glanced at Mary, but all trace of vulnerability had vanished, her face now as stony as one of Moses's tablets.

A Visitor (or Two)

Unsettled by the morning's discussions with Mrs Bennet and Mary, I once again found sanctuary in my study. It offered a more functional refuge than the library, providing a home for everything from bills to billhooks. Ledgers, letters, pots, and trays filled a labyrinth of shelves in a chaos where everything and nothing had its place.

My gaze roamed the room in search of distraction, eventually resting on the tallest cabinet present and the various items that stood atop it. Reaching up, I found and pulled down a rosewood box, a tell-tale letter V burnt into its side. A rub of my cuff soon revealed the dark grain beneath the dust, though the lid took some prising off, as if the contents within feared exposure to the light. Inside, a piece of charred wood left black marks on my fingertips and coaxed the crackle of flame and broken timber from my memory. The noises faded at the cold touch of an old hip flask. I traced the dents in the metal—scars left by a musket ball that had stained my shirt with brandy but not with blood. Beside the silver vessel lay the large pebble I had picked up before boarding the ship back to England, each day at sea marked by a scratch in the stone's grey surface. Each scratch had torn away another layer of tension until only vague shadows of fear remained—dark shapes I once thought banished by the sight of England's coast and the clamour of the docks at Liverpool.

Returning the box dislodged some cards, sending one to spin down to the floor and land at my feet. Abigail's faded name on the front brought a wry smile to my face.

"It seems there is no escaping you," I said.

The back of the card revealed my own handwriting—a date and departure time. That coach had left on schedule all those years ago, though too late for my purpose. Or so I had thought. My life might have followed a different path had I travelled earlier that week. Or had I ignored the gossip spread by my fellow passengers and put my question to Abigail anyway, without care for honour and pride, and hoping to persuade her to make a different choice to the one they said she had already made. She might have succumbed to my pleas and would now bear a different name to that of Hayter.

How often I had cast such regrets to one side, yet they always returned, unshakeable as the devil's own hellhound. I let the card fall onto the desk. This was not the distraction I had sought, for it led only to more memories. The teashop again, her hand stretching towards mine. Her words.

I loved you, you know.

But I had not known. Not for sure. And, so, I had allowed the opportunity to slip beyond my reach, leaving a trail of regrets in its wake.

Fielding was quite correct—to conquer one's fears, one must meet them head on. All I could do was resolve to face my own test of character at Rudford with fortitude, should Abigail be present. And a small part of me whispered words of truth and betrayal—did I fear her presence or secretly hope for it?

Abigail's card now lay next to John's letter. I had found contentment in helping my young friend achieve a happiness denied me. Perhaps, then, there was relief to be had in repeating the exercise.

"I might prove my wife wrong, after all," I murmured.

One of Mr Spigott's thin monographs lay on the other side of the desk. My mind drifted back to Mary. I had been ever present in her life and yet also entirely absent. The same was true of Kitty and Lydia. My two youngest, however, could do without my help; they had time—and Mrs Bennet—on their side.

"Why not?" I said out loud. "Why not, indeed?

~ ~ ~

It seemed fate had waited only for my resolve, for no sooner had I decided to become active in encouraging Mary and Mr Spigott than I found myself awaiting the curate at my house once more. He accompanied my neighbour, Sir William Lucas, who must have recently returned from Hunsford.

"I had best relieve him of his gossip, lest he explode from the strain of containing it," I muttered at Hill, our housekeeper, who came to warn me of the two gentlemen's approach.

The returning traveller stood in the back garden, explaining the architecture of my roof to his companion. My whispered prayer to the heavens gave thanks as much for Mrs Bennet's absence as for Mr Spigott's presence. My wife took any interest in our home from the Lucas family as a sure sign of delight at their good fortune and our lack of it. Sir William's daughter, Charlotte, had risen from burdensome child to prospective mistress of Longbourn in the time it took to accept an offer from Mr Collins, on whom my estate was entailed. I bore the Lucas family no ill will, though. It was I—not Sir William—who had failed to sire a son.

"Mr Spigott," I said. "It is good to see you again."

"I had some business with Sir William, and he asked if I might accompany him."

"And how glad I am that he did. And dear Sir William—how was your journey? How is your daughter? How is *my* daughter? How is our dear Mr Collins?"

Unfortunately, questions were like glasses of brandy to Sir William—too many at once blunted his faculties. He stood with his mouth half open, eyes blinking rapidly.

"Your journey was tolerable?" I said.

"It was!" Sir William smiled.

"And your daughter—she is content?"

"She is!"

"And her husband—did Mr Collins prove an obliging host?"

"He did!

"And Lizzy—she has settled into Hunsford life?"

"She has!"

Having answered all my questions to his obvious satisfaction, Sir William was now free to address the more important aspects of his recent trip, particularly his encounters with Mr Collins's patron, the great Lady Catherine de Bourgh.

"Lovely little village, Hunsford. Capital place! Rosings Park. Delightful! Quite a family, there. Lady Catherine. Capital woman!" Sir William was a man of few words but many sentences. And fond of capitals. He embarked on a series of anecdotes, expressed with such excitement that I feared he might exhaust Meryton's entire supply of exclamation marks before dinner. Mr Spigott listened to Sir William politely, his shoulders straighter than normal, though his gaze often wandered to the garden. Eventually, our loquacious knight could find nothing new to say about Lady Catherine.

"It is a fine day, gentlemen," I said. "Shall we remain outside a while? We might take some tea later. I fear you have missed the rest of the family, who left earlier for Meryton. Mary, in particular, would have enjoyed a curate's conversation." I glanced at Mr Spigott, but he was staring across my lawn, deep furrows carved in his forehead. "You are distracted, Mr Spigott. Something presses on your mind?"

"Those rhododendrons. Sorry, no, my…my apologies. It is just…" The curate's eyes brightened. "I have some liking for gardens. And for nature. Sir William tells me you have fine views across the fields from beyond the hedge. Perhaps…I mean, might it be possible to…" Mr Spigott looked at me like a cornered poacher might view the gamekeeper.

"You would like to take a look? Of course."

We strolled down to the border of old yew that marked the edge of the rear garden. As we passed through the gate buried within it, the curate ran his hand across the surrounding foliage, pausing once to rub the soft waxy needles between his fingers. The path continued directly down to the stream, but I took my guests off to one side, the ground soft but not muddy, up toward a rise that afforded a better outlook.

"Tell me a little more of Mrs Collins, Sir William," I said.

"Ah, yes, now, well, Mr Collins has given my Charlotte a good home. We may be grateful for her situation and her excellent prospects." My neighbour coughed, cheeks colouring. "That is. I mean to say…I did not intend. Is that a chaffinch?" He pointed to where a flash of russet and black dipped its way across a meadow and disappeared into a small copse.

"Do not be concerned on my account, Sir William." I hoped my smile would put him at ease. "All here know the terms of the Longbourn entail. But is married life treating her well? I daresay her husband and the affairs of the parsonage keep her busy."

"It is far from easy being married to a man of the cloth, as no doubt our friend here will confirm." Sir William looked at Mr Spigott, but the curate offered no such testimony. Either he felt unqualified to comment or the fearsome sight of my neighbour's prodigious eyebrows, in whose bushy interior a badger might well have found refuge, had silenced him. "Busy, busy, Charlotte is," continued Sir William. "Always off here and there. I cannot imagine how she will find the time for her sister and Miss Elizabeth."

"A rector manages the affairs of the parish," I said. "But his wife has to manage those of the parishioners. It is much to ask of her. She must be at ease in all manner of company, from the lords and ladies down to the poorest labourer. Mrs Collins is a sensible woman, though, and practical with it. Not prone to flights of fancy. My Mary shares similar qualities." I cleared my throat. "No doubt, Sir William, your daughter makes an excellent job of her new role."

"She does. She has the Lucas spirit, just like her sister Maria and all our younger ones." Sir William stole a quick look back at Longbourn before pulling his gaze away as his cheeks reddened once more. Sometimes my wife's suspicions were not entirely misplaced.

By now we had reached the top of the rise, where a slope curved down to meadows and pastures below. In the distance, the silver thread of the stream and the call of some river bird brought back memories of the time John Barton and Anne Hayter—as Mrs Barton was then called—had visited. How John and I had thought ourselves so very clever in our machinations, when we were mere puppets in the hands of Lizzy and Miss Hayter.

Though Mr Spigott took in the requested view, murmuring his approval, his head kept turning back to Longbourn, his brow still furrowed, his lips pursed. In concern? In contemplation? In calculation? I could not say. The absence of certainty caused me to pause in thought.

I had seen Mr Spigott often at church during Reverend Toke's absences and listened to his sermons. But he was a distant figure, a mouthpiece for scripture; I had never considered what lay beneath the mantle of his office, never sought to understand his true nature. And yet here I was, ready to push Mary upon him at a whim. I, who had once considered Mr Collins's poor character sufficient grounds to deny him Lizzy's hand, despite the security such a match would have brought my family. Mary had the right of it—she was nobody's favourite. I resolved to learn more of Mr Spigott.

The sky seemed to mirror my thoughts as cheerless clouds to the west carried the promise of rain.

"Shall we return for tea?" I said, my smile somewhat forced.

Officers!

To properly understand the character of a man, one must either fight him or dine with him. Since a duel with Mr Spigott seemed somewhat inappropriate, an invitation to dinner offered a more sensible alternative. I had hoped Mrs Bennet would prove a willing ally in such an undertaking. Unfortunately, the opposite proved true.

"I have no time to bother with Mr Spigott," she said, as we discussed travel arrangements for our forthcoming trip to the Bartons. "There is much to do. Besides, any dinners we host before leaving must be for the officers."

"Why the officers, my dear?"

"Oh, husband, must men be so ignorant of such matters? Is it not obvious?"

"Not to me."

My wife put down the list of all we needed to take with us. Judging by its length, we would be staying with John for five months, rather than five days.

"Mr Spigott has little to recommend himself," said Mrs Bennet. "Which means there is no urgency to secure him. He shall still be here on our return. And still in need of a wife. But the officers leave for Brighton soon, and we should have them at Longbourn as often as possible before we depart. They do so admire Lydia and Kitty, and this must be encouraged."

"What about John's eligible gentlemen?"

"You do not throw away your stick until you have crossed the stream, Mr Bennet."

"But why not invite the officers *and* Mr Spigott?"

"Lord, give me patience." Mrs Bennet picked up a pen, dipped it in ink, and began adding more items to her list. "Have you no understanding of courtship?" she muttered.

"Apparently not."

"He is a curate, Mr Bennet. They are officers." No other information was forthcoming.

My wife paused for a moment, dipped her pen in the inkwell again, then added a single word to the paper.

"Why are we taking flowers with us?" I said, peering over my spouse's shoulder.

"Flowers? Such nonsense. Why would we take flowers?"

"You have written garlands." I pointed at the word.

"*Gowland's*, Mr Bennet, *Gowland's* lotion." Mrs Bennet motioned toward the door. "Perhaps I had best do this alone. Do you not have a book to read?"

"I still do not understand dinner arrangements, my dear. The curate is a decent fellow."

Mrs Bennet sighed. "It is no reflection on Mr Spigott, but you cannot expect him to compete with officers. Better he is not there at all than to suffer by comparison. Nor do we want him inhibiting lively conversation."

Mrs Bennet was drawn to braid like a magpie to silver; the dark coat of the clergyman could never hope to compete with the bright red of an army uniform. In my experience, neither garb recommended the wearer to others. The cut and colour of a soldier's jacket disguised many a failing. I had spent enough time among officers to know their real character emerged only when danger demanded the truth of people. As for clerical frocks and vestments, I was sure there were many fine men in the church. Unfortunately, I had yet to meet one. Perhaps Mr Spigott would be the first.

~ ~ ~

"We are fewer than normal, gentlemen," I said, a day or two later. "My eldest daughters remain in London and Kent. And your number has dwindled, too, since we last dined together. Has there been some conflict of which we have heard nothing? Do not say Meryton is lost to England?"

"It remains in safe hands, Mr Bennet," said Colonel Forster from the other end of my dinner table. "You need not fear the arrival of French troops just yet. Several officers have gone ahead to Brighton to make preparations for our redeployment in May. These are dangerous times, and I would have us ready for all eventualities."

"And we must buy all the best wines before another regiment does so." Mr Wickham rarely ignored an opportunity to sail a conversation into shallower waters, his manner as assured as his smart clothing, though the rain that plagued us had left a damp patch on his breeches.

The subsequent talk meandered from the banal to the trivial, tackling subjects of great importance but no value. I paid scant attention to the chatter beyond that required of a diligent host. Whatever Mrs Bennet might have hoped, I knew my daughters would fail to interest any of the assembled gentlemen. Colonel Forster had married only recently; his twice refusing an offer of more wine suggested no sign of dissatisfaction with that state of affairs. Mr Denny barely had need of a razor. And though Mr Wickham possessed an engaging charm and an eager eye, he was clever enough to know he could use both to catch richer fish than those available in Longbourn's waters.

Mary, too, played little part in the general conversation, her demeanour not cold but absent, as if her soul lay elsewhere. She took her time with eating, first rearranging the food on her plate in an orderly fashion.

"Oh, we shall miss you all so." Mrs Bennet drummed out a lament on the tabletop with the end of her knife. "Meryton will not be the same without you officers."

"That is certainly true," I said.

"Must you go?" said Lydia. "Brighton is so very far away, and I shall have no one to dance with."

"I have no doubt, Miss Lydia, that you will never be short of partners." Mr Wickham bowed as he spoke, earning a coquettish smile from my daughter.

"Oh, Wickham, you are a tease. I shall miss you and Denny, in particular." Lydia turned to her neighbour at the table. "You are very quiet, Denny."

"Hard for me to get a word in edgewise with Wickham here." Mr Denny pointed at his colleague with a knife.

"Let us hope Mr Wickham fights as well as he talks," I said.

"Then we have nothing to fear from France."

"I care little for the French." Kitty stuck her chin out. "If it were not for them, you all might have stayed longer in Meryton."

"You may care little for the people," I said. "But you do care for their fashions. All I hear at breakfast is Paris this and Paris that. When we defeat Napoleon, we must insist on reparations in the form of fabric and fashion plates."

"Your daughter shows taste, Mr Bennet. Fashion is a fine thing." Mr Wickham held up his glass. "Like wine."

"There should be less of both." Mary spoke without lifting her head. "Many ills of the world would be much diminished by their absence."

The moral interjection drew a giggle from Lydia, who then took an unseemly large swig of wine.

"Come now, Miss Bennet," said Mr Wickham. "Would you have us drinking nothing but tea and dressing like servants? How miserable we would all be."

"I merely meant that—"

"Can you imagine it?" continued Mr Wickham. "You might find yourself dancing with the stable boy at a ball and not know the difference. How would that suit you, Miss Lydia?"

"It would not suit me at all. How silly of Mary to say so."

"It was not silly," whispered Mary, knuckles white where she gripped her knife.

"You must allow for a difference of opinion, Mr Wickham," I said, keeping one eye on Mary.

"On some matters I will concede your point, sir." Mr Wickham gave me a small nod of acknowledgement. "There are, after all, those who prefer red wine and those who prefer white.

But against wine itself there can surely be no objection."

"I rather prefer port. It has more depth to it." My eyes lingered a little longer on the lieutenant, before looking over at Mary. "There is something to be said for your idea, child. We would have to judge men on their character and not their clothes."

"An admirable sentiment, Mr Bennet, were not the clothes a reflection of that character." Mr Wickham raised his glass again as if to toast his own wisdom.

"Am I to understand that all soldiers are equally brave, then?" I leant forward. "After all, they all wear the same uniform?"

"A uniform may make a soldier braver," said Colonel Forster. "But it will not make a hero of a coward. That I do know."

"What of the ladies?" said Mr Denny. "I would not have them hide their beauty."

"Well said, Denny." Mr Wickham nodded his approval.

"True beauty would shine through whatever clothes one might wear." Mary looked across the table at me as she spoke. "And a pretty gown cannot hide an ugly soul."

"Nonsense, Mary." Mrs Bennet waved a boiled potato on the end of her fork like Neptune lecturing a sea nymph with his trident. "Why, I have seen the plainest of girls turned out presentably thanks to their choice of fashions. Even Charlotte Lucas looked well on her wedding day. Do not frown at me so, husband, I am only saying what everyone knows. And she is married now, so I am sure it is she who laughs at us."

"What would plain men do if they had no recourse to fashion to hide their defects?" said Mr Wickham.

"They would all look like Mr Spigott." Lydia shuddered. "With his thin legs and—"

"Lydia!" I growled. "It would not hurt you to show a little more respect for a man of the church."

"Just because he is a curate does not make him less plain, Papa." Lydia's traditional pout of defiance accompanied her words.

"He has a strange way of walking," added Kitty. "As if unsure of himself."

"Good for him," I said. "No man should be sure of himself. It only leads to trouble."

"*I* am sure of only one thing." Mr Wickham drew himself up as he spoke. "That the food, wine, and company in this house is of the highest quality and shall be surely missed when we leave for Brighton."

"A sentiment we may all agree on," said Colonel Forster.

As the table raised a toast to false compliments, Mary's glass remained on the table. Her face had assumed its usual impenetrable smoothness, though her cheeks seemed a little paler than usual. I lowered my own glass without drinking.

About Mr Spigott

The following day, the sun had finally squeezed its way past disgruntled clouds to pick out the indomitable march of green across Longbourn's fields. The birds welcomed the return of the insect world with a chorus of joy, which the insects wisely chose not to reciprocate. I had risen early, and the scent of hot rolls and cold pork promised a hearty breakfast enjoyed in isolation. Sadly, unexpected conversation already emanated from the dining room. I slipped inside, lifted the fresh copy of the *Chronicle* from its place, then settled into my usual chair at one end of the table.

"You are sure, Mama?" said Lydia.

"Quite certain," said my wife. "Mrs Philips tells me that azure and lilac are very much the fashion, ever since Lady Powlett's appearance at the Rochester. Who knows what gentlemen John may have gathered up in Gloucestershire? You must look your best."

"Good morning," I said.

"Good morning, Papa," said Mary, after a short pause.

"You, at least, can see me, Mary? I thought I might have passed away in the night and now pursue a ghostly existence, charged with spending eternity listening to talk of balls. Does the

Bible mention such a purgatory?"

Mary simply continued eating her roll, spreading butter and jam evenly across its surface, as if unwilling to show favour to any one part of the bread.

Mrs Bennet stared at me intently. "You look perfectly well to me, husband."

"So, your gowns are to be blue and purple?" I said. "How fortunate I neglected to inform John of the need for yellow decoration."

"It would not do for the girls to appear in an unfashionable colour." Mrs Bennet jabbed her spoon at me as she spoke. Strawberry preserve flew indelicately through the air but found a safe landing place on my shirt. I cracked open the *Chronicle* and sheltered behind its papery barricade.

"You know full well we must make a good impression at John's," continued my wife. "He is a fine gentleman now and walks in the very best of circles."

"My dear, John has always been a fine gentleman. But the only circles he enjoys walking in are around whatever person or object he wishes to paint. Do not allow your hopes and expectations to rise quite so much or you may meet with disappointment in Gloucestershire."

"Nonsense, husband. John is married to a family with a great deal of connections. Oh, do you think Mrs Hayter may be there? She would surely bring a party with her. Imagine!"

My grip tightened around the edges of my paper.

"Now, make haste, girls," continued my wife. "We must see Mrs Bracegirdle this morning and ensure all will be ready before we leave."

"And what about you, Mary?" I glanced around the side of the paper. "Do you look forward to our trip? To balls and bachelors? I suspect not."

"It is all the same to me, Papa."

"Have a care, Mary," said Lydia. "Or you will find no man of note to marry and have to make do with Mr Spigott."

I did not expect Mary to respond, since she had long understood that Lydia attached no weight to words spoken by others. On this occasion, however, a tiny spark seemed to light in Mary's eye. "And what, pray, is wrong with Mr Spigott?"

"Larks, Mary," said Lydia. "Do not say you have fallen for him."

"It is a legitimate question, Lydia." I folded the paper and dropped it on the table. "What, precisely, has Mr Spigott done to deserve your opprobrium?"

Lydia shrugged. "He is just plain Mr Spigott. That is all." She turned her attention to opening a boiled egg, a task she began with unexpected delicacy before simply crushing the poor thing's brave resistance with her spoon. "Oh, look. Now I have bits of shell everywhere."

"How long has Mr Spigott been curate?" I addressed the question to Mary, but Mrs Bennet answered.

"Some three years. Perhaps four."

"So long?" I said. People may be in plain view but never seen. "Where was he beforehand? He has no accent to speak of."

"I am sure I do not know." My wife put her head back and drank the last of her coffee. "No one ever talks about Mr Spigott. Not even Mrs Philips."

Society uses various measures to determine the worth and

status of an individual. Meryton, however, used Mrs Philips. Her lack of interest in a person was a cut few could survive without extensive surgery to their character and position.

"Come now, dear, you must know something," I said.

"I confess, husband, I had never given him much thought until recently. Mr Spigott was always just…there." She stuffed a piece of bread and jam into her mouth.

"His family is from Lincolnshire." All heads turned to Mary, who sat primly, chin slightly raised. "His father has a large estate near the village of Saxilby."

Mrs Bennet stopped chewing at the exact moment the word "estate" appeared after the word "large." She swallowed, then smiled at Mary. "A *large* estate, you say?"

"Yes, but he speaks very little of it. He has older brothers."

"He will not inherit, then." My wife wrinkled her nose. "Still, he will have to do."

"Mama?" said Mary.

"Nothing. Now eat up, girls." My wife took another bite of bread.

"You might have told us this before, Mary," I said.

"You did not ask. Oh, and there is one more thing you might like to know about him, Papa." Mary gazed out of a window edged by the fresh growth of a climbing rose. "He likes to garden. Very much."

"A gardening man? As I recall, he said something similar himself. The more I learn of our Mr Spigott, the more intriguing he becomes. Perhaps I shall pay him a visit now the weather has turned."

"Well you had better be quicker about it than you were with

Mr Bingley last year," said my wife. "Or it will have to wait until after Gloucestershire."

~ ~ ~

I had always considered an interest in gardening a sure sign of an excellent character. An appreciation for nature's bounty and a desire to bend it to man's needs suggest both humility and ambition, not to mention courage. It takes a brave man to do battle with the wanton thistle and its licentious companion, the dandelion. Then I met Mr Collins, whose own interest in horticulture disabused me of all such absolutes.

Despite the salutary lesson of the Hunsford rector, I approached Mr Spigott's cottage with hopeful interest. A poet might have described the curate's home as idyllic, a pretty little thing with a small front garden. But spring idylls offer little defence against winter's chills, and dark evenings pass slowly when you are cold and alone.

Under the thatched eaves of the house, slips of mud hinted at the beginnings of a swallow's nest. I lifted my head at a passing shadow on the ground to catch the dive and swoop of the nest's presumed owners, brief streaks of blue, orange, and white among the drifting dots of flies and other insects.

As I reached for the twisted iron that formed the doorknocker, a distant click stayed my hand. More clicks followed. Instead of knocking, I squeezed through a narrow path alongside the building to find myself behind the cottage, where the curate trimmed the deadwood from a hedge.

"Do excuse me, Mr Spigott," I said. "I heard the shears and wondered if you might be in your…" My mouth stayed open as my eyes widened, my words of greeting humbled into silence.

The garden must have covered just over an acre, ending on all sides at tall hedges of hazel, hawthorn, dogwood, and spindle. They formed a dense thicket even without their full head of leaves; a passer-by would never see the treasures within their wooden walls. A path led from the rear door of the cottage down to the very back of the garden, where it disappeared like a causeway into a sea of apple, pear, and cherry blossom. Smaller paths led off to the sides, marked out in dark, flat stones and bounded by box plants no more than a foot high. I recognised the shale from the quarry over at Shenley. Each path formed a curl around a flower bed layered in tiers like sections of an amphitheatre, each bed full of foliage that promised a summer of colour. Later, each path turned in on itself like the frond of a fern to form a circle, the enclosed space consumed by roses, their tight green buds still hiding the elegant jewels within.

"Mr Spigott, you have brought Versailles to Hertfordshire. How on earth…" My voice trailed away again, lost in the glory of what lay before me.

"Time, Mr Bennet, time. And the generosity of Mr Latham and his gardener."

"Well, of course, Latham's estate is magnificent. The plants were his?"

"Many of them, yes."

"But…how many people know of this?"

"Only those who visit. So…" Mr Spigott shrugged. "Goodness." He wiped a sheen of sweat from his face, then cleaned his hand on breeches whose worn sides spoke of many hours of honest labour. "My appearance…"

"Becomes you, Mr Spigott." I seized his free hand and shook it heartily. "I congratulate you on your efforts. This is all quite wonderful."

The curate took a step back, as if concerned I might explode with enthusiasm. Somehow, surrounded by his garden, Mr Spigott seemed taller and more assured than usual. Perhaps nature had given him some of her vigour.

"I cannot identify everything," I said. "Would you mind…?"

"I would be delighted." Mr Spigott put down his shears, and we began to walk up the main path.

"Your skill astounds me." I paused to admire the geometrical precision of the box hedges. "You have kept this from us."

"Not deliberately, Mr Bennet, though I rarely speak of it. It is my sanctuary, you see."

"Ah." I nodded. "A library built by nature under man's guidance."

"By nature and much hard work."

"And is that, no—it cannot be." I pointed to a small leafy shrub not yet in bloom. "A buddleia?"

"A gift from Mr Latham after his last visit to The Vineyard at Hammersmith."

I turned up the leaves of the rarity. "Oh dear, aphids already. And plenty of them by the looks of it. Does their presence not bother you? I know of a substance. My friend Elliston swears by it. Or there is soap, but then you will know that."

"They do me no harm," said Mr Spigott. "So I do them none in return. The plants flower, aphids or not. Besides, the ladybirds will soon arrive, and then nature shall decide."

I looked at all the different shades of green, flecked with spots of colour that would soon form a mosaic of flowers. "So many different plants. How do you manage?"

"You will consider me strange, Mr Bennet, but I think of them as my children. Each to be nurtured in its own way to fulfil its potential. Some will bloom under my care; others will show merely that I am not a perfect parent."

We walked on to the orchard, where rough bark and old whorls seemed to give the trees the kind of faces that might scare young children at night.

"This was all here before the cottage," said Mr Spigott. "The apples are suited to baking, or so Agnes—my servant—tells me. The pears I give to old Mr Pyne for his cider press."

"And the cherries?"

"The birds take their fill. Whatever I can rescue goes to the workers on Upper Lane."

I clapped my hands in delight. "You are too good to be true, Mr Spigott. A clergyman who follows the word of Christ. I am all surprise."

"I do not know what you mean."

"Oh, ignore me. I am still in shock at what you have shown me." I gazed back down the garden. "But you have not told me where you gained your skill."

For the first time since my arrival, Mr Spigott looked a little like his usual self.

"My apologies if my curiosity seems impertinent, Mr Spigott."

"No, no, it is just..." The curate frowned. "Perhaps you have heard something of my family?"

"Very little."

"I grew up in Lincolnshire on my family's estate near Saxilby. When not at my books or schooling, I followed the gardeners. By the time I was twelve, I was helping the steward plan extensions to the park." Mr Spigott ran his fingers through his hair. "My uncle, God rest his soul, encouraged my interest and took me with him to many great estates of the north. I learned by observation." He smiled. "And now you wonder why I am here in this tiny curate's cottage."

"The thought had occurred."

"My eldest brother, John, will inherit. This leaves my brother William and myself. One for the army and one..."

"...for the church." I finished the sentence for him. "But why so far from Lincolnshire, if I may ask? Why our small village? Why a position as a curate?"

Mr Spigott bent down to retrieve a twig, which he twisted and broke before throwing the remains into the hedge. "My father and I do not share the same understanding of a career in the church. He sees a profession and prospects, whereas I see responsibility and service."

"And a calling, too? You make a most dedicated impression."

"A calling?" Mr Spigott smiled. "No. But I respect my duty as a clergyman."

"Few discharge that duty with such diligence," I said. "But if the gardens at Saxilby are anything like this one, they must be magnificent indeed."

"They are perhaps much changed since I last saw them."

"You do not visit often, then?"

"I do not visit at all." Mr Spigott's countenance and voice revealed no trace of regret. Instead, his chin rose slightly as if anticipating criticism.

"I see. I am…sorry for you."

"Do not be, Mr Bennet. It is my choice. I do not share my father's opinions on what constitute appropriate pastimes for a *married* gentleman." Mr Spigott grimaced, then shook his head as if casting off a veil. "I miss William, though. He is in Portugal, of course." Some of nature's light now seemed to leave the curate.

"Let us hope the war ends soon," I said. "One advantage of five daughters is that the military will never steal a child away from me."

"Miss Mary Bennet tells me you were once an army man yourself."

Now it was I who bent to pick up a stray twig, picking at the burrs and stripping away the thin bark as I spoke. "I was in the army but never an army man. And only briefly. Long enough to know I preferred mulch to muskets. Now, tell me, what do you give those roses to have them so advanced at this time of year?"

Like all good Englishmen, we talked a little longer of those matters that did not deserve the time we gave them and ignored those that deserved more. We debated the best timber for a fork handle, argued over the right manure for gooseberries, and even wondered when we could expect to see youngsters in the swallow nest. Further talk of families and futures was left to another day, as if the hedges around us refused to let life's concerns spoil the tranquillity of the garden. I would not say that Mr Spigott and I became friends, but we were no longer strangers.

A Chance Encounter

A few days later, and the trees and bushes danced madly to the tune of a spring storm outside my carriage. The poplars remained unbending but still trembled in fear as April rain lashed their leaves. The wildfowl practically fell into their ponds, then scurried away to shelter as if to escape the shame of their inglorious landing. And the people walking into Meryton adopted the universal salute of the wet and windblown—one hand fixed firmly on the head to prevent the loss of a hat or hood.

Inside the carriage, a letter from Lizzy kept me company on my last journey into Meryton before we left for John's.

> *...you will be pleased to hear that Mr Collins does not improve on better acquaintance. He seeks constant approval, though mostly from himself, and is particularly keen to demonstrate the felicity of his position, perhaps in the hope I might express regret at my rejection of his proposal. I will not do so, even if he were to become Archbishop of Canterbury. Though I feel sure he will not attain such a position, for it is not in the power of Lady Catherine to give.*

Rosings grows on me with familiarity, even if its occupants do not. I should willingly endure much hardship to be mistress of such an estate. My favourite walk begins at the great gates that guard the entrance off Hunsford Lane, then takes me along the drive and into the woodlands that hide the house from the road. An open grove at one side of the park attracts little attention and allows for some solitude. I have already observed any number of butterflies on the flowers and shrubs within its borders. Perhaps one day you will visit and see for yourself.

But what of Charlotte, you likely ask? I believe we both questioned the wisdom of her decision, but I find myself revising my opinion at each passing day. Her work within the parish, her animals, and her music all bring contentment. Mr Collins spends much of his time in the garden or visiting his patroness, a state of affairs that can only improve his wife's happiness. In short, I believe her more satisfied than I might have considered possible. Perhaps one's choice of partner is not of such great import to one's degree of happiness?

"If only that were true," I whispered. Lizzy's words sent flickers of the past spinning up again: a hint of a smile and the promise it contained, the rustle of a crimson gown, the brief scent of lavender on the cover of a book. I put away the letter, then thrust my head out of the window, perhaps hoping a moment or two of rain might scour away the memories. Ahead, a familiar figure trudged up the road, wet cloak clinging to his body. My swift rap on the roof of the carriage brought us to a stop.

"Mr Spigott?" I shouted.

The figure turned. "Mr Bennet!" A hesitant smile broke out on the curate's face. "Quite a day we have."

"Might I ask what brings you out in such appalling weather?"

The curate struggled toward me, finding some protection in the lee of the carriage. "Mr Mulcaster's Bible meeting. I promised I would attend."

"He cannot expect anyone to travel to him in this storm." A sudden gust rocked the carriage. Above us, clouds did not so much drift on the wind as flee from it.

"You are likely right, Mr Bennet. I gave my word, though."

"But you have such a long journey ahead of you and so little cover on the lane between Meryton and the Mulcaster estate."

Mr Spigott gazed back down the road that would return him to his cottage home, one hand still pinning down his hat. He nodded to himself before looking up at me. "Did not Paul travel from Antioch to Athens to bring people the word of Christ?"

"That he did," I said. "But without the Hertfordshire weather to contend with. Might I at least take you as far as Meryton? I can drop you at the Flighted Duck."

The grateful curate hauled himself up into the carriage, his cheeks white from exposure. He settled down opposite me and tiny pools of water gathered at his feet. Strands of hair stuck to his face, and I could not help but recall Lydia's assessment of his looks.

"You are most terribly kind, Mr Bennet. I would not normally take advantage of your generosity, but I must concede the wind is proving quite troublesome. Twice it took my hat, and it does not do for a curate to appear without one." Mr

Spigott removed the victim of the gale's eager grasp from his head. "What would people think of me?"

"I am sure their opinion would be no worse than it is now. You truly wish to continue to Mr Mulcaster's?"

"I feel it is my duty."

The curate had a stoicism to him that made me wonder if I could ever guess at his true feelings.

"You use the word 'duty' with regularity, Mr Spigott. It has much to answer for, it seems. Still, I cannot fault a man for the exercise of his profession. You will be glad to return home, though."

"Yes, I suppose." Mr Spigott's look appeared almost wistful.

"Pardon my curiosity, but that does not sound like a man who looks forward to his hearth."

"Forgive me. A curate's living does not extend to much in the way of luxury. Or company. Though I have my garden." Mr Spigott straightened his back even as he shivered. "I have no complaints, of course, for the good work of the church is reward enough."

I leant forward. "If it is company you lack, you are welcome at Longbourn at any time."

My travelling companion showed no reaction to the offer, though he was somewhat busy drying himself with a handkerchief so damp, he may have made his face wetter than before.

"My daughter, Mary, often questions me on matters of religion. Yet I fear I cannot answer her well enough, for I know rather more about geese than gospels."

"I would be happy to offer her instruction and insight where

I can, Mr Bennet." Mr Spigott began to wring out his handkerchief but stopped himself, instead tucking it away on his personage with a wince and a sigh.

"Tell me, do you enjoy reading scripture with Mary?"

"Enjoy?" Mr Spigott looked puzzled. "Scripture is my work. But I very much enjoy discussing her other interests with her."

"Other interests? And those would be? I mean to say, which of her other interests in particular?"

"Mainly her love of gardens." Colour seemed to suddenly return to the curate's cheeks. "If I may be so bold as to say so, she has wonderful ideas."

I gripped the edge of my seat as another gust rattled the coach. "You know, when a fellow lacks companionship at home, there is one alternative that comes to mind. Have you ever considered marriage? Find some soul to share your burden on days such as these?"

Mr Spigott looked away, and his jaw tightened briefly. "I could not impose such a life on any woman."

I cocked my head sharply and waited for the curate to continue.

"My work is my chief occupation and consumes ever more of my time. My garden suffers already, and I am not sure I could properly attend to my duties as husband. More importantly, though, you yourself were most eloquent in your description of the difficulties facing the wife of a clergyman. Your wisdom concerning Mrs Collins's position did not go unheeded."

"It did not?"

"No, sir. And I am grateful for your words. They have confirmed my own feelings on this matter."

"Really? Oh dear." I bit my lower lip. "Now, Mr Spigott, while it is true that Mrs Collins faces some not inconsiderable challenges, this has less to do with her husband's occupation and more to do with his…well, particular circumstances. Besides, is it not the express wish of the church that rectors and curates set the example of matrimony in their parish?"

"It is." Mr Spigott pushed the wet hair back from his face and rubbed at his forehead. "The bishop has been quite clear on that matter. Yet I cannot in all good conscience condemn any gentleman's daughter to the trials of such a life."

"Pardon me for saying so, but your wedded colleagues do not seem to share your concerns."

"We must all answer to our own consciences, Mr Bennet."

"And to God, Mr Spigott. You must answer to your God." It was time to bring out the weapons of education, beginning with a carefully aimed shot of Genesis. "Your selflessness does you honour, but does not the Bible say 'It is not good for the man to be alone. I will make a helper who is just right for him?' No?"

"Ah, but I am not alone." Mr Spigott paused for a moment, then raised his finger. "It is written 'Behold, God is my helper; The Lord is the sustainer of my soul.' Psalm 54, if you please."

I turned to Proverbs for my next attack. "And yet, 'He who finds a wife finds what is good and receives favour from the Lord,' does he not?"

Mr Spigott said nothing. Outside, the dark clouds and rain had left Meryton drab and faded, like a landscape painting abandoned in a damp attic. Fresh mud peppered the walls and houses along the road that would take us to the square.

"How could I find favour with the Lord," said Mr Spigott,

eventually, "knowing what kind of life I would give a wife? A life that may be inadequate both materially and in terms of my attentiveness? And, Mr Bennet, who would wish to marry a poor creature like myself?"

"My dear Mr Spigott, you are a man of many qualities. We have established that you are dutiful. Loyal, too, I think. And kind. You may be surprised where you find love. It is a strange thing. For instance, you may have thought it lost to you. Gone. Absent. And yet, years later, you realise it has always been there. In your heart. Not lost, merely ignored." I rubbed the tips of my forefingers together and closed my eyes.

"Forgive me, Mr Bennet, I am not quite certain of your meaning."

I blinked away the memories. "Neither am I. My apologies. I will think on your words. As I said, I am no master of scripture."

Ahead of us, the Flighted Duck came into view, its sign swinging from side to side in welcome, like the tail of a dog on its master's return.

"I shall be some time in the inn," I said. "There is much to discuss with my friends. My driver will take you on to Mr Mulcaster's."

"I could not—"

"You could and you shall. I will not hear of anything different."

As the horses pulled away, I stood alone, the retreating carriage taking me back through the years again until a firm hand on my arm caught my attention.

"Good God, Bennet," said Fielding. "Whatever are you doing, standing quite still in all this wind and rain? Let us go inside at once. Are you unwell?"

"I am perfectly well." We moved under the awning above the inn's entrance. "I was merely distracted by a thought."

I looked back from the doorway and wondered if carriages ever brought good news.

"It must have been a matter of great import to keep you outside like that. Come along, now." Fielding tugged at my sleeve. "Port and cake await."

On Marriage

"Gentlemen, gentlemen, if you please." My words brought an end to the noise at the table, if not at the window, where the rain seemed determined to break through the glass. "There is much for us to do. We have nets to repair." My audience nodded. "Collecting jars to wash." More nods. "Cake to be eaten." Jackson clapped his approval. "Port to be drunk." Mutterings of pleasure filled the room. "And..."

"Go on," said Fielding.

"A bachelor to be guided toward the safe and welcoming harbour of matrimony." My raised glass met only silence.

Eventually, Jackson spoke. "Again, Bennet?"

"It was all well and good helping your Mr Barton out," said Stanhope. "I do not deny that I took great pleasure from his success. But we should not make a habit of it."

"Absolutely not." Elliston glared at me. "When my wife heard the tale, she accused me of hiding a romantic inclination from her. As Stanhope said, we all enjoyed seeing Mr Barton's efforts bear fruit. But I have no wish to raise certain expectations in Mrs Elliston. She has already suggested we take carriage rides for no purpose other than to spend time with each other." He looked at us all one by one. "I jest not, gentlemen."

"My wife," said Stanhope, "has actually taken to putting her arm in mine after Sunday services."

Elliston edged his chair just a little further away from Stanhope.

"Come now." Fielding looked at us over his spectacles like an amused schoolmaster. "Let us not be hasty. As I recall, and as you have yourselves admitted, we did all rather relish the challenge. You, Jackson—it was your intervention that sent Bennet here off to London where he first made contact with the future Mrs Barton. And you, Stanhope—I recall you visiting Longbourn without rhyme or reason merely so you could get a glimpse of the lady. Do you deny it?"

Stanhope gave a reluctant shake of the head. "I do not." He glanced around at our little group. "And, if truth be known, well, I quite enjoy having my wife on my arm."

"Steady on," said Elliston. "This is Meryton, not London. We should not let standards slip."

"Let us at least give Bennet a chance to explain himself." Fielding gestured to me. "Continue, my friend. Of which bachelor do you speak?"

"Our very own Mr Spigott." I waited until the laughing had stopped and found myself quoting Mary. "What, pray, is wrong with Mr Spigott?"

Fielding rested a hand on my arm. "There is nothing *wrong* with him, Bennet. Nothing at all. A decent man, from what I hear. Godfearing and sensible. Not a man of means, though, and—how shall I put it?—not of a cut that would excite immediate interest from the ladies."

"Plain fellow and poor," said Jackson. "We would enter battle naked and with no weapon."

A brief, but unsettling, consideration of my old army comrade without clothes prompted me to take a large sip of port.

"Nobody has a bad word to say of him," I said. "Though, if truth be told, nobody has *any* word to say of him. Yet I have spoken to Mr Spigott myself and found him to be, well, a fine sort of a fellow. You should see his garden; it puts all of ours to shame. He is as a curate should be. And by being so, he presents himself badly for he does not seek attention."

"Still does not make him handsome." Jackson reached for a piece of cake. "Or wealthy."

"You gave John Barton little chance either, Jackson. Yet here I am, off to visit him and his dear wife in Gloucestershire. You are unfair to Mr Spigott." I folded my arms.

Fielding opened a fresh bottle of port. "But why him?" he said as he poured more ruby joy into our glasses. "Young Barton was an old family friend, and you owed a debt of honour there. But this curate? What is he to you?"

"Ah. There I must confess to a personal interest. Mr Spigott would make a promising match for my daughter, Mary. As such, the matter of his income falls aside, for my wife and I have no objection on that front. Mary has no fortune to her name to attract a better kind of suitor. But she is not unintelligent. Perhaps overly fond of certain religions pamphlets, though that would serve her well with a man like Mr Spigott. I believe they might find happiness together. I also believe there already exists a degree of affection between the two, though neither has said as much directly. The seed of love has certainly grown in less promising soil. But it needs nurturing, particularly since neither party seems inclined to romance or excesses of emotion. They need...encouragement."

"You say Mr Spigott has some fondness for your daughter?" said Fielding.

"I believe so."

"Then where is the problem? All you need do is let nature take its course. Perhaps encourage him to visit often." Fielding's words drew nods from the others.

"Well, yes, they have already spent time in each other's company. Unfortunately, Mr Spigott considers the joys of marriage insufficient to compensate for the burdens placed on a curate's wife."

"He is a man of the church." Stanhope shrugged. "Marriage is practically a requirement of the profession."

"I have told him that." I sighed. "He simply insists on sparing a woman the difficulties of a clerical life."

"What fool gave him the idea that a woman might find such a life difficult?" said Fielding. He shook his head and sighed at my sheepish grin.

"Fortunately, Mr Spigott cannot be more than seven-and-twenty and, therefore, not yet fixed in his ways," I said. "All we need do to change his mind is persuade him of the overwhelming benefits of marriage. I thought I might invite him along to one of our meetings. Then you could all impress upon him the pleasures of wedded life."

A general grumbling filled the room.

"You ask much of us, Bennet. Especially of our friend here."

Elliston nodded toward Jackson. "He has no wife."

"Yes, why is that, Jackson?" asked Stanhope. "Must be enough ladies keen to share the riches of your estate."

Jackson shrugged. "Never felt the need."

"Really?" Stanhope jerked his head back an inch or two.

"Let us stick to the matter in hand," said Fielding with more severity than seemed necessary. "This is all perfect nonsense. Your only challenge, Bennet, is to help Mr Spigott and Miss Mary to grow that seed of theirs."

"We shall cross that particular bridge when we come to it. First, we place him on the road to matrimony, then we ensure it leads to my daughter." I tapped my glass with a knife. "Let us make a list. Suggestions, please, gentlemen. The benefits of marriage…"

Nobody spoke. Elliston sat with his brow furrowed and his tongue stuck out one side of his mouth. Stanhope pursed his lips and drummed his fingers on the tabletop. Fielding folded his arms and looked at me as if I were a puppy next to a smashed vase. As for Jackson, he simply continued his skirmish with the cake; such an encounter could only have one victor.

"Well, there is the obvious one," I said.

Feet shuffled and cheeks turned red. "Now, then, Bennet." Elliston waved a finger at me. "Let us not allow this meeting to descend into dissolute conversation."

"Some things are best not discussed in society." Stanhope regarded me with something approaching disappointment. "At least not in *this* society."

"Really, gentlemen." I peered at them all individually shaking my head. "I meant management of the household affairs."

A round of polite coughing spread quickly through the room.

"Ah, yes, of course you did." Relief replaced affront on Elliston's face.

"My dear friends." Fielding spread his arms out wide. "Do we really find it necessary to draw up such a list? The history of England is full of men who declared themselves committed bachelors only to find themselves married. And what caused those bachelors to withdraw their objection? The intervention of love. If I know your Mary, Bennet, she is not one for putting herself forward or presenting herself in a particularly favourable light. I have a high regard for her for that. I suspect Mr Spigott is much the same. Too modest and humble for his own good. That is the problem you must address."

"Very well, I shall think on it," I said. "And perhaps see what might be done with Mary on my return from Gloucestershire."

~ ~ ~

"So, you are to visit the Bartons, after all?" Fielding raised an eyebrow as he handed me another glass of port at our traditional tête-à-tête after the society meeting. He then pulled out a bulging napkin from under his chair and unfolded it to reveal a few slices of seed cake. "I took the precaution of hiding some until the others had gone. You know Jackson. It is a matter of honour for him to leave no plate unemptied."

"You are a wise fellow," I said. "Too wise for your own good, sometimes. But to answer your question, yes, we leave the day after tomorrow."

"And what precipitated the change of heart?"

"There was truth to your words the last time we met. If I am honest, though, the decision was a spontaneous one. Longbourn lacks the comfort of good conversation, and I can only remain locked away in my rooms for so long. So, to Gloucestershire we shall go."

Fielding steepled his fingers. "And your concerns about Mrs Barton's mother?"

"My concerns remain. But I am no foolish young man. Uncomfortable it may be, should she be there, but I may surely survive a few days in the company of one I…"

"Yes?" said Fielding.

"You know what I mean." I helped myself to the cake, then crumpled up the napkin and threw it at my friend, receiving a thoroughly rewarding look of surprise and mild amusement in return. "Fielding, I hope you realise you are the most fortunate of men. There is far more to your marriage than convenience."

"Well." My friend shifted in his seat.

"Our little group may pretend otherwise, but we all envy you and your wife."

Fielding smiled and looked out the window at the town square beyond. "We met at Weintraub's, you know. I am sure I must have told you that. Not long after my return from…you know. It was old Weintraub in the store back then. I was looking over some reds my father wished to purchase. He never trusted anyone else on such matters. 'Servants and horses, my dear boy. Food and fabrics,' he used to say to me. 'Can put 'em all in the hands of others. But wine—that is far too important to leave to anyone else.' He was not wrong." My friend settled back into his seat. "Penelope had accompanied her father, but he had stepped outside to accost some acquaintance. She was not a pretty woman."

"Fielding!" I raised my hands in gentlemanly protest.

"Ah, she was not handsome, and nor was I. There we were equals. You know how we were in those days, drunk with the relief of peace and safety. She proved resistant to my gallant talk and ridiculous attempts to impress her. But she listened to me, and she treated Mr Weintraub with respect and kindness. Do you recall how he struggled with his sight? You would always have to check the colour of the wine before leaving. Love is a mysterious fellow, Bennet. I do believe I loved her within moments of first clapping eyes on her."

I settled back into my chair. "I do not recall where I first met Mrs Bennet." Tapping the table with my finger did little to jog my memory. "At some ball, perhaps. Meryton, maybe. Or...well, it does not matter. Now she *was* pretty, that I do remember. Far too pretty, as it turned out. But you cannot blame a moth for being drawn to the flame, eh?"

"And Mrs Hayter?" The hint of a smile spoiled the look of innocence on Fielding's face.

"Abigail?" I took a few moments to recollect, though I did not need them. "Oh, Bath, presumably. I hardly recall the details." My voice trailed off as I heard again the rustle of carriage wheels on Bond Street and the urgings of my companion, Mr Merryweather. He had wanted to get back to my lodgings so we could start reading the books we had just borrowed. She stood there with her mother, wearing a bonnet trimmed in a blue that matched her eyes. It began to rain. Only slightly, though—not enough to scare us all indoors. I dropped my book as we passed each other, and she picked it up. "Cowper?" she said. "You do not look like a man of poetry, sir."

My fingers rubbed together, recalling the touch of her glove against mine as she handed me my book. "No, as I say, I cannot remember the details."

"Poor fellow, your memory is shot to pieces." My friend reached over and patted me gently on the arm.

"Yes, very well, thank you, Fielding. You have tricked me again into remembrance. Let us talk of other matters better suited to two gentlemen of age and distinction. Or at least of age. Let us speak no more of love. It does not do to talk of food in front of a hungry man. But first, take your glass in hand and wish me luck. By the end of the week, I shall be in Gloucestershire."

Rudford

"We must be there soon," I said. "It is not such a large estate. At least not that I remember. Did it always take so long to reach the house?"

My impatience was of my own making, since we had made quick time up the drive leading from the small lodge, pausing only briefly while a group of labourers cleared away the trimmings from a hedgerow that had strayed too close to the road.

"Do pull your head in, husband. My nerves cannot stand it." Mrs Bennet tugged ineffectively at my coat. "Suppose you were to hit a tree and die? By the time we returned home, Mr and Mrs Collins would have moved in, and oh, it does not bear thinking about!"

"Then do not," I said.

"They will turn us out as soon as possible," continued my wife. "Mr Collins will be making alterations before you are cold in your grave. Did you see how he examined the staircase, girls, the last time he visited?" Neither Mary, Kitty, or Lydia answered, dulled into silence by the long journey and the early start from the inn. My wife dabbed at her eyes with a handkerchief. "Such a cruel world that lets us suffer, so. If only Mr Bingley had made Jane an offer. If only you had forced Lizzy to accept Mr Collins."

"I am not dead yet, my dear. Though the idea begins to appeal. Ah, here we are."

It was not the sight I had anticipated. Scaffolding covered half the west side of the house, the courtyard below it full of barrels, barrows, and pallets, each heaving with stone, tiles, tools, or ironware. Oiled canvasses hid some containers from view and, presumably, from any rain. I caught my breath at a couple of carriages to the east and found myself wondering if any of them might suit a visiting lady from Bath.

We had just disembarked, the three girls and Mrs Bennet now gawping like young children at the circus, when a cry reached us from the main entrance to the house.

A young man leapt across the courtyard, as if crossing a river on stepping stones. As he reached us, he slowed, stopped, and took a deep, theatrical bow, which I returned with all the aplomb of a seasoned Shakespearean actor. John's face seemed fuller and his clothes newer than I remembered, though he still wore his cravat with a reassuring disregard for precise folds. Without thinking, I embraced him, surprising myself and all those around me.

"My apologies, John, but you cannot imagine how good it is to see you again."

"The feeling is entirely mutual. Welcome to Rudford, Mr Bennet, Mrs Bennet. Miss Mary, Miss Catherine, and Miss Lydia, too. Anne will be out in but a moment." My friend looked back in the direction of the house. "Ah, here she is already."

"Mr and Mrs Bennet. And Mary, Kitty, Lydia. You are all welcome to our home." Mrs Barton glided toward us with arms outstretched. "I have given you the best rooms, though you must not tell any of the other guests."

"Oh, you are too generous," said my wife. "Other guests, you say?"

"Why, yes, Mrs Bennet. We have one bachelor here already and more to arrive before you leave." Mrs Barton winked at me.

"Well, I am sure it is all the same to us, whoever they might be," said Mrs Bennet. "Come along, girls. Let us go inside. It does not do to stand around like this. Bachelors, Mrs Barton?"

"Lord Davenport, for example," said John's wife.

"*Lord* Davenport?" My wife fanned herself with a gloved hand.

"Mrs Barton," I said. "You know, I find it hard not to call you Miss Hayter. I bring greetings from my friends at the Society. They still enjoy hearing the tale of your courtship."

"Which they are entitled to hear, given the role they played within it," said Mrs Barton. "We have so looked forward to your visit. We may at last thank you properly for all that you did for us."

"As I recall, most of what I did was done unwittingly and at your command," I said.

"Nonsense." Mrs Barton placed her arm in mine and began to walk me back to the house. Her familiarity sent a tremor coursing up my arm.

The rest of my family rushed forward eagerly, like hounds on the chase—all except Mary, who kept pace with John, Mrs Barton, and myself.

"You and Lizzy led John and me in a merry dance through Bath and Meryton." I walked awkwardly, unused to the touch of a young lady who did not share my surname. "Is he proving worth the effort?"

"I am not minded to exchange him just yet." Mrs Barton locked eyes with her husband, a flicker of a smile on both their faces.

"My dear," said John, "why don't you go inside with the ladies? I would like a few moments with Mr Bennet." His wife nodded and turned her attentions to Mrs Bennet and my daughters.

"Is something amiss, John?" I said, after the others had all moved far away from us. "You are both well, I hope?"

"Quite well. There is simply a matter I wished to talk to you about in private. Nothing alarming, I assure you. But still. Shall we walk?"

John took me along the front of the house, where we picked our way through the wreckage of construction.

"No workers?" I pointed at the abandoned tools of a stonemason.

"Sent away until the guests leave. A little peace and quiet outside is not unwelcome, even if we may not have it inside."

"You have great plans, it would seem."

"Long overdue improvements made possible by the removal of long overdue debts. Mrs Hayter was very generous."

The name seemed to cast a spell of silence over the two of us that lingered until we reached a small square of manicured bushes that rose from beds of gravel and marked the edges of a wood.

John stopped, turned to me, and scratched his head. "I

thought we might extend the path further into the trees." He pointed into the thicket of oak, birch, and beech. "Thin it all out a little. Put in benches. Perhaps some sculptures."

"Out with it, John," I said. "Say what you must say."

"Very well." My friend clasped his hands together. "Now, you must believe me when I tell you that my question is meant with the best of intentions. God knows I have burdened your goodwill enough ever since that day in the Flighted Duck. Anyway, you once told me at Longbourn that meeting Mrs Hayter in Bath had been..." John dipped his head from side to side. "Uncomfortable. That you once thought of her as I do of Anne."

"Go on."

"If you were to see her again—spend time with her—would it be..." John grimaced.

"Challenging?" I said. "Difficult? Unpleasant? Yes, most likely all of these things."

"Oh."

John opened his mouth as if to speak again, but no words came out.

"She is here, then?" I said.

"Yes. Though we did not expect her."

For a moment or two, I stopped breathing, frozen like a soldier in those few seconds between the firing of the enemy's cannon and the explosion of the shot. I took a deep breath to calm the competing flurry of emotions that threatened to flare up inside me.

"Well, it would be difficult, John, but not unbearable." I heard my words, but they seemed to come from someone else.

"My encounter in Bath with Mrs Hayter was a little disconcerting. But I am a married man. An old one, too. I have left the past behind." I clapped him on the shoulder and offered what I hoped he would take to be a reassuring smile.

"Excellent," he said. "Then you will not mind that she has a gentleman with her."

"What?" I spoke louder than intended.

John eyed me carefully. "Lord Davenport. My wife mentioned him."

"A friend?"

"A companion of sorts. To be frank, I am not sure myself."

"Is he...? Are they...?" My head sunk. "Pay me no heed, John. Who Mrs Hayter chooses to spend her time with is none of my business. We are not connected in any way or form."

We stood, now, at the threshold of topiary and woodland, poised between order and chaos, where man and nature were just a step—and a low hedge—apart.

"If I might be so bold, Mr Bennet, it seems the past is not so far behind you as you wish."

"Yes, well, it never is, John, whatever people may claim." My sigh felt old and worn. "Forgive me—I shall give nobody cause for concern. You may rely on me."

"Of course. But you may like to know..." John glanced about him before continuing. "Lord Davenport is a bit of a fool. He is all talk and little else."

"Good," I said. "I mean, poor fellow. And poor Mrs Hayter." With our laughter, the tension fled from our conversation as swiftly as a startled pheasant. "My apologies, John, for the delay in responding to your invitation. It was due to nothing but my own indolence. Not to mention cowardice. But I am here, now. And to find you and Mrs Barton so obviously happy, well, it brings me much pleasure. I have missed you both. You stand forever high in my estimation, my dear friend, and if a few uncomfortable moments with Mrs Hayter are the price to pay for seeing you again, then so be it."

"The pleasure in your visit is all mine, Mr Bennet." John's eyes seemed ready to burst with delight and anticipation. "I owe all my happiness to you and hope to pay some of the debt with company and entertainment during your stay."

"Entertainment?"

"Yes. I thought we might walk the estate tomorrow." John pointed to a small gate further up the hedge. "Then perhaps a trip to Gloucester."

"Fine suggestions," I said.

"Then a dance the following evening with some of local society."

"Ah." I picked up some gravel and pretended to throw it at my young companion. "Not so fine a suggestion. It seems I misjudged our friendship after all. I might forgive you for Mrs Hayter's presence, but dancing? And people?"

Confusion crawled its way across John's face. "I do not understand. Your letter included an express wish for just such an occasion. Did you not write 'Mrs Bennet respectfully asks that you hold a ball?' I will not go so far as that, but I trust a dance will suit her just as well."

"The perils of written communication." I juggled the gravel in my hand. "I did not for a moment imagine you would take me seriously."

"I always take you seriously, Mr Bennet."

"Then you are as much of a fool as Lord Davenport. Still, my wife will certainly be pleased. As will my daughters—two of them, at any rate. And I daresay you and I shall survive the ordeal. In fact, the only way you could make Mrs Bennet happier is to say that half a dozen bachelors will attend."

"There may be as many as eight."

"Eight? She will faint with excitement. And Kitty and Lydia will have even more excuse to embarrass me." I gave my friend my most earnest look. "Do not say there are officers."

"No officers."

"Well, that is something." I dropped the stones and brushed the dust from my hands. "Come, my journey was long, and the others will begin to worry. Let me see this home of yours and face whatever challenges might lurk within. How much must have changed inside since my last visit." I turned to wander back through the clipped lines of the bushes.

A deeper truth now fought its way into my consciousness as John and I reached Rudford's paved forecourt. For along with fear, shame, and guilt came another emotion, one driven by an old love that resisted all that honour, loyalty, logic, and faith could bring against it: longing. The confusion of feelings proved almost overwhelming. So, I did as all good Englishmen do in troubled moments and affected an air of implacable disinterest.

Mrs Barton sat on the steps leading up to the main entrance of the house but stood and walked toward us as we approached. "You have told him?" she asked.

"I have," said John.

Mrs Barton placed a hand on my arm. "Husband, would you

go on and see to Lord Davenport? He has another problem he needs your counsel on. I will escort dear Mr Bennet inside."

John walked on, but I did not follow.

"Your husband seems well." I made no attempt to move, my feet seemingly stranded in the quicksand between dread and desire.

"He is." Mrs Barton released my arm and tipped her head to one side, a disarming smile playing across her face as if she faced a shy child. "We are blessed, Mr Bennet. All that remains to complete our happiness is for him to concede that I am right in all matters."

I recalled their initial meeting in Bath, a teashop conversation full of misunderstanding and disagreement that proved the first clumsy steps on a path to the altar.

"You still argue then?" I said.

"About most everything. Though on one matter we are agreed."

"Neither of you can abide Wordsworth."

"You remembered!" Mrs Barton's smile was now one of delight.

"I did not think you would ever find common ground. Let alone a future together. It teaches one to hope. I believe you will both enjoy a long and pleasant marriage."

"A belief I share. Did you know we are planning a trip to visit John's father in Vienna? Perhaps in a summer or two, depending." Mrs Barton's hand caressed her waist for a moment, and she glanced up at a window I knew looked out from the old nursery rooms.

"Rudford brings back many memories," I said.

"John told me you and your family often visited when his mother was still alive. I wish I might have met her."

"She would have approved of you; of that I am certain. And not just because you have brought John such joy." Mrs Barton seemed to glow at my words.

A distant neigh reminded me of Fielding's words and John's painting back at Longbourn, the thoughts drawing a sigh from my lips.

"It is time to get back on the horse." I waved toward the house. "Shall we go in?"

"If that is acceptable?"

"My dear Mrs Barton, your concern does you credit. But I cannot stay out here for five days."

John's wife reached up, adjusted my cravat, then stepped back. "There, *now* we may go in."

We both turned to find a woman had appeared at the door.

"My dear James, how wonderful to see you again."

My foot caught on a flagstone, almost sending me stumbling to the ground. Mrs Barton reached out quickly and kept me upright, though. I pulled myself up straight, put something resembling a smile on my face, and failed miserably to look Abigail in the eyes.

"Abigail…Mrs Hayter…yes…that is…I mean to say, a pleasure to see you again, too."

"Such a poet with words, James. Are you well? You seem to have some difficulty lifting your head."

"Quite well, quite well."

I looked up. Abigail stood there, arms folded, head angled to one side in that challenging way of hers.

My mother used to say there is beauty in everyone, if you look hard enough for it. However, some are blessed with a beauty that cannot be hidden, nor stolen by age. The kind that carries off a man's reason and leaves him ignorant of his loss. As my eyes finally met Abigail's, I knew this visit could not end well.

"There you are!" My wife called from the entranceway and bustled down the steps. "You have found him, Mrs Hayter, how clever of you. You must come and see the house, Mr Bennet. So many improvements! I am filled with ideas. And your Lord Davenport, Mrs Hayter—what a delightful gentleman he is. I feel sure we shall all become very well acquainted."

Tea and Pigs

"You have met Lord Davenport, then, Mrs Bennet?" I descended the stairs from my room after changing. My clothes exuded an air of assured confidence, even if their wearer did not.

"Oh, indeed," said my wife. "Such a pleasant man. He is about your age, so quite old." Her playful slap on my arm stung more than it should have. "He suffers a little from rheumatic infirmity, so will surely wish a young wife to care for him. Kitty will suit him better than Lydia, I think. They say he has six thousand a year."

It remained a mystery to me how my wife knew so much about the finances and character of people she had barely met. If my passing left her impecunious, she could always find useful employment in a bank.

"You were right to bring us to Rudford," continued Mrs Bennet. "What a good father you are! To think I thought you uncaring of our future. Mrs Hayter is a very fine woman, too. I wish we had seen more of her in Bath. Though she seems rather close to Lord Davenport. We should not let either of them out of our sight. Come along." My wife walked away with something approaching a flounce. "We are expected for tea."

The inside of the house had changed greatly since my previous visit. A sense of delight coursed through the place that had little to do with the fresh carpets from Bristol or new furnishings from London.

As it turned out, the word "tea" had clearly felt too constrained by a mere three letters and become an early dinner of baked fish, roast beef and pork, bread, and a selection of pastries that would have set Jackson quivering in anticipation. Footmen fidgeted in their uniforms, while hushed conversations beyond the door leading to the kitchens also spoke of the uncertainty of new staff.

John sat at the head of a table clearly arranged under Mrs Bennet's mystical influence. Kitty occupied the most promising position, seated between John and Lord Davenport, with Abigail and Mrs Barton completing that side of the table. Opposite them, Mary sat between John and my wife, with Lydia perched at the far end across from Mrs Barton. This left me directly opposite Abigail. If dark magic had placed Kitty so fortuitously, then I would pay Satan's price.

Lord Davenport bore all the tell-tale signs of an English gentleman brought up on overindulgence—his cheeks florid, his waist expansive, his mind empty. Still, he endeared himself to me with his enthusiastic, if vacuous, conversation; I was not in the mood for any intellectual discussion, and Lord Davenport proved an able ally in that regard.

"Mrs Hayter, you must visit us at Bransfield Court. We have the finest stock in the country. My man, Wilberforce, now he knows his pigs. And Mrs White is a fine cook. We'll have a porker trussed and stuffed for you."

"What lady could resist such an offer?" said Abigail. "It sounds like heaven."

I avoided looking at Abigail as she spoke, wary of revealing more than I cared to.

"Excellent," said Lord Davenport. "Excellent!"

"Do tell us more about Bransfield." My wife began to circle her prey. "Is it a large estate?"

"Large enough, Mrs Bennet. The times are fortunate—I get an excellent price for my wheat."

"Many folk struggle to pay for bread." This was the first time Mary had spoken at the table. "Few benefit from higher wheat prices."

"Happily, I am one of them." Lord Davenport raised his glass, apparently oblivious to Mary's implied criticism.

"Lord, Mary, what care we for the price of bread?" Lydia poked at her food like an overfed crow and made no attempt to hide a yawn.

"Miss Bennet makes a fair point," said Abigail. "War begets further hardship, and so we must live in fear of a popular uprising."

"I see no cause for complaint in Hertfordshire." My wife helped herself to some fish. "Our servants grow fatter by the day. Cook will require a bigger apron soon."

"Longbourn is a little piece of paradise, Mrs Bennet," said Mrs Barton, frowning at her mother.

"The men of power and wealth wring their hands and argue," continued Abigail. "But a lasting solution escapes us. Like many men, they presumably hope a problem ignored is a problem solved."

I chanced a look at Abigail as she spoke and found her staring directly at me, causing me to avert my eyes like some embarrassed child caught spying on his betters.

"London is the problem, Mrs Hayter." Lord Davenport now waved his glass about him. "Too many distractions for politics. Full of clubs and what not. Tell me, Mr Bennet, do you ever get down to the capital?"

"Not if I can help it."

"Oh, but you must, sir! Join me at the Ramsden for a few rounds of cards and a flutter or two, eh? Take in a dancing show."

"I fear such days are beyond me now, Lord Davenport. Perhaps if I were single. I must pursue more appropriate pastimes for a married man."

My words almost mirrored those of Mr Spigott, spoken a few days earlier. For a while, the conversation continued without me as I found myself ensnared by the memory of my encounter with him in his garden.

I think of them as my children. Each to be nurtured in its own way to fulfil its potential. Some will bloom under my care; others will show merely that I am not a perfect parent.

So had the curate spoken, a man who truly understood duty and, it seemed, parenthood. I thought of Jane and Lizzy, two young women of astonishing character. One all grace, kindness, and beauty, the other all sharp wit, intelligence, and secret charm. I studied Mary, who sat primly, her eyes focused as if reading an imaginary book. Opposite Mary, Kitty ate clumsily but earnestly, her silliness an honest one, bereft of malice. As for Lydia, I could not call her character bad, nor could I call it good.

Next to me, Mrs Bennet continued to work her way through her food, mouth in constant motion with chewing and chatter, eyes truly alert only when talk of fashion, men, and society came to the fore.

If I do not address such matters with urgency, Mr Bennet, then who shall?

Whatever our past failings, my wife, at least, continued to work for her daughters and their future, however ineffectually.

On the other side of the table, Abigail ate slowly, listened acutely, coaxed conversation from those around her, and offered words of wisdom mixed with those designed to tease and provoke. And she often sought to draw a reluctant Mary into the discussion.

I looked from my wife to Abigail and back again, thought of a kindly curate back in Longbourn, and knew then where *my* duty lay—not with my heart.

"Tell me, dear Mr Bennet," said Mrs Barton. "With the change of season, will you be out collecting butterflies?"

"Butterflies?" said Abigail. "Chasing beauties across heath and meadow? It has a familiar ring to it."

"Well now, Mrs Barton. As it happens, the Society has a small trip to Dorking planned in August for that very purpose. I have resolved, however, not to bring back any captives."

"Why ever that, husband?" My wife squeezed the words out between mouthfuls of pastry.

"Something I was told by a young lady changed my opinion on such matters. I shall appreciate nature's grace and charm at a distance."

Mrs Barton nodded at my answer, her broad smile ample compensation for any number of pinned butterflies.

"I can quite understand your reluctance," said Abigail. "Once captured, pretty things fade, do they not?"

"On the contrary, Mrs Hayter." I took hold of my glass of wine with both hands. "My butterflies at home still bring me considerable joy. I merely have no wish to add to their number."

My eyes met Abigail's across the table but gave no quarter this time; perhaps the wine gave some strength to my resolve.

"I wonder whether you do not find more pleasure in those butterflies that remain free." Abigail took a sip from her glass, her plate of food still largely untouched. "Those that elude you and your little net."

"Little?" squealed my wife. "Why, Mrs Hayter, you should see his study. It is filled with nets of such a size. He and his friends order more muslin than my girls." Laughter echoed around the table either side of Abigail and me.

"The butterflies that retain their freedom often do so for good reason." I still held Abigail's gaze. "Perhaps there is some flaw that makes them less attractive to the collector."

"Or perhaps," said Abigail, "they are simply too clever for you."

"Good luck to you, sir." Lord Davenport waved a knife in my direction. "I cannot say that butterflies excite me, but I would never stand between a man and his interests. I prefer my animals large, roasted, and covered in gravy."

"Talking of butterflies, how are the gentlemen of your natural history society, Mr Bennet?" said Mrs Barton.

"All well. They remember your wedding fondly, particularly the cake."

"You did not introduce me to them that day," said Abigail. "It was remiss of you. I should have liked to have met your friends. The company a gentleman keeps says so much about his character."

"The same might be said about a lady." I turned my head toward Abigail's neighbour. "Tell us more about your pigs, Lord Davenport. Berkshires?"

"Of course. Though Wilberforce wants me to get new stock in from Leicestershire. You have pigs here at Rudford, Barton?"

"We're eating one now." John pointed down the table at a tray piled high with crisp porcine delights.

"You are such a kind man, John," said my wife. "If only my own daughters were as fortunate as yours, Mrs Hayter. But we live in hope." Mrs Bennet cast her eye about the room, as if she might spot a willing bachelor sitting undiscovered in a corner somewhere.

"Let us not trouble the table with tales of daughters and marriage, Mrs Bennet," I said. "I am sure Mrs Hayter has no wish to learn of Hertfordshire intrigues."

"Well, I hope the county bachelors behave as they should," said Abigail. "There is nothing worse than a man who promises more than he delivers."

"Is that not the very definition of a man?" Mrs Barton smiled as she spoke.

"Perhaps women demand more of us than we have to give."

I looked up the table at our host. "John, what say you?"

My friend thought for a moment before answering. "If I promise more than I deliver, then it is only through a wish to please my wife. Though what a man promises and what a woman hears may be two entirely different things."

"Wise words," I said.

"Wise or not, I cannot say I understood any of them, but I'll drink to them all the same." Lord Davenport raised his glass again.

"Men and their drink." Abigail pushed her own glass away from her. "They say some prefer it to their own wives. What do men see in port and brandy, Mr Bennet?"

"Their own reflection, mostly, Mrs Hayter. Though drink does not judge us or oblige us to make conversation. It takes us as we are. And port does go rather well with a fine stilton. For my part, I would not choose drink over my wife. I would not choose anything over my wife."

"Oh, Mr Bennet!" said the subject of my compliment. "You have had too much wine!"

I had not had nearly enough.

Revisiting the Past

Rudford sat on a small plateau, its gardens bounded by woodland that led down a slope to a patchwork of meadows, pastures, and field crops, all stitched together with hedgerows. The house might have looked like some ancient hill fort if viewed from above, surrounded as it was by a natural palisade of timber. A hearty breakfast and fresh morning air had cleared my head of the previous day's indulgences, and I stood on the path that marked the boundary between trees and grassland. In the distance, the season had brought forth farmers and livestock from their winter shelter, and both busied themselves with the time-honoured tasks that would eventually draw vegetables, meat, and grain from Gloucestershire's rich soils.

"Do you mind if we visit the Sackrees, tenants of mine out on the edge of the estate? It is some walk." John used his hand to shade his eyes from the bright sun.

"The longer the walk," I said, "the more content I shall be."

"If I did not know better, I might think you sought to avoid the house."

"As you well know, it is not the house I wish to avoid, but the people in it."

"One person in particular?"

"You saw what happened at dinner last night."

"I did. It reminded me of some ancient wall paintings I once viewed in Italy. We should put you both in an amphitheatre and give you each a gladius." John feigned a sword fight, swinging his arm with enthusiasm.

"Yes, all very amusing I'm sure. Though at least then I might call on the blessing of the Roman gods. Janus, in particular, might be quite sympathetic to my situation."

As we walked, memories of my previous visits to Rudford rose and fell unbidden: the laughter of John as a small boy, delighted by the stick I found for him; the firm touch of his mother's hand on mine, as she implored me to look after her husband; the scent of jasmine that hung about her. One memory held its ground: John waving to us as we left, his mother's hand resting on his young shoulders. Henry's arms had been wrapped around his wife—a futile gesture built of love and defiance, as if his own will and body might defy fate's curse. "It will not be long," my wife had said. I had kept silent, not wishing to acknowledge the truth.

The gruff call of a crow jolted me back to the present, and a good hour later we reached the Sackrees. Their farm barely deserved the name, being little more than a cottage, two small fields, and a pigsty. I remained outside, perched on a low wall, taking the occasional sip of water from a bottle, and watching a blackbird grub for worms with the patience and dedication of a young mother.

"I wonder that such a farm can make a living," I said, once John returned.

"It cannot."

"Then how do they pay the rent?"

"They do not." My friend shrugged. "They have very little; it is not my place to take that from them. Do not look so, Mr Bennet—a few pennies of rent from the Sackrees could not have prevented the land sale last year. That bill we may lay at the feet of my father and his travels."

"You say he will not return?"

"He enjoys Vienna too much and the prospect of revisiting his past too little. And he has developed a fondness for Beethoven, so there is no better place for him to be." John looked across his estate and perhaps far beyond its borders. "I often wish he would join us, though, so he might meet Anne and see what we have made of the estate."

"Do not think badly of his decisions. The pain of the past may still be felt keenly in the present."

We followed a circular route that first took us up behind the Sackrees' holding. Down below us, an elderly man and woman sat together, her head on his shoulder, both seemingly oblivious to the whirl of chickens around them in what passed for a garden. We walked on slowly; neither of us seemed in any hurry to return to Rudford.

"A man might endure much hardship knowing that such happiness awaits him." I pointed back at the Sackrees. "You will recall my friend Fielding?"

John nodded.

"We were together in Virginia. Neither of us had a lady back in England. I thought I had lost the only one there could be, but Fielding believed we would both find love, eventually. It seemed to help him. And his faith kept me from falling into irreparable melancholy."

"When I visited Italy," said John, "I painted buildings. I could *see* buildings—follow the lines and shadows, the form of a curve, the pattern of the stone. I did not paint people, because I could see their shape but not what made them."

"And yet your portrait of Kitty is excellent."

"That was after Bath and Anne. Love opened my eyes to people. I believe that even a love lost leaves its mark. A heart that has opened once remains open forever."

"I am not so sure. Perhaps it closes itself off, unwilling to risk further injury." I tapped my side and grimaced. "A man wounded in battle does not rush toward the enemy with quite the same vigour as before."

"But he still enters battle, does he not? There is always the chance of victory."

"This is why I enjoy your company, John. You possess so much optimism, I need have none of my own."

Our journey continued to reveal spring's gifts to the estate. Small blooms of yellow and purple lined the side of the path; flashes of white darted among them as young rabbits fled our steps. Calls of alarm from mother birds broke through the constant bleats and low groans of lambs, ewes, calves, and cows. Above us, a crow flapped gracelessly between two companions, drifting from one to the other as if torn by divided loyalties.

"What is it like?" asked John. "To love so long and without hope?"

"What a question to ask of a man." I might have been affronted had I had less experience of John's naïve honesty.

"The curse of the enlightened artist, Mr Bennet. To observe.

You owned to a previous regard for Mrs Hayter, and I do not think time has lessened it. At breakfast, you watched her like you might view a painting of a childhood haunt, seeking out every detail and yearning for a time past."

"Hmph." I made no further comment until we reached a stile that would take us through a hedge and back in the direction of the house. Standing on the small step, I turned to look down on my young friend. "It is a battle, John. Between loyalty and love. Between reason and need. The battle rages within, neither side giving quarter. And though your actions may remain honourable, there is always guilt. You are damned either way. Ever does the heart weep and cry out 'what might have been?' Hold on to your love for your wife, John. Hold to it like a drowning man to a log. It is a rare and precious thing."

My friend did not reply but simply came up to me and gripped my hand with both of his for a few short moments.

The rest of the walk we talked of other things. Of my friend's time in Jamaica and Vienna, of the estate and his plans for the future, of Longbourn and London, and even of Bath. We made no mention of Abigail. Nature had us wrapped in her gentle arms, and I let her ease my spirits for a few short hours.

~ ~ ~

I rose early the next day, ate a hurried breakfast before the others, then went outside to enjoy the choral greetings of Rudford's songbirds and the tranquillity of a landscape still emerging from night's embrace. The numerous paths through the trees made chance meetings near impossible, especially if you ducked behind a leafy shrub at any sign of other visitors. On my return to the house, a footman informed me that, having failed to find me, the rest of the guests had left for Gloucester without me.

Denied the pleasure of social obligations, my feet took me to the one place able to offer more peace than even the most serene of woodland glades. John's father had a love of history, and the shelves in the library heaved with opportunities to learn from the past, but also tales of the many monarchs and military leaders that had failed to do so. A sprinkling of newer tomes on nature and philosophy spoke of Mrs Barton's own love of books.

I had barely entered the room, rubbing my hands at the prospect of an undisturbed day spent dipping into stories of Rome and Greece, when the door opened again behind me.

"I thought I might find you in here. You always did like your books." I froze at the voice, as paralysed as any victim of the Gorgon's gaze. "You may turn around," continued Abigail. "I am no Medusa."

"And I no Perseus." I turned to face her. "I did not expect to see you, Abigail."

"I have seen so little of you, James, I might almost think you are avoiding my company."

"You have not gone with the others to Gloucester." I hoped my face did not betray the truth of her words.

"How clever of you to notice. I see now why men rule the country. One of the advantages of my age is that the young are all too ready to believe how easily infirmity may strike. I pleaded a poor head. Are you pleased?"

"Yes—no—I mean…" I looked behind her. "Lord Davenport is not with you?"

"I persuaded him to accompany the rest of the party. I believe the presence of a particular gun shop in town eased his regret at our spending time apart."

"So, it is just the two of us?" I almost reached out in search of a chair or table that might help me steady myself.

"Yes, just the two of us. Alone. All alone." Abigail took a step toward me, and I forced myself not to take one back. Perhaps the books gave me a little of their strength. The great kings of the past found reassurance behind thick castle towers; I found encouragement within thin library walls.

"We should talk," I said.

"We should."

Neither of us moved or spoke. Abigail folded her arms and smiled. She knew who would give way first.

"I am not the confident young man you once knew."

"We have all lost the confidence of youth, James. Intelligence and wisdom are equal parts bane and boon. People like us can never bathe in blissful ignorance and certainty. We know what might have been and thus must also know disappointment."

"Yet you must, surely, be happy for your daughter. If anything is certain, it is John's devotion to her."

"They are blessed." Abigail tugged at the sleeve of her gown. "But may I not take pleasure in the joy of others while recognising the lack of it in my own life? It is a duality I must live with as a widow and mother. I have all that society deems necessary for contentment. Wealth. Position. Acquaintances. My health. Yet I am not...entirely satisfied." Her voice seemed softer, lacking its usual rigid self-confidence.

"You seek companionship?" I asked my question hesitantly, not knowing what answer to expect or wish for. "A man?"

Abigail's eyes narrowed. "Strange how men believe they are always the solution to a woman's needs."

"That is not what I meant."

"Well, let us leave that argument for another day." Abigail reached across to close a book that lay on a table next to her; the cover held her attention for a moment. "Perhaps we suffer from the same ailment. Your position is one that should give pleasure and yet..." Abigail lifted her shoulders with a half shrug.

"Oh, I am not unhappy. My family, my friends, and my butterflies are enough. More than I deserve."

"How easily lies come to us." Abigail frowned. "And I had hoped we might be honest with each other. We are alone, after all. I miss the simplicity of truth. In society, every word seems laced with undertones and subterfuge."

"I have not given such matters much thought. I tend to avoid society as much as possible."

"Perhaps you will do me the kindness of honesty for some minutes. The man I once knew in Bath was so full of life. I do not see that in you now. Why?"

Now it was my turn to give a shrug. "Time has left its mark, Abigail. You know of my service and why I entered it."

"I do not believe the youthful James is gone forever, though. There is still something there of him. I saw it at dinner, two days ago. There was fire in your eyes during our conversation."

"Conversation? That is not the word I would have used. John described it in terms of gladiatorial combat."

"And did I cut deep?"

I did not reply, though at least I managed to avoid lowering my eyes.

"No answer for me, James? Are we to leave honesty for another day, then?"

I had a thousand words for her but nothing to say.

"Very well. So be it." Abigail pulled herself up, clasping her hands in the time-honoured pose of the polite lady of society. "You know, I spent some time yesterday with Miss Mary Bennet. I am much enamoured of her."

"Really?" I found my voice at last.

Abigail gave a wry smile. "You seem surprised."

"Yes and no. I have no claim to understanding Mary's character. She is one of my many regrets. I have been remiss with her and should endeavour to make up for lost time."

"She is a kind girl at heart. It cannot be easy standing in the shadow of all her sisters. She wears her Bible and morals like armour, though you might be surprised at what lies beneath were you to peel it all away. You are not the only one who uses books to hide from the world. And from yourself." Abigail picked up the book from the table and handed it to me—a copy of Homer's *Odyssey*. "I shall leave you to them. Let them enjoy what it seems I cannot."

As Abigail moved back toward the hall, a familiar confusion of relief and disappointment washed over me. Then she paused and turned in the doorway.

"Perhaps you might do one thing for me, James. A dance tomorrow? Just the one. Enjoyed as we once did in the Assembly Rooms all those years ago. It is all I ask of you."

I nodded. "I believe I might manage that."

After Abigail left, I felt almost as if I had passed a test. Then the air seemed to change—a slight shift that might have gone unnoticed by anyone whose life had not once depended on such things in the woods of Virginia.

"Is someone there?" I called out.

No reply came, but I began walking up the library toward the two huge leather armchairs at its far end, the nearest with its back to me.

Bookcase after bookcase, oak guardians for a treasury of words, slipped past, their contents charting a journey through time: Brown's treatise on Augustine, Norrie's collections of Norse myths, Crowley's monographs on medieval devil lore, all the way through to Botley's review of the reign of George II, which Botley wrote for the sole purpose of obtaining favour from George III.

Once past the first armchair, I lowered myself into its twin and sat with my chin resting on my hands, fingers intertwined.

"I am so sorry, Papa." Wide eyes stared out at me, all Mary's usual hardness lost in the awkwardness of her situation. A mosaic of emotion shimmered across her face, all framed by a quite inelegant shade of scarlet.

"It is not seemly to eavesdrop," I said.

Mary looked down. "I did not…I mean, I was here when you came in and—"

"How much of our conversation did you hear?"

"Very little, Papa."

"But enough to startle you, it would seem. You have questions, perhaps?"

My daughter gathered herself together. "You and Mrs Hayter, were you…?"

"We had some kind of an understanding. Many years ago, and

long before I met your mother. But our lives took different paths."

"Does she…? Do you…?" There was no certainty in Mary's voice.

"Whether we do or do not is no concern of yours."

Mary's face blossomed red once again. "Of course not, Papa."

I tapped my two forefingers together. "You heard how Mrs Hayter spoke of you? Does she know you better than your own father? Have we left you in the shadow of your sisters?"

Mary remained silent.

"No matter." I watched her for a while, noting the slight tremble in her frame. "It is perhaps for the best if you say nothing of this to anyone. People might misunderstand, read more into what was mere coincidence. You know how your sisters think."

Mary nodded, her throat catching as she struggled to speak. "Who?" she forced out as she stood.

"What do you mean, 'who?'"

"Who would I confide in, Papa? Who would pay me any heed here?" The questions came out in a rush.

Now it was I who flushed scarlet, embarrassed by the realisation and revelation of Mary's loneliness—her words always heard but never listened to. She fell forward into my outstretched arms, clutching me like a rescued child.

"My dear girl," I said. "What have we done with you?"

No answer came, but Mary buried her head deeper into my chest. After a minute had passed, I gently pushed her away, held her head in my hands, and brushed the wetness from her cheeks.

"You may confide in *me*, Mary. I may not have been a good father, but I will strive to become one. I will not have you stand in anyone's shadow. I would have you come out into the light. This promise I make."

The Dance

Late the next day, I watched the servants at work from outside the windows of the grand saloon, where the steps led down to the rear garden. At some point, Mary joined me with a book, which she read while sitting against a pillar. We did not speak at first, testament to the fragility of our newfound connection.

"Might you play for us tonight?" I said after some minutes had passed.

My daughter closed her book, marking the page with a pressed cornflower. "As I recall, Papa, you prefer to let the other young ladies have time to exhibit."

My mouth twitched at the memory of the Netherfield Ball back in late November. "Well, that was then, and this is now. I have heard you practice at Longbourn and would not deny John's guests the chance to hear your skills. Anyone who wishes otherwise has neither taste nor sense."

A smile flickered across Mary's face.

"This business of becoming a better father," I said. "You will tell me when I commit an error?" Mary nodded. "And also when I appear to be succeeding?"

"I am fine, Papa, really. You need not concern yourself with my well-being. You have been a good father."

"And how am I to know you are not just saying that because of scripture? 'Honour thy father and thy mother: that thy days may be long upon the land which the Lord thy God giveth thee.' Is that not how it goes?"

"Mr Spigott says the fifth commandment demands nothing more than obedience. Praise is not required."

"Well, if Mr Spigott says as much, then I must take your words as a compliment and endeavour to remain a good father for at least the course of this evening. Now, much as I am enjoying our conversation, it is perhaps time we prepared ourselves for the coming entertainments."

John may have described the occasion as a dance, rather than a ball, but that did not dampen Kitty and Lydia's enthusiasm. The two girls had watched the comings and goings through the day, their squeals rising in pitch with each fresh delivery boy. Barrows and boxes brought eggs, milk, vegetables, and joints of meat for Rudford's kitchens and flowers for its rooms. In the saloon, servants had created a ring of chairs and tables around the space left for dancing. Twists of Virginia creeper climbed the door frames, wildflowers tied into their foliage. The glasses and punch bowls lay in a bed of peonies and primroses, while vases of lilac and bluebells set off white tablecloths. As such, the room offered a colour for every gown, an egalitarian state of affairs destined to leave Mrs Bennet both pleased and disappointed— pleased to find Kitty and Lydia's own attire in harmony with the decor, but disappointed that the same might be said of every other woman at the dance.

The evening entertainments held little attraction for me, though they did offer one singular opportunity for a gentleman interested in the natural world: the chance to indulge in scientific observation.

Some ladies wore gowns designed solely to attract attention, into which category my youngest daughters fell most conclusively. Kitty and Lydia left nothing to chance, of course. Where their gowns failed to elicit appropriate interest, their behaviour more than compensated. A better father might have taken them in hand and sought to temper their conduct, but I persuaded myself that time would do the job just as well. Besides, both were of an age that provided a ready excuse for much impropriety.

Other ladies wore gowns designed most decidedly to avoid attention. Mary, for example—a worker bee to Lydia's peacock butterfly.

And then there were those women with a grace and presence that no gown could enhance or diminish. Attention flew to them as if drawn by a celestial light. Only two such ladies graced the Rudford dance floor. John had the good fortune to have married one of them, while Lord Davenport clung to the other like a lamprey.

The gentlemen, on the other hand, largely distinguished themselves through attitude rather than attire. Some sought to impress with swagger, others with nonchalance, while others understood that their income and status trumped all. Few differences were evident in their clothes but for the structure of that capricious beast that is the cravat; its symbolism remained as mysterious to me as Egyptian hieroglyphics.

John drifted through the assembled company with a gentle

confidence that comes from a marriage based on true love and abiding respect. Some of the uncertain artist remained in his stride and shy chatter, but much of his wife's self-assurance had found its way into her husband's heart.

As for myself, I resolved not to dance, unless with Mary or my wife, though the half-promise to Abigail sniped at my conscience. A man of my age had enough ways to make a fool of himself without adding dancing to the ignominious list. Fortunately, Mrs Bennet seemed equally averse to a cotillion or two, presumably since dancing would have meant relinquishing hold of her cup of punch. She traversed the room like a frigate at the leading edge of a raiding party, ever alert for heavily laden merchantmen.

The dances progressed under the stony eyes of the Greek statues that occupied niches along the wall opposite the broad windows. Apollo and the muses either inspired or intimidated, depending on the confidence and education of the observer. Both ends of the room had balconies above them, one of which housed the musicians. The other stood empty, but for long twists of wild vine interspersed with rose buds, some still closed and unwilling to reveal the treasures within. For a while, I watched Kitty and Lydia apply themselves on the dance floor with their usual enthusiasm, moving about the occasion with all the subtlety of foxes in a chicken coop. Then I made my way up to the unoccupied balcony, all the better to observe—and evade—the silliness underneath.

Below me, gowns spun and twirled like birds of paradise, each patch of colour tied by some invisible string to a column of black and white formed by a jacketed gentleman. Abigail moved with the grace of old, each of her steps seeming to carry me further into the past until it was I who held her hand and brought the smile to her lips. I could even smell lavender.

"I thought I might find you here. There is no escape, you know."

I turned to find Mrs Barton leaning against a pillar on the other side of the balcony.

"Escape, Mrs Barton? From what?" The heat of the saloon could not entirely explain the flush in my cheeks.

"From dancing."

"You must forgive the attempt." I lowered my head in mock shame. "I enjoy dances as little as funerals. They both involve the same forced conversation and dishonest compliments. Only the music differs."

"Nevertheless, it would be quite improper to go the whole evening without at least one set with your hostess." Mrs Barton held out her hand with a natural authority that brooked no dispute.

"I thought myself safe up here. How did you think to look?"

"This is the only place you can see but not be seen."

"You are too wise for your age, Mrs Barton. Poor John never had a chance, did he?"

By the time we reached the floor, the musicians had readied bows against strings, and we took our place in the line. But then John appeared at his wife's side to whisper into her ear.

"Oh dear," said Mrs Barton. "It appears you may enjoy a reprieve, Mr Bennet. Though perhaps you will do me the honour of a later dance?"

"Only if I can find no excuse."

"I will take that as a yes, then."

After bowing, I lifted my head to discover I had leapt from the frying pan into the proverbial fire, albeit one dressed in a pale blue gown.

"Alone on the dance floor, James? Then let me be your white knight. We might even try conversation again."

As always, Abigail's voice was a siren call to a poor Odysseus; the battle between longing and restraint started afresh. Before I could collect myself, the music began, and I had little choice but to take both Abigail's hand—warm and gentle—and my chances on the dance floor.

"If you only wished to speak with me, you might merely have asked," I said. "There is no need for dancing."

"*Au contraire*, my dear James. There is no place quite so private as a dance. Each couple has eyes and ears only for each other. And what could be more natural than to converse with your partner? Besides, you promised me this." The formation took her briefly from me, but she continued on her return. "And here I have you at a disadvantage. You cannot parry my words and dance at the same time. That is too much for any man."

"You may be surprised." My feet almost missed a turn.

"The music seems most apt," said Abigail. "The same as our last dance together in Bath. Mrs Murray's evening entertainment."

"Is that so? If I were possessed of a suspicious nature, I might consider this all some prearranged plot between you and your daughter."

"And are you suspicious?"

"Where you are concerned, always." The exertion of the dance, and the nearness of a presence denied so long, ensured my words came out between hurried breaths.

"You have been avoiding me again ever since our meeting in the library. Are you so afraid?"

"It is not that simple."

"Oh James, I hope you do not intend to be churlish. You avoid the truth and will not play the games you once so enjoyed."

"What do you want of me, Abigail?"

"Want? From you?" Abigail's grip on my hand lost its delicacy. "Nothing. There was a time when I might have. But it is gone."

"Then why tease me so? It does not become you."

"I do nothing of the sort." The hardness in Abigail's touch now spread to her face. "Have you considered it might be *you*, James, who teases *me*?"

"I assure you nothing could be further from the truth."

"Yet you contrived to meet me in London. You did so again in Bath and now here in Gloucestershire. You seek my company and then apparently resent it. How am I to understand you?"

"I did not and do not seek your company at all."

"How very gallant."

"No, you misunderstand me."

"Then enlighten me, James. What am I to think of you? Of us?"

"Of us?"

The music stopped. I bowed, but Abigail left in a rush of fabric, her retreat hurried and graceless. Too hurried, it seemed; a small brooch lay on the floor where she had last stood. I bent down and closed my fingers on a silver swan, whose neck arched gracefully above open wings; a jewelled eye glittered in the candlelight. Two raised initials flanked the clasp set into the back of the brooch—one a J, the other a B.

The clamour of the room seemed to close in, voices merging into a tumble of sound that grew ever louder and insistent, driving me away through the throng and out of the door in search of cool air and quiet. Though the sun had not yet fallen below the horizon, torches lit a way along a path guarded by laurel and ancient yew; a pale blue gown moved away in the distance.

Love, Honour, Pride, Duty

At my approach, Abigail turned sharply, hands dropping from her face. The torches sent flickering shadows across the small grove where we stood.

"Your brooch." I held my hand out.

"Keep it. I have no need for it." Abigail spoke quickly. She seemed somehow less composed—less a lady and more a woman. Her hair had come loose, threatening to tumble down in dark locks threaded with silver. I fought a sudden urge to take her into my arms, and she took a step back as if reading my intentions.

"I asked for honesty in the library, James, but you did not offer it. I ask for it again now, when no one can hear or see us. If not now, then when?"

"Honesty?" I said. "You might not like honesty."

"Try me."

"Very well. Why did you come with Lord Davenport? The man is a fool. I did not think you so vain that his interest would have such a marked effect on you. You seem to enjoy his company and his conversation, yet I cannot believe it of you."

"At least he offers me company and conversation."

I took a step closer to her. "And that is all you seek from him?"

"What else would I seek?"

"Marriage." I regretted the word immediately.

"Marriage?" Abigail gave a snort of derision, her composure returned. "Why do men assume marriage is all we women wish for?"

"Do not judge all men the same."

"Yet you seem willing to judge all women. According to you, only men and marriage can complete us."

"I merely—"

"I need not explain myself to you, James Bennet. Especially not you. You gave up your right to comment on my choices when you turned back that day in Bath. You call Lord Davenport a fool, but was there ever a greater fool than you?"

"I do not understand."

"Or do not wish to understand." Abigail took half a pace toward me. "Do you regret nothing?"

Spoken from her mouth, the question pierced all defences carefully built through the years. "Where shall I begin? That I left Bath when I did. That I lacked the courage or wisdom to make you an offer. That I submitted to a misguided sense of honour and pride. Oh, the list is long. You cannot imagine how such regrets have been my constant companion."

Without my noticing, the distance between us had grown less. I could have reached out and touched her.

"I have shared those regrets and others," said Abigail.

"Others?"

"That I gambled with your feelings. That I did not give you

longer to express them. That I did not seek you out, however improper that might have looked." Abigail hesitated. "That you never kissed me. Though that, at least, is one regret easily remedied."

If the silence had continued a moment longer, I might have moved, might have taken another decision to rue later.

"But that would not be honourable, would it, James?"

I let out a breath, grateful she had made the choice for me.

"Tell me," continued Abigail. "Why *did* you turn back that day in Bath?"

"In the coach, they told me you were already engaged."

"Yes, but if you had loved me—truly loved me—you would have ignored honour and pride, begged me to break my promise to another, assured me of your love even if you were denied me. But you did not. You left. What love is that, that withers so fast?"

"Is that what you believe of me?" I turned away to leave but then swung back around, my face now mere inches from Abigail's. "You cannot know the depths of my love for you. You cannot know the days, weeks, and months of despair. The years."

"And yet love did not return you to me."

"As I said, I regret my decisions. But I cannot undo what is done. And more than honour holds me fast, now. I have a duty to my family."

"You think I seek to seduce you? To engage in some tryst or affair like so many others among the seemingly moral?"

"All I know is you flaunt Lord Davenport in front of me. You cannot throw yourself away on such a man."

"Throw myself away?" Abigail practically shouted the words. "Who are you, James Bennet, to judge what I may or may not do?"

"That is not what I meant."

"Then what did you mean? Who should I throw myself away on? On you? Will you save me from my tristesse? Of course you will not." Abigail's lips were a hand's breadth from mine. "Do you still love me?"

"What?" I froze for a moment. "No, I will not answer that question. My regrets do not end with you, Abigail. I have given my wife little of that which she is owed. But I will give her my loyalty. She deserves that much from me."

"You choose honour, loyalty, and duty, James, but I choose love. In the library, you wondered what would satisfy me. To know that I am truly loved by another. To know that I was not wrong about you. Will you give that to me, James? I ask only for a word, nothing else. To know the truth. So, will you be true now to your love?"

"Do not ask it of me," I said. "I cannot. I will not."

"Then leave."

I did not move.

Abigail's face softened. She placed her hand on my cheek and left it there.

"All I ask is that you say you love me still."

"I cannot."

"Why not? You have a duty to the truth, too."

I leaned even closer to Abigail, drawn to her by a promise, by a memory, by unfulfilled dreams and desires, cast back to days of joyful youth, before war, before everything.

"I...cannot," I whispered, then eased her hand from my cheek, the parting of our fingers slow, reluctant, and final.

Abigail backed away from me.

"Then do not speak to me again, James. I never wish to be reminded of your false pride, your misplaced sense of duty and honour that causes you to deny a truth so evident in your eyes and your behaviour. Leave now. And let us never speak again. Not ever."

Lost

No path seemed open to me that would not end in regret, guilt, or shame. Another time, such insight might have brought some kind of acceptance. Instead, my despair grew with each step I took toward the copse that adjoined the gardens. Not even the knowledge that I had stayed true to my wife offered any respite.

The trees left long shadows as night began its triumph over day, drawing me further into the woodland until I fell to my knees, the mossy ground giving way beneath me. I stared at my hands in the failing light; my palms, smooth and almost unblemished, told of a gentleman's life. Only the slash of white running from the base of my left thumb across to my little finger spoke of hardship. A knife held in fear, its owner lacking the strength to pull the blade from my desperate grip. He must have been no more than a boy. Just a farmhand caught up in the broiling insanity of conflict. I could not recall his face, just the sharp pain of the cut and the cries as he fell away, Jackson's sword tearing a rip in his stomach.

Self-pity claimed me in its poisoned grasp as the sun finally abandoned its effort to see through the tangle of leaves and branches. I peered through the trees, feeling the sense of disquiet rise like it used to do in Virginia, when the darkness fell, and our demons rose. The shadows seemed to shift in the gloom.

"Is anyone there?" I called out, thinking I saw a light. "Show yourself."

A twig cracked, the retort sharp as a musket shot.

"Mr Bennet?" A familiar outline emerged from the shadows.

"Gods, John, whatever are you doing?"

"Looking for you. One of the footmen saw you walk in this direction. I feared you might have become lost in the dark."

"Lost? Yes. Lost. More than you can know." I stood slowly as my friend came nearer, the flames of the torch revealing John's face creased in concern. Some piano piece, played with spirit and accuracy, carried to us from a distance—I had not wandered far.

"Well, I must look a fool, no?" I continued. "I felt the need for some time to myself. The ground is very soft here." John's expression did not change at my gabbled excuse, nor did he support it with meaningless words of comfort. "It seems Mrs Hayter troubles me a little more than I anticipated."

"I thought that might be the case and came prepared for that very eventuality." John reached behind him to pull around a bag. "Sit, Mr Bennet, if you would." He motioned with the torch to a fallen tree that formed a natural bench of sorts. Then he pulled out a bottle and two glasses. "One considerable benefit of my marriage has been to the quality of my cellar. There is something to be said for marrying into the wine trade. I am told this port is a particularly good vintage."

I looked at my young friend. "You are much changed, Mr Barton. Where is the confused young man I once knew?"

"Oh, he is still here."

"You know, I envy you so. I am happy for you, too. Such a woman as Mrs Barton. But envious. Oh, so envious."

"I do not deserve her."

"No, you do not." I tapped my young friend on the chest. "But you are married to her nevertheless."

We sat on the log, glasses of port as dark as the wood around us, the torch thrust into the ground to offer some light. John said nothing. He, too, had learnt the ways of prying secrets from others: do not ask them to reveal them and let silence do the bidding for you.

"I am unsure I have lived a good life," I said after half a glass of port.

"Come now, Mr Bennet."

"No, John, hear me out. I have not led a wicked life. But a good one? No. I have allowed my past to define my thoughts and actions. And even though I made many a solemn promise to abandon regret, it returns to haunt me at all times." I touched John gently on the arm. "Do not misunderstand me—I did not marry badly, but I made a poor choice. Though not as poor as Mrs Bennet's. She might have married someone better able to sweeten her days and remove the burdens that task a mother of five daughters. But how are we to know this when we are young? I have not done well by those daughters, either. At least not by all of them, though this is something I endeavour to correct. Unfortunately, some actions cannot be undone, no matter what we might wish."

"You speak of Mrs Hayter?"

"I do. You know the story of my carriage ride to Bath?"

"Yes, and you cannot blame yourself. If she was engaged, there was no honourable course of action you might have taken."

"I wish that it were so, my young friend. There might have been had I spoken to Abigail earlier. Goodness knows, I had ample opportunity. If I had stayed in Bath, convinced her to break off her engagement. It would have been a minor scandal, but such things pass with time." I winced. "Such a proud fool I was."

"Some might call your regrets churlish. You have much to be grateful for." John did not look at me as he spoke.

"You sound like my friend Fielding. But both of you loved well and with success. Neither of you know the bitter taste of a love thwarted by fate and circumstance, two demons whose tridents poke in the embers of my life with unfortunate regularity."

"But you may, at least, rejoice that you have tasted true love, no?"

"That is what the poets would have us believe, John, but they are wrong. I would rather suffer an ephemeral love—the wound would heal and leave no scar." I rose from our wooded seat and drained my glass. "Still, port always helps. I believe its absence would be the biggest regret of all." I sensed rather than saw his smile, the torch having grown smaller and weaker. "My friend Fielding would now tell me to face my fears. So, we must return to your home, and I must smile, dance with your wife if it is not too late, and make conversation of little substance while all that is important remains unspoken."

"I rather think that is the definition of a dance, Mr Bennet."

I clapped him on the shoulder. "I have taught you too well, it seems. Your friendship is a true boon, John. Was it Cicero who said, 'Friendship improves happiness and abates misery, by doubling our joys and dividing our grief'? Come, let us return and see how much trouble my daughters have caused. I shall leave regret here in the dark woods, at least for now."

By the time John and I returned, the musicians had already put away their instruments. Small groups had formed at tables, each guest retiring to the bosom of old friends, too tired to attend to the formality of conversation with unfamiliar faces.

"Wherever have you been, husband? We quite missed you. And the state of your breeches! Lord Davenport has been telling us all about the shooting on his manor."

"I sought a little fresh air, that is all, then found myself lost once the sun went down. John here saved me."

"And just in time, too, for Mary is to play for us." My wife pointed across to a pianoforte, where my daughter sorted through sheet music. Perhaps Mary felt my eyes upon her for she looked up, her smile a lone beacon in my darkness.

"Finally, some joy tonight," I said and meant it.

"Oh, you delight in sarcasm, Mr Bennet. Tell me, Mrs Hayter, was he so in Bath? Did he tease you so, too?"

Abigail turned toward me as if we were just two loose acquaintances at a public engagement. There was hesitation in her voice and a touch of red to her eyes, or perhaps my imagination played tricks in the candlelight. "I do not recall our conversation in Bath, Mrs Bennet. It was so long ago. Your husband was a man of few words back then. I often thought he should say more, but he did not."

That was the last time she spoke in my presence until we left for Longbourn.

A Young Gardener

"When you pick up Lizzy and Jane in St Albans, treat them to a decent meal at the George. I know the inn well, and they do an excellent ham." I raised a finger. "I also know that a milliner of some repute resides in that town. Do not spend the money on ribbons, bonnets, and whatever else takes your fancy, do you hear?"

"Yes, Papa." Kitty and Lydia spoke in unison as they settled into my carriage.

I turned to my wife. "Perhaps you should accompany them?"

"I cannot, husband, for I am to visit Lady Lucas. Though she will be all Lady Catherine this, Lady Catherine that. What do I care for Lady Catherine in her big house? She has only one daughter. Her troubles are nothing compared to mine."

"If such conversation is so displeasing, I wonder you go at all," I said. "Were your nerves to make a timely appearance, this would excuse your absence."

"Of course I must go, Mr Bennet. How else am I to learn the news from Meryton if I do not visit?"

"As you wish. Stay or go, it is all the same to me." I turned back to the carriage. "Now, girls, take your time. Lizzy and Jane will be tired. Have them rest up at the inn for a while before continuing. We shall not expect you back too soon."

As the vehicle pulled away, neither daughter leant out of the window to wave farewell and I felt only relief at the prospect of their absence. My wife left for Lucas Lodge a few minutes later. I recalled Lizzy's departure of a few weeks ago. That one I had regretted. A letter from her had greeted me on our return home from Rudford.

> ...we have dined several times at Rosings, and you cannot imagine who has joined us there. None other than Mr Darcy! It seems he is intended for Lady Catherine's daughter. I have written little of Miss de Bourgh for want of any substance to write about. She rarely speaks, which Lady Catherine attributes to an unfortunate constitution. I suspect a malaise brought on by knowing the identity of her future spouse. With such a small party, Mr Darcy is forced to converse far more than he ever did in Hertfordshire, but I might almost say that, unlike Lady Catherine, he improves with time. He may yet become almost tolerable.
>
> My companions do not share my opinions of Mr Darcy, for they hold him in the very highest regard. It seems ten thousand a year compensates for many a character flaw, an understanding I feel sure Mama would share even though I know you do not. I must, however, at least give our Derbyshire acquaintance credit for his choice of companion. Colonel Fitzwilliam is a fine

gentleman, able to converse freely without giving offence—an accomplishment neither our host nor Mr Darcy can claim…

I might have enjoyed Lizzy's wry observations had they arrived before our trip to the Bartons, but Rudford cast a long shadow. Longbourn seemed somehow different, now, as if an inferior copy of the original—the detail less clear, the colours drab, the sounds dull and distant.

Menander once wrote that time is the healer of all necessary evils, but some wounds perhaps demand more time than we have left to us. Wise men encourage us to learn the lessons of the past, but I had only ever learnt the futility of trying to do so. Of late, the rich soil of remorse had yielded its regular harvest of good intentions. To be a kinder husband and a more considerate father. But these shrivelled once more in the glare of a self-pity given new life two weeks previously in Gloucestershire.

Was there ever a greater fool than you?

Abigail's question produced no great epiphany. It merely served to remind me I had lived a foolish life.

Some better part of me refused to fade, though, clinging instead to the one responsibility I could not ignore: my obligation to my middle daughter. I had made her a promise. And there was still the matter of Mr Spigott.

"Papa?" said Mary, as the two of us walked back toward the house. "Why did you give Kitty and Lydia such an amount of money?"

"Was it so much? I hardly took note. Well, perhaps they will spend it and spare me their usual carping. A father should be treasured in his old age, not badgered and put upon." I tugged roughly at my cravat, which felt too constrained. "Oh, forgive me, child. You give me no cause for complaint. Now, tell me, how shall we while away the empty hours before your sisters and mama return?"

"I will read."

"And may I ask what grand moral tome has your attention today?"

Mary held up a slim volume. "Blake's *Milton*."

"But that is not religious at all. Or is it? Sometimes it can be hard to tell with such authors."

"It depends on your interpretation, Papa."

I placed a hand on my daughter's arm, causing her to stop and look at me, her forehead creasing at my earnest expression. "Mary, I have not forgotten our conversation in the library at Rudford. So, while I applaud the newfound variety in your reading material, may I urge you to leave Blake for later? Let us rather take a turn about the garden."

Curiosity passed across Mary's face, but she said nothing and offered no resistance as I drew her gently around the side of the house. We crossed the back lawn, and I stamped hard on the grass to remind the leatherjackets that I knew they were underneath and disapproved.

"I have not seen Mr Spigott since our return," I said. "Has he run out of pamphlets?"

"His work with the church keeps him from us." Mary's voice offered no clue as to whether she viewed this state of affairs with displeasure or indifference.

"You know this or choose to believe it?"

"The former." My daughter did not explain how she knew, and I did not ask. If you let people keep their small secrets, they may reveal the larger ones to you.

"Perhaps we should invite him for dinner," I said. "A curate deserves a good meal now and then. What say you?"

"I am sure he would be grateful for the invitation."

"Would you like to see him at Longbourn?"

"I am happy with whatever decision you choose to make, Papa."

The English are masters of deception. We are able to talk of everything but say nothing. Or talk of nothing yet make our meaning quite clear. Equally, we spend much of our lives in hiding, keen that our words and actions do not betray our true thoughts and feelings. But few of us can lie without consequence. Our souls will not allow it. And so we may offer a clue to our discomfort. My dear Lizzy would rub the fingers of her hand with a thumb. According to Fielding, I poured myself a glass of wine or port when denying the truth. Mary never lied, but when she did not speak the whole truth, she offered up something between a smirk of triumph and a shy smile of apology.

"I said you might confide in me, Mary, yet you do not. I have broken many promises in my life, but I intend to keep the one I made you."

Mary stopped. "It is easy to invite confidentiality."

"Ah," I said. "But harder to deserve it. Your point is well made." I pointed across to a distant patch of the garden filled with rather scrawny shrubs, their leaves more yellow than green. "I am of a mind to remove those insults to the name rhododendron and redesign that part of the garden. What are your thoughts?"

"You wish my opinion on the garden? But I know nothing of gardens."

"I think you do. I think you very much interested in them. Something you have kept from me. I had to discover this interest from none other than Mr Spigott."

A gasp escaped Mary's lips. She covered her face with Blake's poetic efforts. "Have you talked of me with him?" came a muffled voice from behind the book.

"Calm yourself, child. Just chitchat when we found ourselves travelling in the same direction."

The book lowered. "I did not keep my interest from you. You never asked."

"Still, you might have spoken up," I said.

"And you would have listened?" The crimson touch of anger caressed Mary's cheeks. "You have Lizzy for advice in the garden and leave no room for another. I cannot be Lizzy. Nobody truly listens to what I wish to say, anyway. Nobody, except for…"

"Mr Spigott?"

Mary's resentment seemed to dissolve at the name. "Yes." She looked down. "He is gentle and kind and encouraging, and he does not lecture me. But nobody cares about him, either. He is 'just plain Mr Spigott.'"

"My dear Mary, you have a talent for imitation. I might have laughed were I not determined not to do so for at least a few days more." I lifted her chin so she would look at me. "You should know that I care about Mr Spigott. Even like the fellow. And I care about you, too." I pulled my hand away and cleared my throat. "So let us begin again. I thought to replace those shrubs with box and roses, a possibility inspired by your kind curate himself. What is your opinion?"

My daughter tapped her lips with her finger. As she pondered my question, a blue tit burst out of the shrubbery with a chirrup of annoyance, perhaps equally disappointed at the lack of botanic effort from the rhododendrons. "Box can accept a lack of sun," said Mary. "It should grow tolerably well there, even in the shade of the yew."

"Excellent. You *do* have an eye for such things. I do not suppose you have an interest in insects, too?"

Mary shuddered.

"No," I said. "Perhaps that would be too much to ask. Now, come along. We have many years to catch up on and only a few hours until the others return."

Lizzy

Coach wheels, giggles, and my wife rushing toward the door announced the arrival of the four girls. The two youngest barrelled past me, each bearing a band-box that suggested my financial instructions had fallen on deaf ears. I did not care.

"My dearest Jane," I said. "Returned at last." The city had not diminished my eldest daughter's beauty, though her cheekbones stood out more than I remembered, her skin as pale as Dover chalk. "How was London?"

"Diverting, Papa, but I am glad to be home. There is nothing quite like the comfort of Longbourn."

"Let us go through to the drawing room," said my wife as she pulled Jane away, barely allowing her time to remove her cloak and hat. "You must tell me all about London. How is your uncle? How is Mrs Gardiner? How are the fashions?" As they passed, my daughter gave me a desperate smile of apology.

I found Lizzy sitting outside on the doorstep, watching the unloading of the carriage and the release of the horses from their harness. She seemed somehow diminished, and I recalled how her final letter from Hunsford had lacked her usual esprit:

...the few days until my return to Longbourn seem interminable, Papa. I have had enough of great houses and great people. I yearn for the sanctity of Longbourn and our books. Mr Collins's own library is severely lacking in that regard. There is the Rosings library, of course, but to use it means to visit with Lady Catherine and her guests. I shall miss only Charlotte and perhaps Colonel Fitzwilliam...

"My dear girl, what is a father to think of a favourite daughter who will not greet him on her return?"

Lizzy stood at my words and brushed down her front. "My apologies, Papa, but it has been a long journey. I am not quite ready for Mama's questions."

"You need not worry yourself on that account. She has taken Jane aside and has a whole capital city to get through before she arrives at Hunsford. But you will not mind the odd enquiry from your father?"

"Of course not." Lizzy took my hands in hers, tilted her head, and smiled. The brown of her eyes seemed lighter, almost hazel, an impression I put down to the contrast with the dark lines beneath them. And those same eyes seemed somehow older, though I could not say why.

"Let us walk," I said. "Colour has returned to the garden, and I have plans for the shrubbery that I would value your op...well, never mind."

Moments after we passed the drawing room window, Mrs Bennet came rushing out. "Lizzy, Lizzy, you are hiding from me. Oh, you will need care and attention after so long with Mr Collins.

How is Mrs Collins? Half an eye on Longbourn, no doubt."

Lizzy gave me a tired smile.

"My dear, you may ask all the questions you like of Lizzy a little later. For now, she is mine to interrogate."

"Jane never saw Mr Bingley," continued my wife. "But then I expect you know that already, Lizzy. I always said those sisters of his were not to be trusted, did I not, Mr Bennet?" She hurried away without waiting for my confirmation, hesitating once as if she might turn back, caught between sources of gossip like a cat between two saucers of cream.

Lizzy and I took the same route I had followed with Mary just hours before.

"How is our dear rector?" I said.

"He is well. As long as he enjoys the patronage of Lady Catherine, he will ever be so."

"He remains constant in his character?"

"Very much so."

"I feared as much. Still, at least we may credit him with a tenacity of purpose. Few individuals are capable of such diligent pursuit of all that is ridiculous in a man. I almost miss him."

"He spoke quite fondly of you, Papa."

"Did he now? Then we must add an alarming lack of judgement to his many qualities. And how is Mrs Collins?"

Lizzy paused before giving a slight shake of her head. "I cannot rightly say. She seems content, and yet, as much as I know that to be true, I cannot help but wonder."

"Happiness may be found in unusual circumstances, even in the house of one such as Mr Collins. Do not judge so swiftly, my dear girl."

Lizzy looked up at me sharply, as if I had affronted her in some way. "I do not judge, Papa. I am uncertain, that is all. My experiences in Hunsford showed me that opinions once held with conviction may not hold fast under closer consideration."

"Steady, Lizzy. You cannot suggest we allow such trivial matters as facts to sway our opinions? That way lies madness."

We walked on, her arm now in mine, enjoying a renewed bond that required no words. Yet the silence seemed heavier than normal, as if that bond between us had frayed at its edges. We stopped on reaching the end of the lawn, and I reached up to my daughter's forehead to tuck a stray hair into place. It is our blemishes that make us beautiful. Perfection is not true beauty but merely the pretence of it. There is much to admire in the lines and curves of a landscaped garden, but a woodland glade is where we may taste of heaven.

"You have not slept well," I said.

"The Kent air did not agree with me wholly."

"The air or the company? Do not say you argued with Charlotte? I know you disagreed with her choice of spouse, but she has always been a good friend."

"She remains a good friend. We did not argue. Though she showed herself alarmingly adept at ensuring Mr Collins rarely has time to spend in the house. I had not considered her so cunning."

I shrugged. "She is, after all, a woman."

"And now who is swift to judge? And an entire sex, too." Lizzy's accusation took me back to Rudford and my conversations with Abigail. Another lesson of the past left unheeded. "Do not look so contrite, Papa, I am only teasing you. Besides, how can men be as cunning as women? They have not the intelligence for it."

"Lizzy, you have been gone too long from Longbourn. I have missed the sharpness of your tongue and mind. But Hunsford has not served you well. You are not so ready to smile as I recall. Perhaps we should invite the officers to Longbourn. You always enjoyed the conversation of Mr Wickham, I believe?"

Lizzy turned abruptly to me, "Oh no, Papa, no Mr Wickham, no officers. I mean, not yet. I have been in company for so long, I yearn for its absence. As for smiles, you forget Jane and I spent the last few hours in an inn and carriage with Lydia and Kitty."

"Of course. That would drain the humour from the best of us. You cannot know how I have suffered." The sun seemed to diminish for just a moment, as if in sympathy with my thoughts. "Come, let the flowers restore the smile to your lips. We shall sit by the rose beds while the light remains good."

The May warmth had enticed clusters of dark reds and pale yellows from the roses, and Longbourn looked decidedly tranquil from our small white bench.

"Tell me more of Rosings," I said. "How unbearable is Lady Catherine? I would hear of her flaws. Since she pays Mr Collins such attention, they must be many."

"Who am I to pronounce on others, Papa? Though I suspect her kindness to Mr Collins is for want of an alternative when Rosings has so few guests. The estate is quite a sight. My cousin did not exaggerate on that front—so many windows. But it seems so empty with just Lady Catherine and her daughter inside."

"But your letters talked of visitors. Mr Darcy, of course. And a colonel."

Lizzy shifted on her seat, perhaps seeking a more comfortable spot. "Colonel Fitzwilliam was quite the gentleman—easy to converse with and pleasant company."

"Whereas we know Mr Darcy to be quite the opposite."

"Yes." Lizzy's jawline seemed to harden, and her thumb picked at her forefinger. "I had little to do with him, if truth be told."

I did not pry further. To be slighted by a man of great standing is one matter, as Lizzy had experienced last October at a Meryton assembly. To be reminded of it through his constant presence quite another. I had not considered my daughter so sensitive, but the more thought I gave to people and character, the less I understood either.

"Well, I am sorry for you, Lizzy, to have such a man there. It must have been quite distressing. But you are rid of him now and need never think of him again. I am sure your mother has been tireless in her search for bachelors that do not possess Mr Darcy's talent for poorly chosen words."

"You cannot possibly imagine, Papa." Lizzy's eyes closed for a moment. "But Jane and I are not the only ones returning from travels."

"Ah, yes, no doubt the girls told you all about our trip to Gloucestershire?"

"They did. But they talked mostly of dancing, the town, and a collection of bachelors entirely unsuited to their proscribed role as suitors. Are John and Anne well? Do they still fight?"

"They are both well, more than content, and still argue. The latter seemingly contributes to their state of happiness. Mrs Barton misses you and sends her particular love."

"My sisters mentioned various guests," said Lizzy. "Of the bachelors at the dance, I have already learned all I wish to know. But what of the others? Mrs Hayter brought a companion?"

"Mrs Hayter, yes." I reached forward to pluck out a weed. "I must speak to Alfred. A lawn is like the soul—we must endeavour to keep it pure."

"Who was her companion?"

"Look, another one. A thistle. Really, this is quite intolerable."

"Papa, is there something offensive in my question?"

"Oh, no. Not at all." I waved my hand at her. "A Lord Davenport. Nobody of any note."

Lizzy cocked her head at me. "You did not like him?"

"Like or dislike, I cannot say."

"If you cannot say whether you liked or disliked him, then I suspect the latter to be the case."

"Ah, now that is the daughter I remember. Very well. Let us say he is not blessed with too sharp an intellect. And he suffers from a heightened sense of self-importance entirely unjustified by his character and accomplishments."

"If I was not resolved to avoid casting judgement on people, I might say you have done little more than describe most every man of my acquaintance."

"Goodness, Lizzy, has my sex wronged you so greatly? I might almost call you bitter. No, I think what displeases me most about Lord Davenport is that he does not care for butterflies. An unforgivable trait in a gentleman."

On cue, a brimstone danced its way out of the roses in a flutter of iridescent yellow.

"And how is Mrs Hayter?" said Lizzy. "She was most kind to me in Bath."

"I did not speak much with her."

"Come now, Papa. Did you not reminisce about the days of your youth?"

"We did not talk of the past. Or anything of import."

Lizzy's brows furrowed. "You surprise me, Papa. I would have thought you keen to renew your acquaintance."

"I believe I spoke with her as little as you with Mr Darcy."

Lizzy held my eyes for a moment. Or perhaps I held hers. It felt like entering a dark room, reaching out for something, but not knowing what and never quite finding it.

"Shall we go inside?" I got to my feet. "You have not seen Mary yet. She saw much of Mr Spigott before our trip."

"Mr Spigott? Kitty mentioned his visits, but by the tone of your voice…surely not? Are you suggesting…?"

"I suggest nothing, dear girl. I merely note that Mr Spigott seems to have an unusually extensive supply of pamphlets, and Mary an unusually large appetite for consuming them."

A Dinner

All the Hunsford adventurers had enjoyed a brief supper with us on the day of Lizzy's return, but it was only a matter of a week before they assembled at Longbourn again for a proper debriefing...or dinner, as Mrs Bennet would put it. Ever eager to hasten the demise of two birds with a single stone, my wife insisted we invite the militia, too, despite Lizzy's lack of enthusiasm for military guests. The soldiers' imminent departure for Brighton added urgency to my wife's wishes.

Kitty and Lydia treated the impending loss of officers as an event worthy of Revelations. I found myself casting glances to where the stream ran, half-expecting a beast to appear "with seven heads and ten horns, and upon his horns ten crowns, and upon his heads the name of blasphemy." Instead, we had Mr Denny and Mr Wickham appear on horseback, each bearing nothing more dramatic than a shako upon their heads.

Sir William and Lady Lucas arrived with Mrs Collins's younger sister, Maria, who had been with Lizzy in Kent. The presence of so many ladies at table had, at least, allowed me to persuade Mrs Bennet to invite Mr Spigott. It seemed the curate's alleged ability to discourage lively conversation proved no hindrance when that conversation included Sir William.

I had largely let nature take its course with Mary and the curate. My *laissez-faire* approach aligned me with the mothers of Meryton. They followed a simple philosophy when it came to encouraging an understanding—if two people are placed in the same room often enough and for long enough, then marriage becomes inevitable.

My relationships to my daughter and Mr Spigott had not yet the intimacy required to gauge their affection for one another with confidence. They saw each other too often to suggest a mere acquaintance but not often enough to imply a fixed attachment. My questions to Mary on the matter only met with evasion. I suspected both felt certain of their own feelings but not sure enough of the other's to declare something more than a friendship.

Mr Denny and Mr Wickham collected at one end of our table with Mrs Bennet, separated by Kitty and Lydia. My youngest daughters had an unerring ability to insinuate themselves into a nest of soldiers like cuckoos, demanding food, wine, and attention with equal vigour.

At the other end of the table, either side of myself, sat Sir William and Lady Lucas with their daughter, along with Lizzy and Jane. Mary and Mr Spigott occupied the neutral territory between the two groups, being party to neither.

Cook surpassed herself, as if wishing to show that Longbourn could match anything Rosings Park might produce, with rabbit and onion, pigeon, wild duck, and a haunch of venison, all accompanied by fresh vegetables, tarts, and cheesecakes.

My wife regarded gossip much like Jackson regarded Mrs Tincton's efforts—one helping could never suffice. Although stories from Kent had enlivened the breakfast table for several days, Mrs Bennet still questioned Miss Maria Lucas and Lizzy on all matters to do with Hunsford and Rosings. Eventually, though, talk began to include other subjects.

"Did you attend any balls or assemblies while in London, Miss Bennet?" asked Lady Lucas.

"Very few," replied Jane. "I was quite content with the company of my cousins."

Sir William, who had been uncharacteristically quiet, came alert at the mention of London. "When I attended court—"

"More potatoes, Sir William?" I pointed at a plate of steaming Lumpers topped with fresh parsley.

"Potatoes, yes. Capital vegetables!" My neighbour leaned toward me and assumed a knowing tone. "You can take the measure of a man in his choice of vegetables."

"Really?" I said. "I have never greatly enjoyed peas. To which flaw might I owe such a preference?"

"I cannot speak to peas," said Sir William. "But a man who likes potatoes, well…"

"Is a man of capital character?"

"Precisely, Mr Bennet."

"Do you enjoy potatoes, Mr Spigott?" I was keen to include the curate in our conversation.

"Potatoes?" Mr Spigott looked for a moment as if I had asked him to explain the Papal Schism of 1378. "Yes. I suppose I do."

"Boiled or roasted?" asked Sir William.

"A slight preference for roasted."

Sir William nodded and leant back in his chair, giving me an approving look that seemed to suggest the curate's preference for roasted potatoes indicated a superior nature.

"Maria, how did you find your sister?" I said. "She has a busy life, but I understand from Lizzy she is quite content as the wife of a rector."

"Oh, yes." Maria nodded with some enthusiasm, perhaps relieved at the simplicity of the question. "Quite content."

"We Lucases are as robust as they come." Sir William helped himself to another slice of venison. "A little inconvenience does us no harm at all. Why, when I was at court—"

"More carrots, Sir William, with your venison?" I pushed the pot of orange delights toward him.

"Carrots, why yes, don't mind if I do."

"How were Mr Collins's sermons, Maria?" asked Mary.

"Very long."

Lizzy put her hands together in mock prayer. "It is fortunate our Lord did not deliver the commandments to Mr Collins instead of Moses, or we should have a good three dozen of them."

"Lizzy!" I dipped my head in the direction of the Lucases.

"Oh," My daughter put a hand to her mouth. "I did not mean…" She looked about her as if seeking a saviour.

"I suspect Miss Elizabeth simply meant that Mr Collins was most diligent in his readings and keen to find a deeper truth in scripture."

I had not expected Mr Spigott's intervention but was all the more grateful for it. Perhaps Mary's presence gave him confidence. The two of them talked rarely, and the casual observer might have thought them simple acquaintances. But close study revealed more.

They shared the same choice of food, each serving the other with the naturalness of an old couple. And they looked at each other far less often than mere acquaintances might, as if each had something to hide from the other.

"My son-in-law is a fine man," said Lady Lucas. "His exuberance does, however, lead him to talk at length on certain topics."

"Once gave me an hour-long lecture on the care of laurel hedges." Sir William let out a deep sigh. "We do not even have any laurel at Lucas Lodge."

"Well, nobody may accuse him of frivolity," I said. "Charlotte has chosen well." At that moment, Mrs Bennet seemed to swallow something the wrong way and busied herself with a bout of coughing.

And so the conversation drifted on to safer ground, slipping through the fields and meadows of Longbourn, meandering along the streets of Meryton, and finding its way eventually to the one person in our midst whose nature and life we knew of the least.

"What of yourself, Mr Spigott?" said Mrs Bennet. "Do you have any family in these parts?"

"Not in Hertfordshire. Only in Lincolnshire and some cousins in Herefordshire. Are you, perhaps, familiar with those counties?"

"I cannot say that I am." My wife shook her head. "Are they near Derbyshire?"

"Not particularly."

"That it is to their credit." Mrs Bennet nodded in apparent approval. "I once met an unpleasant gentleman from Derbyshire, and I cannot think well of anything from that county since. Mr

Wickham excepted, of course." Mrs Bennet patted the lieutenant's sleeve. "He is such a dear."

"Thank you, ma'am." Mr Wickham seemed content to allow the dinner conversation to proceed without his usual ribaldry. He had spent much of his time eyeing Lizzy with a thoughtful look on his face, though she had not returned his interest. As host, it should have been my duty to ensure the officers joined the general conversation. But few obligations held any appeal since Rudford.

"Mrs Bennet, you speak of the esteemed Mr Darcy?" I said.

"Esteemed!" cried my wife. "Perhaps his manners are the kind to please folk in Derbyshire, but he does not have the gentlemanly manner of a Mr Bingley. It will not do for Hertfordshire. Mr Darcy should take a lesson from Mr Wickham and Mr Denny."

Lizzy winced at the suggestion, but she said nothing.

"And both you officers so soon to Brighton where you will be sure to find wives and not miss us for an instant. We will be obliged to seek young men elsewhere." Mrs Bennet took out her frustration on a baked onion, layer after layer surrendering under the assault of her fork. "Such a pity John and Anne Barton live so far from us. Still, we could invite them, and perhaps John would bring some gentlemen with him. Like that Lord Davenport. Mind you, he had eyes only for Mrs Hayter. I cannot understand why; she has a hardness about her as if suffering from some great disappointment. I enjoyed her many stories, though. You did not tell me you knew her so well in your youth, Mr Bennet. Did you think I would be jealous?"

I ignored the question, preferring instead to rescue the last of the potatoes from the admiring gaze of Sir William.

"I fail to see what she can possibly be displeased about," continued my wife. "She survived two husbands with her wealth intact and her daughter married well. Mrs Hayter has no need of anything. Shall we invite her to Longbourn, too?"

"Certainly not." The vehemence of my answer drew a sharp look from Lizzy. "I will not have that woman near my house."

"Why, Mr Bennet, you astonish me," said Mrs Bennet. "Whatever can you have against Mrs Hayter?"

"I do not like her views on butterflies."

"Well, no matter." My wife looked at the two officers and sighed deeply. "Besides, nobody can make up for dear Mr Wickham and Mr Denny. Your absence will vex me so. How my nerves will suffer!"

"Rest assured, my dear, that we will suffer with them," I said.

"Mrs Bennet, we shall be truly sad to leave your company." Mr Denny raised a glass of wine toward my wife, then did the same to me. "And your table, sir." The young man was one of the more tolerable officers, though the distinction came easily, given the nature of most of his colleagues.

"And as to finding a wife, Mrs Bennet, you need have no concerns there." Mr Wickham's gaze drifted around the table. "We are married to our duty and our tasks. In Brighton, alas, we shall have little time for entertainments and even less for ladies."

"How easily men lie when they seek to beguile us," said Lizzy after the laughter had ended. "It is most unbecoming of you, Mr Wickham."

The poor light prevented me from seeing Mr Wickham's reaction in his face, but he dabbed at his mouth with a napkin as men do when hiding their embarrassment. "I fear Miss Elizabeth has a poor opinion of men," he said.

"Not of *all* men, Mr Wickham," said Lizzy.

"I wish you luck of Brighton, gentlemen," said Sir William. "They say it is nigh on impossible for a man to escape the town without a wife, for it is full to the brim with young ladies!"

"Heavens!" My wife threw up her hands. "I knew it. If only Mr Bennet would take us all there. But he refuses, even though it has long been my most earnest wish to go to Brighton. I am not one to grumble, mind. Never once have I complained on that score."

"How very true, dear," I said. "You have never complained once. Nearer a hundred times would be my estimate."

"Allow me to put you at ease, Mrs Bennet." Mr Wickham adopted a serious tone. "Marriage is not a soldier's due. At least not for those of us below the rank of colonel. We may offer too little of good character for matrimony."

"I believe," said Jane, "that marriage draws out the best in both partners, so that they may grow together in time, even where circumstances did not allow for much consideration of character before the wedding."

I looked across at Mrs Bennet, who was now busy dismembering a pigeon with all the grace of a drunk buzzard.

"What about you, Mr Wickham?" Lizzy sat with her arms folded. "What could ever induce you to marry? What should a wife possess? Looks? Character? Or wealth?"

I could not be sure, but my daughter seemed to place a peculiar emphasis on her final word.

"It is not something I have greatly considered, Miss Elizabeth. A man of my means cannot hold great hopes."

"Then you must rely on your character to marry well. How fortunate that you have the benefit of such a charming disposition." Lizzy took up her knife and fork and began to cut vigorously at a piece of duck.

"Lizzy, you are so serious today." Lydia frowned at her sister. "You should enjoy life more."

"And what would you know about life, Lydia?" I said.

"Papa, I am sixteen in June."

"And none the wiser for it."

"Oh, husband, you and Lizzy make quite a pair," said my wife. "You will frighten Maria. Now, where were we?"

"Discussing marriage." I turned to the curate. "What say you, Mr Spigott? What is the church's view on the topic?"

"Marriage is an object of approval, Mr Bennet. The church is quite clear on that, but—"

"Well said, Mr Spigott, well said." I nodded my head enthusiastically. "Look at Sir William here. And dear Mrs Collins, happily married in Hunsford."

"But did you not say—" began Mr Spigott.

"Ah, that silly conversation about the difficulties of a rector's wife?" I waved my hand dismissively. "That all depends on the location. Longbourn is such a fine village with the best of people. A curate's wife would have an easy life of it here, no doubt. Not like in Kent, with its proximity to London."

"We are but a few miles from London ourselves, are we not?" said Mr Spigott.

"Indeed, we are," I said. "But on the *right* side of London. You cannot compare the two. And Charlotte manages quite well, does she not, Lizzy?"

"She does, Papa."

"Tell me, though, Miss Elizabeth." Mr Spigott paused, as if wishing to select his words carefully. "Would you say Mrs Collins found her responsibilities as a clergyman's wife burdensome?"

"Burdensome but not a burden, I think. Charlotte is practical. Sensible. A credit to her family. An excellent wife and a blessing for Hunsford."

"Tish," said Lydia. "Who would marry a clergyman? You must make do with so very little. Charlotte is only content because her husband will inherit Longbourn."

Silence descended on the room as most of our guests developed a sudden and close interest in the contents of their plates.

"Lydia," I said. "Have another slice of tart."

"But I am not hungry, Papa."

"Have a slice anyway." I motioned to Mary to pass her sister the serving plate. "And remember to chew slowly."

Brighton and Daughters

The consternation and frustration at Longbourn peaked a day or two before the date of the militia's departure. Shakespeare once wrote "The better part of valour is discretion; in the which better part I have saved my life." I had enough discretion to remove myself to the library, its book-bound walls proof against familial opprobrium. Lizzy joined me, perhaps seeking solitude in my company. I hoped it might provide an opportune moment to talk with her about her apparent change in character since Hunsford—a conversation we had not yet quite managed since the day of her return.

Despite my intentions, the seductive pull of our books found both Lizzy and me sitting in silence, transported to literary destinations. We returned now and then only for a sip of tea or a bite of a biscuit before sailing forth once more on a sea of vowels and consonants. I found my pleasures in Matthiessen's exposition on coastal birds. The Lord had seen fit to send us a veritable multitude of different ones, and I was determined to learn more about the beasts since Jackson's sighting of a gull on his estate. Hertfordshire's inconsiderate lack of a coast made direct observation largely impossible.

After some time had passed, I put my book to one side, swapped intellectual nourishment for the more prosaic kind, and took the opportunity to observe my daughter closely. Although the lines had faded from beneath Lizzy's eyes, she still seemed to have left her ready smile in Kent. She twisted that lone strand of hair as she turned the pages, mouth sometimes twitching at the words on the paper before her.

"You have been strangely quiet of late, Lizzy," I said. "Has an officer captured your affection, yet shown no sign of reciprocating? Mr Wickham, perhaps? He seems the sort to play fast and easy with a girl's heart."

Lizzy fixed me with a stern look. "Mr Wickham is *not* an object of my affection."

"And yet you used to speak so well of him. Some other fellow, then?"

"It is nothing, Papa. Perhaps Mr Collins tired me out so and I have yet to recover."

"That is a possibility I can give credence to. I wonder we bother with elixirs of jasmine and camomile when a good half hour with Mr Collins has a similar soporific effect."

My daughter surprised me by leaning forward to take my hand and kiss it. "I am glad to see you in good humour, Papa. You have not been yourself of late, either. You seem reluctant to find joy in anything. And you are especially harsh with Lydia and Kitty."

"Harsh?" I frowned. "I only treat them as they deserve; they grow sillier with each day."

"They are no more silly than they have always been," said

Lizzy. "It is not they that have changed."

I pulled my hands free of my daughter's. "Perhaps my patience is at an end, stretched thin across too many breakfast table conversations about balls and bonnets."

"They will not improve without proper discipline, Papa."

"And why should I waste what little time I have left on such a futile undertaking? Tell me that. Besides, what has discipline and good manners brought you or Jane? A single proposal from an utter buffoon."

Lizzy stiffened. "That is not fair, Papa."

"Fair or not, it is true. So, I shall let your sisters be but find some relief in chastising them for their excesses. It may all prove better in the long run; I was once a man of education and honour, and it brought me a fool's life. Perhaps they will fare better with a lack of both."

"I was mistaken about your good humour, Papa. You are truly not yourself." Lizzy's stance softened; her voice spoke only of concern. "I cannot believe you hold such opinions. Are you unwell?"

"Have no fear, I am perfectly well. Sound of body, at any rate." My anger drained away on seeing the distress in Lizzy's eyes. "Forgive me, child. With each passing year, the burden of life grows heavier. I count my failures more than my successes."

The touch of Lizzy's hand on mine offered some reassurance, though it reminded me of Abigail and the dance at Rudford.

"I envy you your youth," I continued. "You may take everything in your stride. No uncertainties. Few disappointments. And no great secrets to hide." My daughter looked away, perhaps embarrassed for me. "But the more we know and experience, the less certain we become."

At this point in our conversation, a mix of exultation and wailing breached the defences of the library walls. I could distinguish the voices of Kitty and Lydia, with an occasional high-pitched intrusion from Mrs Bennet.

I had long learnt that no argument between my youngest daughters ever required fatherly intervention. Their animosity rarely survived for long, soon dissipated by the sighting or promise of a new bonnet or bachelor. Contrary to expectations, however, the cacophony outside increased in volume until the door burst open. Lydia and Kitty tumbled through, closely followed by my wife.

"Papa!" said Lydia.

"Papa!" said Kitty.

I held my hands up to demand a silence that never came.

"Say I may go, Papa, please!" Lydia held her hands together in supplication.

"Such news, husband, such news!" said my wife.

"Enough, enough!" I cried, to some effect. My two youngest daughters stood with their cheeks flushed and pronounced, as if words piled up inside them. "Now explain yourselves." I held a finger up. "Mrs Bennet?"

"Oh, Mr Bennet, such good fortune. Mrs Forster has written to Lydia." My wife paused to clutch Lydia's hands. "She has invited my dear girl to stay with her in Brighton."

"And Colonel Forster is to bear all the expense," said Lydia.

"*All* the expense," I said. "Then I can think of no immediate objection. But give me some time, and perhaps I shall find one."

Lydia did not wait for me to do so. Instead, she rushed out of the room, waving her arms in unadulterated delight and closely pursued by a gleeful mother.

"Papa?" Kitty trembled, as if holding back tears desperate for permission to pour forth. "May I not go to Brighton with Lydia? I am two years older than her."

"Has Mrs Forster invited you, too?"

"No."

"Then you have your answer. Now be off with you, cry elsewhere, and leave your poor father in peace."

Lizzy closed the door behind a tearful Kitty, then turned. She strode forward and knelt before my chair. "You cannot seriously entertain this notion."

"Why ever not? You should be pleased. If Lydia goes to Brighton, I cannot be harsh with her."

"If Lydia goes to Brighton, her behaviour can only worsen. Mrs Forster is younger than I am. She will have no control over my sister's excesses and may even encourage them. Lydia will fall to every temptation, and her reputation—our family's reputation—will suffer accordingly. She will make a fool of herself and of us all."

"As she already does in Meryton," I said. "The difference being that I shall know nothing of what passes in Brighton. Her chatter and nonsense will travel with her, sparing me both. And Kitty will be the better for her sister's absence. My life can only be improved. Besides, Mrs Forster may be young and naive, but Colonel Forster is not. He shall see that Lydia comes to no harm. What is the youngest daughter of Mr Bennet of Longbourn to the officers in Brighton, when they may pick and choose from the garden of English society? No, we need fear no rogues looking for wealthy prey. Your sister may discover her own insignificance—let that be a lesson to her. And should she expose herself in some public place, then so be it. It matters not to me."

Lizzy's eyes narrowed "Why do you care so little, Papa?"

"Why do you care so much?"

My daughter turned her head away from me briefly. She would always be my little Lizzy, but she was no longer a child. One or two tiny wrinkles had already begun to gather around her eyes, as the patina of age and experience took its inexorable hold. Though far too early in one just twenty years of age.

"What passed in Kent, Elizabeth?"

"What passed in Gloucestershire, Papa?"

I gripped the arms of the chair tightly. As for Lizzy, no painter could have captured my daughter's face at that moment. So many emotions seemed to pass across it. She knelt before me with her chin lifted slightly, her cheeks pinched, and her lips narrow and near bloodless. Her eyes spoke of some kind of yearning, though, and, in that moment, I did not know her. The tension slowly seeped away in the silence, as if we both agreed it would be better to leave our questions unanswered.

"If Lydia disgraces herself," said Lizzy at last, "then she will bring disgrace on us all, if she has not done so already with her antics. What have we if we do not have our reputation?"

"I ask again, Elizabeth, why you care so much for our reputation? Has Lydia's behaviour changed our standing in Meryton? Are we not invited to dine throughout the county? Why, now, this great interest in our reputation, which seems to me as admirable as it always has been? Or have you felt some personal slight? Has Lydia frightened away a gentleman, perhaps?"

"Not at all." Lizzy's thumb began to draw circles on her fingertips.

"If she has, think nothing of it. True affection cares little for such matters. No man worth the name falls in love with a reputation. Or out of love for the lack of one." I placed a hand on my daughter's cheek, but she did not move. Perhaps she was too angry to lean into its touch but not angry enough to pull away. "And you may be assured that the behaviour of your sisters can never, and will never, diminish the respect with which you are held by the world. These sentiments apply equally to Jane."

"But—"

"No buts, Lizzy. Lydia will learn her lesson in Brighton, and I shall have some peace at Longbourn. Kitty may gain some sense without her sister, and Mary will have less reason to rail against the immorality of society. I could not have arranged things better myself. My good humour may return after all."

A Change of Mind

I would not say I set out to the Society with optimism but perhaps with less pessimism than usual. Without Lydia, Longbourn contained one less reminder of my shortcomings as a parent. Her absence also improved the quality of conversation, notwithstanding those rare times when she deigned to send her mother a letter, whose contents were then repeated ad nauseum around the dinner table.

The weather made its own contribution to my improved demeanour. The June sun did not have quite the warmth of high summer, but it had the promise of better to come. August always strikes a more desperate tone, knowing its days are numbered and that chill winds and autumn rains have risen to the north and begun their slow journey southwards.

With blue skies above, I even allowed myself to walk the final yards to the inn. As I did, a familiar figure approached on the other side of the road. Mr Spigott moved just a little faster as he passed Weintraub's, as if the devilish influence of drink might be felt from spending too much time in its vicinity. The curate's hat perched precariously on his head, held up there by faith, hope, and God's own will, for it seemed as if the merest breeze or throw of the head would send it tumbling to the ground.

"Mr Spigott! A fine day, is it not?"

The curate seemed lost in contemplation. So much so that he might have missed me had I not called out to him again. He stopped, looked across to me, then seemed to argue with himself a little before straightening and crossing the road.

"Mr Bennet! You have been much in my thoughts." From his uncertain bearing, I was unsure if this was a good thing.

"And what thoughts might those be?"

"I have spent a great deal of time recollecting your advice to me on marriage and reflecting on the wisdom contained within."

Hope peeked out from my heart, like a shy mouse at dusk. I had continued to encourage Mr Spigott's visits to Longbourn and half-expected him to make an offer for Mary's hand before the summer was out.

"I find myself…" Mr Spigott paused to look skywards, perhaps seeking heavenly approval for what he was about to say. "I find myself in agreement. I should like to marry."

"Why, this is excellent news, Mr Spigott."

"Of course, much would depend on the right choice of spouse. Given my position in the church and all that is required of me, I could not simply follow my heart." The curate spoke less to me and more to the ground, as if still justifying the decision to himself or out of shame for his previous recalcitrance. "I mean to say, it is my responsibility to make an offer to someone who could manage the responsibilities and not fear the absences or hardships required by my work and lack of income."

"You have someone in mind?"

Mr Spigott looked up at me. "No. I do not." His cheeks

seemed somewhat more reddish than before.

"Truly?" I took a step back. "Nobody of your acquaintance who would be sure to accept an offer? Nobody you might feel affection toward? Surely you jest, Mr Spigott."

"I do no such thing, Mr Bennet."

"But...Mary?" I spoke the name with care.

The curate winced as if a dart had pierced his side. Then he pulled himself up straight. "Miss Mary Bennet is...Miss Mary Bennet and I..."

"Yes?" I said.

"She is a lady of Longbourn. I could not ask it of her. To bring her so low."

"Mr Spigott, I hear your words but cannot believe them to be yours. Are you suggesting material concerns?"

"I cannot offer her the comfort she is used to. And my understanding of..." Mr Spigott swallowed then hopped from foot to foot. "My understanding of your...situation."

"My situation?" I narrowed my eyes.

"That she cannot depend on your largesse in the future."

"I beg your pardon?"

"It would not be right, you see." Mr Spigott walked backwards away from me, shaking his head. "It would not be right. Not right for her. Not fair. I cannot ask it of her. I will not ask it."

"Mr Spigott! Wait!" I called out to him, but he turned and hurried away.

Any joy I might have felt in the day skittered away like a cockroach from the light.

~ ~ ~

"I bring unfortunate news, gentlemen." I stood with my back to the committee in a room on the upper floor of the inn, staring out of the window at the spot where Mr Spigott had spoken to me. A cat sat there now, washing its paws in blissful ignorance of the drama it had missed a few minutes earlier.

"Well?" said Fielding. "Do not keep us in suspense like some cheap play."

I returned to the table, thumped down in my seat, and quaffed an entire glass of port in one draught. "Our hope that Mr Spigott would come to see the value of matrimony has borne fruit."

"What did I tell you, Bennet?" Fielding slapped my knee. "It was only a matter of time. Though, given your lack of enthusiasm, I sense there is more to this revelation than meets the eye."

"There is." I held my head in my hands. "He has no wish to make an offer to Mary. Indeed, he is quite determined not to do so."

"What?" said Elliston.

"Why?" said Stanhope.

"How can that be?" said Fielding.

I waved away their questions, though I was quietly grateful for their concern. "It is my own fault. You will recall his source of unease was the great degree of responsibility and hardship placed on the wife of a clergyman?" Heads bobbed about the room in acquiescence. "It seems he does not wish to expose Mary to such a plight."

"But what of his affection for her?" said Fielding. "Were you mistaken in that regard?"

"I do not think so. In fact, I rather believe this very affection leads him to reject the notion of marrying Mary. He does not wish to condemn her to a life without the comforts she is used to. Youth and their misguided concept of love!" My statement drew grumbles of approval and sympathy from around the table. "Still, all is not lost; his eye has yet to fall on an alternative. We have time to persuade Mr Spigott to listen to his heart and not his head."

"We?" Elliston opened his arms out wide. "Look at us all, Bennet. *We* are men of reason, not romance. How should we speak to a clergyman on such matters?"

"There is only one among us who might fit the bill," said Fielding.

All heads turned toward me.

"Gentlemen, really." I scolded the gathering with a raised finger.

"Was it not you who brought Mr Barton to his senses when he was resolved to forget Miss Hayter?" said Fielding.

"And you read the most books," said Stanhope. "Some of those words must have stuck."

"I read guides to butterflies," I said. "It hardly qualifies me to talk of love."

"Old friend." Fielding looked me directly in the eyes. "You know it to be true. We all know it to be true. There is no one better to talk to a young man of love and the pain of regret." He placed rather too much emphasis on that last word for my liking.

~ ~ ~

"I am tired, Fielding." A thick slice of Mrs Tincton's sponge cake, the lone survivor of Jackson's appetite, lay untouched on my plate.

"Well, 'every man desires to live long, but no man wishes to be old.' Be of good cheer, my friend. All will be well."

"Will it?"

"Think of your Mr Barton. We had little hope for him, yet he now enjoys all the comforts of a happy marriage."

"Ah yes," I said. "Which reminds me. I have yet to tell you all of what passed in Gloucestershire. Another tale of unbridled delight that has left me full of rapturous optimism." I reached for a glass of port.

"I did not wish to ask for the details. Your general disposition these past weeks told me enough." Fielding peered over steepled fingers but said nothing more. Outside on the window ledge, a lone crow sent out regular caws of distress as if to mark the time of our silence.

"I expect you wish to know about Abigail?" I said, finally.

"Only if you wish to speak of it."

"I suppose you will not be satisfied until you know all of it. Though I had better have another glass of port first." I leant back in the chair and looked across at my old friend. "I do not know where to begin."

Fielding opened his mouth as if about to reply.

"Do not say begin at the beginning or some such nonsense," I said.

"I was merely going to ask if you even saw her."

"Would I be fumbling for words if I had not?" The irritation in my voice left no mark on Fielding, who continued to stare stoically at me. "Forgive me, old friend. As I said, I am tired. And perhaps angry. Not with you but with myself. For allowing feelings to overcome reason. Or perhaps the reverse."

Fielding raised an eyebrow. "Tired and quite possibly confused."

"She was not kind to me." I twisted my glass in my hands, watching the port swirl around the sides. "And I was not kind to her. She wished for the truth, but I did not wish to give it."

"The truth being?"

"That I love her." I closed my eyes for a moment. "Which is part of my confusion. I loved her then. I do now. I always will. Irrevocably. Even without hope of kindness or understanding from Abigail. She despises my cowardice, my lack of regard for honesty, my unwillingness to admit my love." My hand trembled as I swallowed the remains of my drink. "But I could not say the words to her."

"Goodness." Fielding refilled my glass. "This is more serious than I imagined. And may I ask why you could not, at least, tell her of your love?"

"Perhaps I *am* a coward."

My friend frowned. "That is one accusation that may not be levelled."

"You know as well as I do, Fielding, that courage in the field is not the only bravery. But, no, it was not cowardice. I have come to respect my wife. I do not love her, that you know. But I am indebted to her. I owe her my loyalty. She does not deserve to be slighted by me in such a manner. It would be a small betrayal but a betrayal none the less. Consider it a shred of honour I will not yield up."

My companion scratched his head. "You know, I simply expected you to say you felt a little uncomfortable in Mrs Hayter's presence. We walk on unfamiliar ground, dear friend. I shall need some of that port, too." He helped himself to a glass.

"You say she despises you? You do not think she may still be in love with you?"

"Possibly. But her anger tells a different story." I sighed. "What does it matter? I am too old for all this nonsense."

"We are never too old for nonsense." Fielding steepled his fingers once more. "The wisdom of age is often a lie we use to keep the arrogance of youth in check. Mr Toke would urge you to give up all thought of Mrs Hayter. But the reverend knows nothing of love's hold on a man or the pain it brings. The door to the heart cannot be opened or shut at the turn of a key. If fortune favours us, we may love openly and be loved in return." Fielding tapped his waistcoat pocket, where I knew he kept a miniature of his wife. "If fortune does not, we may love in vain. And the most pitiable among us will never love at all."

"John made a similar point," I said. "Yet I wish I did not love."

"Not a choice you can make, my friend."

"You tell me nothing I do not already know, Fielding. There is no path open to me but to forget. But in the attempt to do so, I merely strengthen the remembrance. And goodness knows we have enough trouble at Longbourn without my agitation. Jane's bloom shall surely turn soon and her hopes of marriage with it. Lizzy will never find a suitable partner, not with her mind and spirit. Lydia and Kitty? The world rarely saw such foolishness. Mary may surprise me yet, but if our hopes lie with a shy and misguided curate, then we are in a fine state. Though, to be honest, I find it hard to care. I sup from a cup brimming with indolence and self-pity."

I stood and went over to a small glass cabinet filled with shells and stones, a present to Mr Tincton from the Society.

"Mrs Bennet chides me for failing to secure my family's future. I find myself thinking that once I am dead, my family's financial condition will not trouble me at all. Perhaps this makes me a bad man." Fielding said nothing as I cast my eye over the cabinet's contents: the long twisted whorl of a wentletrap; a nugget of pyrite, tempting the uneducated with its golden sheen; the carapace of some crab, caught on a coastal excursion. My eyes settled on one half of a tiny geode, the surfaces of the amethysts within smooth and true, shot through with purple and white. "What are women to rocks and minerals?" I said.

"Harder, Bennet. They are harder," said Fielding. "They have to be. Rocks need not cope with the vagaries of a husband. But if you cannot forget Mrs Hayter, then accept it. If I may offer a comparison, I cannot forget the stew that kind farmer's wife made us back in Virginia."

"The rabbit one? With cabbage?"

"Best meal I ever had." Fielding patted his stomach. "Though I rather think any meal would have been considered so, given the fare we survived on for so long. But my point, Bennet, is this: I do not need to forget it. I may even enjoy the memory of it. But I leave it in the past, and my enjoyment of good Hertfordshire food is none the worse for it. You love Mrs Hayter. But you do not have to see her or have anything to do with her. Cherish the memory but do not allow it to consume you."

"That, my dear friend, was a terrible analogy."

"I know," said Fielding with a laugh. "But the best I could think of at such short notice."

"I do not know which was worse—her cruelty toward me, or

mine toward her," I said. "Every word she spoke seemed designed to pierce. Though perhaps I allow my memory to cloud my present judgement. Incidentally, a Lord Davenport accompanied her. A more fatuous character you will not find in all of Gloucestershire. Her behaviour toward him was quite inexplicable, bordering on improper. The foolishness of her choice! I expected better of her."

Pity and compassion laced Fielding's hearty laugh. "That affection might last so long," he said. "How many years have passed? I do declare you both still very much in love."

"And yet we act so badly toward each other."

"My dear Bennet, you can be remarkably dim sometimes for a man of letters."

"My dear Fielding, if I had wanted to subject myself to the abuse of others, I would have remained in Gloucestershire."

"What are friends for, if not to remind us of our foolishness?"

"I have my life for that. My friends I rely on for good port and better conversation."

"Then let us drink another glass and talk of other matters." Fielding reached for a bottle. "There is nothing I can say, and little you can do, other than stay as far away from Mrs Hayter as possible. At a distance, sense rules your heart. In her presence, your heart makes no sense at all."

"Well, I shall at least direct my attention to helping those for whom it is, joyfully, not too late." I held out my glass to receive the consolation of port. "God has blessed Mr Spigott with His word and not much else. But he has a goodness in him that deserves its reward, as I believe does Mary. I suppose we have the advantage that he is now, at least, persuaded of the benefits of marriage. All that remains to do is persuade him of the benefits of marriage to my daughter. It is time for me to become more active. And there I might engage the help of a particular ally."

A Plot and a Painter

"Anne!" The arrival of Mr and Mrs Barton at Longbourn accomplished the task of bringing joy to Lizzy's countenance. "We had no warning of your coming. Did you not write? What is your purpose?"

"We come at the invitation of your father," said Mrs Barton.

"I thought you might enjoy the company, Lizzy, so I took the liberty of inviting Mr and Mrs Barton as a surprise."

Some sparkle had returned to my daughter's eyes. Perhaps I was not such a bad father after all.

"Does anyone else know of their coming?" said Lizzy.

"Your mother," I said. "So presumably half of Hertfordshire, too. And your sisters. We all kept it secret from you."

"Thus denying me the pleasure of anticipation." Lizzy's frown was entirely benign. "I shall forgive you, Papa."

I could not reveal the other reason behind inviting the Bartons until later that day. Mrs Bennet and my daughters fussed over the young couple, pestered them with questions, and plied both with enough food and drink to sink a ship of the line. Our two guests bore it all with good humour, knowing the consideration was rooted in genuine interest and friendship.

By the evening, though, Mrs Barton had answered all questions on Gloucester fashions and John all enquiries on the health of his father, the guests from the Rudford dance, and even his pigs. Once Mrs Bennet satisfied herself that her next visit to Gloucestershire would involve rather more of the right type of bachelor, the assembled company dispersed a little. I persuaded John, Mrs Barton, and Lizzy to walk with me beyond the back garden. "For old time's sake," I said.

We found our way down to the stream, just before the bend that saw it turn toward Meryton. Fallen leaves swirled around the slender wooden fingers of a willow, the current quickened by the previous day's rain. Dimples peppered the water, as all manner of insects commemorated the glory of the summer, at least until a trout rose in a burst of ripples to bring an unfortunate end to the celebrations.

As a child, I had named the large stones that lined the side of the stream nearest to us the "old men." Seemingly bent and broken by time, they made excellent places to sit and talk. John, sketchbook in hand, carried on a little further to where the rustle and shift of the reeds suggested some creature making its way along the banks.

"I used to sit here as a young boy." The surface of the stone felt cool beneath my palms. "I never imagined I would one day do so with Henry Barton's daughter-in-law. Henry would come here too, mind you, when he visited with John's grandfather. I would look out for fish, still and quiet, but he would always be whittling away at a piece of wood or poking at some pebble with a stick." The memory brought a wistful smile to my face. "Always a man of action was Henry. I think that is what did for his spirits in the end, when there was nothing he could do for his wife. Forgive me, Lizzy, Mrs Barton. It seems the further I become removed from the past, the more I find myself falling back into it."

Mrs Barton used a handkerchief to wipe a stone clean before she sat down on it. "John speaks often of your friendship with his father."

"Ah, but it has faded with distance. He keeps himself holed up in Vienna of all places. And I am still sitting here, just as I did all those years ago. What does he see in that city? It may offer the finest musical entertainment, but I cannot imagine they have very good tea."

"They say the Emperor enjoys gardening as a hobby," said Mrs Barton.

"Really? Excellent. Then Vienna has my unreserved approval after all."

"So, Papa, what is it you wish to say to us that no one else should hear?" said Lizzy from her rock.

I straightened on my own stony seat. "Now why would you ask that?"

"Mr Bennet, your efforts at manipulation are as transparent now as they were when John and I were courting." I had forgotten that Mrs Barton rarely felt the need for conversational delicacy—another trait she had inherited from Abigail.

Lizzy leaned forward to pat me gently on the arm. "Subterfuge is not your forte. Most of the time we cannot be sure quite what you are thinking, but whenever you engage in any disingenuous scheme, well…" She shrugged. "Your efforts to hide your true purpose achieve quite the opposite."

"Do not despair, Mr Bennet," said Mrs Barton. "You cannot help that your daughter is a quite excellent judge of character."

"Do not say that, Anne." A hint of sharpness coloured Lizzy's voice. "Perhaps once I was such a judge. At least, I always believed it of myself. But recent events have shown me that I, too, may allow prejudice to cloud my opinion." She shook her head, as if waking from an unexpected slumber. "So I am resolved not to judge so quickly ever again. I make an exception for you, though, Papa."

"That is most kind," I said. "And perhaps for Mr Collins?"

"Yes," said Lizzy. "A man whose character is entirely transparent. At least until Lady Catherine suggests he hide it."

"A little respect for my dear cousin, if you please." I shook a finger at my daughter, smiling as I did so.

"Papa, I grant him precisely the respect he deserves. Now, what do you wish to say?"

I pursed my lips and drummed out a little rhythm on the stone with my fingers. "Do not misunderstand me, either of you. I have not brought you to Longbourn, Mrs Barton, under false pretences. Lizzy, you have been quite out of sorts since returning from Hunsford. I thought you in need of Mrs Barton's particular companionship. You have your elder sister, of course, but Jane is far too good-natured and sympathetic to be of any use when a young woman requires distraction."

"Am I to understand, then, that I am neither good-natured nor sympathetic, Mr Bennet?" Mrs Barton set her hands on her hips.

"Quite the opposite. But you understand that kindness and

sympathy alone are sometimes inadequate. Lizzy needs your lively conversation. I admit, however, to a further reason for my invitation—Mary."

Lizzy leaned back, one eyebrow rising slowly as if unsure whether it should first wait for more information. The two ladies then listened attentively as I outlined the situation with Mr Spigott.

"So, your curate loves Mary but does not wish to marry her." Mrs Barton gave me the kind of look I reserved for Mr Jones's delivery boy when he brought us a new kind of nerve tonic for my wife. "That does not sound like love."

"Mr Spigott is, unfortunately, a good man," I said. "And good men do not act for their own pleasure. Their concern is for everyone but themselves; they do what they believe to be right and sensible, with no hope of personal reward. Therein lies the problem with Mr Spigott. It is out of love that he does not wish to marry Mary."

Lizzy shook her head. "That makes no sense, Papa."

"Let us assume I am correct in my assumption that my daughter and Mr Spigott share a mutual affection. As you know, Lizzy, Mary does not declare her feelings openly, though she makes an exception for her disapproval. If I have read the signs correctly, Mr Spigott is not confident enough of Mary's love to expose his own. More pertinently—and to answer your question—he does not see such an offer worthy of her. And so we must act."

"You think Mary suits the role of a curate's wife?" Lizzy's eyebrow began to climb again.

"You underestimate your sister," I said. "Her qualities are

subtle. She may surprise us once she removes herself from Longbourn. Take the bud out of the shadows, and it may flower with enough love and attention."

"Have you tried talking to him, Papa?"

"I thought we might first offer him more evidential proof of Mary's affection. Somehow encourage her to reveal her feelings and willingness to make do in a curate's cottage. Then I shall talk to him directly."

"And for this you brought dear Anne all the way from Gloucestershire?"

"As I said, it was not primarily for this purpose. But given the events of last winter, I thought you both would make ideal protagonists for this venture."

"I was quite happy to play a game in my own cause," said Mrs Barton. "But I would feel uncomfortable doing so for another's. Is it not a presumption to interfere in the happiness of Mary and Mr Spigott, when neither has requested such intervention?"

"My dear Mrs Barton, the entirety of English society is predicated on such interference. Besides, if I am wrong, then Mr Spigott may marry someone else, and no harm is done."

"Except, perhaps, to Mary's feelings," said Lizzy.

"Which is why I call upon the delicacy and—dare I say—deviousness that you showed in John's case."

"I do not know if I should be flattered or offended." Mrs Barton looked across at my daughter. "What do you say, Elizabeth?"

"Does Mama know?"

"Not directly." I grimaced. "She would welcome such a match, but Mr Spigott's current reluctance would only remind her of my failure to secure the future financial security of you girls. I would rather avoid another one of those conversations. But we may rely on her support when push comes to shove."

"And Jane?" said Lizzy.

"I do not wish to talk of love and courtship with your sister, given her recent disappointment. Besides, Jane is not suited to the dark arts of which you are the masters."

Lizzy stood and dusted herself down. "You wish us to present Mary in an even more favourable light and convince her to make her feelings clearer to Mr Spigott?"

"In a nutshell, yes."

My daughter's mouth twisted in apparent thought. "Charlotte would certainly encourage us to do so. I recall her words at the Netherfield ball: '...there are very few of us who have heart enough to be really in love without encouragement. In nine cases out of ten a woman had better show *more* affection than she feels.' If Jane had taken this advice, how different things might have been with Mr Bingley." She sighed. "We will see what can be done."

Lizzy and Mrs Barton decided to return to the house, so I made my way over to where John was standing at the edge of the stream, looking across the meadow.

I pointed to a low hill. "That rise offers the best partridge on the estate. Have you sketched it?"

"No." John held up his paper.

"Good Lord."

"You do not like it?"

"I sometimes forget your skill as an artist, John. Such a remarkable likeness. Although...do I really look so old? You have drawn Lizzy and your wife in the bloom of youth, but me?" I raised a hand to my cheek, let my fingers search for the wrinkles in John's portrayal. "Have I aged so much?"

"You do not grow older, Mr Bennet, just wiser."

I could not help but smile at his kindness. "Quite the reverse, I feel. And if I have grown wiser, it is too little and too late."

John said nothing.

"How is Rudford?" I asked.

"Fine, fine. The extensions near completion and the curiosity of the county has abated, so we may begin to enjoy the best sort of company: our own."

"You are alone there?"

"Well…almost."

"You may mention her name, you know, John."

My friend coloured and turned his head away in that shy way of his.

"Have no fear," I continued. "I shall not repeat any of those sentiments that I expressed on the night of the dance. The sanctity of Longbourn protects me."

We began to walk along the bank, the stream growing darker as the sun's descent sent rivulets of orange coursing through the low cloud. All was still but for the occasional splash when our progress sent some bird or animal scattering into the safety of the water.

"Dusk must be an excellent time to paint." I nodded at the sunset. "All the colours."

"The fading light gives an urgency to the canvas," said John. "I become conscious of all that remains incomplete, all that I must accomplish before the darkness comes."

"Are we still speaking of painting?"

"Of course. What else? Oh no, I would never presume to comment on—"

"My dear friend, I am teasing you. My melancholy has not yet reached such depths." I stooped down and lifted a beetle off our trail, laying it gently to one side, where it bumbled its way into the undergrowth. "Dusk is my time. The house is quiet, and I may read by candlelight. An expensive pursuit neither easy for the eyes nor good for them. But, at such times, the world consists only of words outlined in a patch of light. I may abandon myself to tales of travel, science, and history without fear of distraction. Now, tell me, is that not an exquisite sight?"

John followed my outstretched arm to where two swans drifted down the stream, heads tucked into their feathers, unconcerned by the spin of the current, like a couple at the fair dancing to a slower tune than the fiddler's song.

My friend turned to me. "Your visit left its mark on her, you know. She talks of you still."

"No doubt to rue the day she placed any faith in me. Or is it to criticise my apparent loss of liveliness? The list of flaws and failures must be large in her eyes." I suddenly felt unusually fatigued. "Forgive me. It seems I am not safe at Longbourn after all. Heed our lesson, John. Perhaps both Mrs Hayter and I have let disappointment and anger rule our hearts. Whenever we spend time with each other, it ends in ill-chosen words and more regrets."

"Shakespeare knew," said John.

My tongue will tell the anger of my heart,
Or else my heart concealing it will break,

And rather than it shall, I will be free
Even to the uttermost, as I please, in words.

"Well said. Though I hope I have behaved better than Petruchio. Is Mrs Hayter with you much?"

"Yes. She misses Anne's company and lively mind. Though she bears me no ill will for stealing both from her. Indeed, I could not wish for a more condescending mother. It is a comfort, given…well, you know my story. Still, we have encouraged her to travel to London, where she has a house, her sister, and friends, as well as books and plays to please her mind."

"Then our paths will not cross soon. London is the very last place I would choose to go of my own volition. It has its books and plays but rather too many writers and actors. They are almost as annoying as artists."

A slow smile formed on John's face. "You are teasing me again."

"Good man," I said. "You learn quickly."

Secrets and Lies

Naturally, Mrs Bennet's pleasure at the Bartons' visit depended less on their presence and more on how many people knew of it. Accordingly, an ever-changing cast of ladies and gentlemen passed through our doors. This gave me the opportunity to suggest we invite Mr Spigott to dinner again. My wife offered no protest since our curate still claimed that particular qualification that raised him up from his fellow man—he was in need of a wife, even if not in possession of anything approaching a good fortune.

"Now is the right time for it." Mrs Bennet stood over her collection of dinner menus, eyes focused like a hawk before the kill. "And we shall seat him close to Mary at the end furthest away from the window. Then he cannot observe her complexion too closely."

"My dear," I said. "Mr Spigott is not so shallow."

"Indeed not." My wife returned to her notes, finger running down the page in search of those dishes that would place Longbourn and its daughters in the best of lights. "But if you wish to sell the flower, then you must hide the chips in the vase."

"So, you would approve if Mary and Mr Spigott developed an understanding?"

"You know I would."

"And yet we have not invited him to any dinners these past four days."

"There has been little opportunity to do so, what with all our other guests. And tomorrow the Gardiners arrive to take Lizzy away with them. So, it must be today."

As a curious amateur in the business of matchmaking, I felt the need to dip my toe further into the pool of Mrs Bennet's matrimonial wisdom. "But he might have joined any one of those previous dinners."

My wife's finger ceased its endless roaming, and she stood up straight. "Not again, Mr Bennet. By now you should know to leave such details to me. To invite him earlier would have been most inauspicious."

"I do not understand."

"Hill!" cried my wife. "Tell Cook it shall be the mousse. But do not use as much cream. Mr Spigott should not think us extravagant."

Hill's face appeared around the edge of the door. "Yes, ma'am. I understand Mr Spigott is partial to an apple crumble."

"We shall have a crumble then, too." Once Hill disappeared, Mrs Bennet returned to her lecture. "I had already planned for this dinner from before the day of John's arrival. Oh, do not look so confused."

I turned a chair and sat myself down in the reverse direction, arms crossed over the top of the back. "Explain yourself, my dear."

My wife sighed. "We could hardly invite him on the day of John's arrival. I must be the first to hear all gossip, so I may share it with Mrs Philips and Mrs Long and see their faces at the novelty of my news. The Lucases visited on the second day. That was their right as our closest neighbours. But Lady Lucas now wishes to see Maria follow Charlotte into a suitable union. Given Maria is no less plain than her sister, they will limit their expectations to the likes of Mr Spigott. And so I will not now have the Lucases and the curate at the same table. Then, on Thursday, we dined with Mr Fielding and his wife. With you and your friend present, Mr Spigott would have little chance of joining the conversation and showing himself favourably."

"Why ever not?"

"Mr Bennet, you spent twenty minutes debating whether the Hairstruck butterfly—"

"Hairstreak, my dear."

"Hairstreak, Hairstruck, however you call it." My wife shrugged. "You spent twenty minutes arguing whether it had ever been seen north of Derby."

"But yesterday...the Weatherheads and their daughter, Anne. She is promised to a Mr Freeman, I believe. She would offer no temptation to Mr Spigott."

My wife sighed again. "Anne Weatherhead is promised, but Mrs Long tells me she stood up three times with Mr Freeman at the last Meryton Assembly before any formal understanding had been reached. And Mrs Weatherhead had several admirers before she accepted her husband's offer. As a man of the cloth, Mr Spigott could not be expected to sup at the same table as a source of such scandal and intrigue."

"Scandal and intrigue?" I felt my understanding of the words slipping away from me like a greased pig at the fayre. "Might I remind you that *you* had several offers before you accepted mine? Are you equally as scandalous as our poor Mrs Weatherhead?"

"Certainly not!" Mrs Bennet wagged a finger at me. "I was a beauty, whereas Mrs Weatherhead was quite plain. One might ask how freely she gave her affections to encourage such offers."

"My dear, I think you—"

"Now just Mr Spigott and the Bartons attend our table. He shall be able to speak freely, and we may talk of all those matters that he enjoys. Like those pamphlets. I shall rely on you, husband, to steer the conversation appropriately."

Well," I said. "I believe you may be the Machiavelli of marriage, my dear. It is a wonder none of our daughters are yet married."

"They might have been, if only you had persuaded Elizab—"

"Yes, I know, I know." I threw my hands into the air.

~ ~ ~

In the hours before dinner, I found Lizzy perusing maps of Matlock and surrounds in my study. I hoped her next departure from Longbourn would bring her more pleasure than the previous one. It seemed likely, given her forthcoming journey with the Gardiners would take her far away from Kent and Mr Collins.

"Derbyshire, eh, Lizzy?" I said. "You must call in and see Mr Darcy. Does he not own half of it?"

"I shall do no such thing, Papa."

"Come now, perhaps you may find his estate tolerable,

though not enough to tempt you." I winked at my daughter.

"Tempt me into what?"

"Goodness, Lizzy, has humour abandoned you entirely? Perhaps I should warn Mr Gardiner."

Instead of a smile at my suggestion, I received an admonishment. "Please do not talk of Mr Darcy, Papa."

I caught my daughter's arm and drew her to a chair. "Right, sit yourself down, young lady. I have had quite enough of this silence on Hunsford. Is there something you wish to tell me about Mr Darcy? Did he insult you once more? Well, we knew him to be an arrogant sort, but I assumed he had the manners to at least converse cordially with others. I suppose he thinks you below him in circumstances, does he?"

Lizzy flinched at my last observation.

"I thought as much. I would not tear up the order of things like the French, but rank comes with obligations, particularly to one's lessers. And the least we may expect of such a man is respect." I began to pace up and down, ignoring my daughter's protestations and attempts to gain my attention. "Pride is a terrible thing, and it will have its tribute. Mr Darcy would do well to heed that lesson. Miss de Bourgh has my pity. I might ask what she has done to deserve her fate. Married by Mr Collins to Mr Darcy. Imagine!"

I finally stopped, seeing my daughter bent over with her head in her hands.

"It is not what you think, Papa. Or rather…oh, I cannot explain." Lizzy straightened, wiped her eyes, then clasped her hands together on her lap. "Pray do not press me for details, for I cannot give them. Mr Darcy has done nothing that need concern you. He has merely revealed prejudices I did not think I had and caused me to reflect on my own beliefs, my own character. Nothing more. But that is enough when you have lived your life in the certainty of your judgement."

"My Darcy is the one who should reflect on character," I said.

"It is not as simple as..." Lizzy paused, then threw up her arms. "There, I have finally spoken of Hunsford. Let us say no more of the matter."

"Mr Darcy, indeed. If I were twenty years younger, I wou—"

"Papa!"

"Very well. I shall hold my tongue."

"And perhaps," said Lizzy, "you will now tell me of Gloucestershire."

I caught my breath, straightened my cravat, and then sat down. "This is no marketplace. We struck no bargain or exchange."

Lizzy arched her eyebrows. "I would have thought it a matter of respect, which I am told is essential in a gentleman of rank."

"Hmph! It has come to this, has it? You would use my own words against me?"

The shadows could not hide the challenge in her eyes. *Ut imago est animi voltus sic indices oculi.* Cicero knew that the eyes tell all. A twist of fabric protruded from my chair, growing in length as I teased it out. I held up the strand to the light from the window.

"Take some advice from your father, Lizzy, and never pull at old threads. They come apart."

"Papa? Gloucestershire?"

"Yes, yes, I am searching for the right words, so there may be

181

no misunderstanding." I tucked the strand behind a cushion. "There was a time when Mrs Hayter and I were close. But our friendship ended badly."

"How so?" Lizzy leant forward in her seat.

"Oh, you know how these things are with friends. I did not agree with a decision she once made many years ago. We are perfectly capable of being cordial with each other. One might almost say we have renewed that friendship. But our truce remains brittle, and we argued at Rudford. A misunderstanding. And I am sorry for it."

"That is all? A little altercation among friends? And this is what you wished to keep from me? This is what has you so dispirited?" My daughter did not seem convinced—further evidence of her intelligence. I regretted having let her spend so much time with my books.

"It is not what Mrs Hayter said or what I said. It is how she made me feel. She reminded me of my past, and you know there are events, people, and times I do not wish to speak of."

"The army?"

In not answering my daughter's question, I did not lie. Though I did not tell the truth.

"Oh, Papa." Lizzy moved to kneel before me, resting her head on my lap.

"But see, now it is I who has lost all humour," I said. "My concerns are nothing that a few glasses of port and the company of my friends cannot remedy. And, much as I love Lydia, her absence from Longbourn has allowed me a little more tranquillity. Your worries on that account proved unfounded. In fact, I do declare Brighton to be one of my better decisions." My daughter's hair felt soft beneath my touch. "You are young and so full of promise, even if Mr Darcy may make you question yourself. I have half a mind to send your mother up to his estate. She would teach him a lesson or two."

Lizzy lifted her head. "I am not sure she would, Papa, though she might frighten him into his library where he might never come out."

"Well, there are worse fates than a life in a library. Now, tell me of Mary. Have you spoken with her?"

"We have."

I lowered my voice. "Does anyone else know of our plot?"

"Only Jane," whispered Lizzy. "I could not have kept such a matter from my sister. She does not condone such interference, but she approves of the sentiments enough to ensure her secrecy."

"Excellent. And what am I to expect at dinner?"

"Mousse, Papa." Lizzy tapped her nose. "But with less cream than usual. Or so Hill tells me."

Another Dinner

"Mary looks well tonight, does she not, Mr Spigott?" My wife was the battering ram of Longbourn conversation.

"Why, yes, Mrs Bennet. May I compliment all the Bennet sisters? And Mrs Barton, of course. And you look most well, too, Mrs Bennet." Mr Spigott coughed. He had survived admirably through the first part of the dinner, revealing no apparent awkwardness, though he rarely looked at Mary; they never spoke directly to each other, as if some weight lay heavy on their previous familiarity. I felt sorry for putting the curate in this position after our conversation in Meryton, but needs must when the devil drives—and when a daughter's happiness is at stake.

"You are very kind, Mr Spigott," said Mrs Barton. "A lady enjoys a compliment as much as a man enjoys a glass of wine."

"We men are not averse to receiving a kind word or two, either." John affected a wounded look. "They are made all the more valuable by their rarity."

Mr Spigott continued eating his mousse, but my family paused to watch the drama unfold.

"You must try harder to deserve the compliments," said Mrs Barton.

"But how shall we know what to do, dear, when we receive so few compliments as to guide our behaviour?"

"If you must ask how to behave, husband, then you deserve no compliment for having done so. A compliment must be earned, not handed to you on a plate."

"Mr and Mrs Barton." I clapped my hands together. "You will scare our guest. He is not used to your ways."

"Forgive me, Mr Spigott." Any discomfort the curate might have felt could never have survived Mrs Barton's apologetic smile, honed in the salons and teashops of Bath. "My husband and I enjoy teasing each other. The day we no longer do so is the day I know he no longer loves me."

John took his wife's hand and kissed it gently. "My dear, that day will never come."

"Good," I said. "Though we do not want Mr Spigott here thinking that argument is the way to a woman's heart."

"Well, Papa." Lizzy held up her hand. "Since you imply expertise on the matter, might you tell us just how a man should win a lady's affection?"

"With the size of his income," said Mrs Bennet from the other end of the table.

"I shall not answer your question, Lizzy." I knew a trap when I saw one. "It is not for me to speak for a woman's heart. Your own sex had better do so. If I recall, we had just such a conversation once before. Something about selfless affection, is that not so?"

"Yes. I would only add that the gentleman in question must

accept her as she is. All of her. Her character, her reputation, and even her family." Lizzy twisted in her seat to look at Mary, who sat with her lips parted, as if wishing to say something but lacking the confidence to do so. "What do you say, Mary?"

Mary cast her eyes around the table, dropping them as her gaze reached Mr Spigott. He was, I noticed, all attention now, though whether out of politeness or personal interest, I could not say for sure.

"He must be of strong morals," said Mary.

"Oh, how tiresome." My belief that Lydia's Brighton stay might improve Kitty had proven true, but she still seemed to feel the occasional need to make up for her sister's absence.

"Now, then, Kitty, give Mary a chance," I said. "She has not finished."

Mary nodded slowly, as if giving the matter considerable thought. "He must act for others and not for himself."

"Very honourable," I said. "Yet you must allow a man a little selfishness. That he might choose the woman who would bring him the most contentment. Is that not so, Mr Spigott?"

The curate did not answer, his attention still fixed on Mary.

"He must be kind. He must read scripture." Mary's breath now came in gasps. "And he must like gar—" Her voice broke off for a moment. "Excuse me, Mama, Papa." She stood, attempted what I assumed was a smile in the direction of Mr Spigott, who sat quite still, then rushed out of the room.

"Well, I never," said Mrs Bennet.

"Lizzy," I said. "Will you see to your sister?"

"I shall go with you, Elizabeth." Mrs Barton rose hurriedly. "Should you need something fetching, I may be of assistance."

"More mousse, Mr Spigott?" My wife waved a serving spoon.

"Or perhaps some crumble?" I gestured at a large tray of dessert, where the occasional piece of apple poked through an undulating landscape of baked topping.

No more than half a minute later, my daughters and Mrs Barton returned. Mary approached her chair, smiled awkwardly at Mr Spigott again, then, in what might have been an attempt to behave coquettishly, twisted a curl of hair, trapping her finger in the process. As Lizzy attempted to repair the damage, Mary turned a shade of red that would have put a cherry to shame and, as soon as her finger was free, rushed out once more, gamely pursued by Lizzy, Mrs Barton, Jane, and Mrs Bennet.

I swallowed. "Perhaps, gentlemen, we had best retire to my library."

"But what about me?" Kitty sat alone, surrounded by the aftermath of dinner.

"Have some more mousse," I said.

~ ~ ~

"I do hope Miss Mary Bennet is not unwell. Her behaviour was...somewhat unusual. Is there anything I might do?" Mr Spigott stood at one of the bookcases, tapping the floor with his foot, and casting occasional glances at my collection of volumes on gardening.

"She is in good hands." I refrained from offering an obvious and pointed riposte to his question. "But I thank you for your concern. Mary will be glad to hear of it."

"You have many books, Mr Bennet." The curate looked around the walls. "You must truly have little need of my pamphlets."

"Goodness, no, I can always find a use for your pamphlets." With some effort, I avoided looking at the fireplace.

"Do you write them yourself, Mr Spigott?" John knelt by the smallest bookcase in the room, the one dedicated to art and poetry. He picked out a tome and blew dust off its top.

"No, no. The bishop has them sent down to me. I read them all, though. I cannot expect others to do what I have not done myself. Though of late…" Mr Spigott's voice trailed off, his gaze still wandering through the room.

"Port?" I asked, expecting the usual refusal. On this occasion, though, the curate nodded, took the glass, and drank the liquid down in one.

"You seem pensive, Mr Spigott." I refilled his glass. "Can I help in any way?"

The curate looked over to where John had buried himself in a book of Venetian sculpture. My friend traced lines and curves across an engraving, his mind perhaps back on his travels through Italy.

Mr Spigott leaned over to me. "I have had second thoughts," he whispered.

"About what?" I pulled him further away from John and tried not to allow hope into my voice.

"About what makes a good wife, Mr Bennet. How should a man choose? What weight to give duty and what to give love? I am all confusion."

I took the glass from the curate and left it on a nearby table, then placed my hands on his shoulders and pulled him up straight. "It is, perhaps, time for you to stop behaving like a man of God and start behaving like a man. May I be so bold as to ask what your heart truly wishes?"

Mr Spigott seemed on the verge of replying when the door flew open, throwing Kitty into the library.

"Kitty!" I released the curate from my grip. "I realise you lack a formal education, a fault for which I am to blame, but I presume you understand the role played by a closed door?"

"I am sorry, Papa." My daughter spoke between quick breaths, her cheeks flustered. "But Mary will not come from her room, and Mama's nerves, and Jane thinks we might call for Mr Jones. You must come."

"John," I said. "You know where there is more port should another bottle be required. Do not drink it all. I have a feeling I shall need some before the day is out."

By the time I returned, Mr Spigott had left for home.

Wisdom in Cake

The Bartons left early the next day, their departure overshadowed by the arrival of Mrs Bennet's brother and his wife. Mary refused to leave her bedchamber, but she did emerge, briefly, to greet her relatives in the evening, her face pale but not marred by the tears I half expected. She did not speak to either Lizzy or me before returning to her room. I wished to finish my conversation with Mr Spigott but would not do so until I had spoken with Mary. However, I left her to first find her own way to whatever destination her thoughts would lead; the journey would take her several days. Mr Spigott did not call, no doubt overwhelmed by his infuriating shyness and uncertainty, to which we could now add confusion. He did, though, send a note thanking us for the dinner and asking after Mary's health.

Mr and Mrs Gardiner travelled onward not a day after their arrival, taking Lizzy with them to the north and leaving behind four nephews and nieces in return. It was not a fair exchange; I regarded young children much as I did our Prussian allies. Their existence was of great comfort to me, but I did not wish them in my home. As so often, I found regular refuge in books.

A week had passed, and July stood at the threshold of August when the library door creaked open. Glancing over the top of Sheen's treatise on Welsh minerals, I could see nobody enter, yet the patter of feet spoke of an invader in my inner sanctum. The footsteps stopped in front of my armchair, and I lowered my book to reveal a small face with large eyes. A trembling arm held out a plate with a square of cake on it, one small corner missing, as if a child had taken the very tiniest of bites.

"Julia, is it not?"

The face nodded.

"This is for me?"

Another nod.

"There appears to be some missing."

To Julia's credit, she did not flinch, though the trembling now migrated to her lower lip.

"Do you know the best thing about eating cake?"

"No," whispered my niece.

"Sharing it with others."

I patted my knee and, after handing me the plate, Julia clambered up in relief.

"Let me give you some advice, young lady, that will serve you well in years to come. If you are going to share a sponge cake, then do not always cut from top to bottom." I lifted off the upper portion of the piece to reveal the jam-lined centre. "Give the top half to your companion and keep the bottom half for yourself. That way you get all the jam."

I winked, took a bite of the upper part of the cake, and held out the jam-laden remains to my young companion. Her face glowed.

"And if one day a young gentleman should offer you the bottom half of his cake, as I have just done, then think well of him. Now, be off with you."

A few minutes later, the door creaked open again.

"More cake?" I said.

"No, Papa."

Mary walked into the room, her face composed, but her steps hesitant, as if unsure the floor would bear her weight. She would normally perch on a seat, unwilling to submit herself entirely to its comfort. On this day, however, she melted into the armchair opposite my own. Perhaps she needed the physical reassurance of the chair's upholstered back. I marked the page in my book and placed it to one side, then watched her over steepled fingers. After a minute or so, Mary took a deep breath before closing her eyes for just a moment. Then she spoke.

"Papa, you recall when I overheard your conversation with Mrs Hayter in the library?"

A prickle of embarrassment threatened to make its way to my cheeks. I forced it down, reminding myself that my actions that day had been entirely honourable.

"I do."

"You said, then, that I might always confide in you."

"That is true. Though, here at Longbourn, you claimed that confidence had to be earned."

"I know." Mary hesitated. "But I must speak with someone."

"Then confide away."

"I made a fool of myself." Mary did not need to say when. She seemed smaller than ever in the depths of the huge chair.

"My dear girl, you were not foolish. Even if you were,

Longbourn has seen much worse. Do not trouble yourself."

"But I *was* foolish. Not just in my actions but in allowing my own judgement to be overruled by others. Lizzy and Mrs Barton encouraged me to behave...flirtatiously." My daughter spoke the last word with some difficulty. "Mr Spigott's regard for me will have declined. That is not something I wish."

"What *do* you wish, then?"

"To have Mr Spigott's good opinion for who I am and not who I might pretend to be."

"Do not be harsh on yourself or on Lizzy and her friend." I picked at a hole in the armrest, the passage of time measured out in missing fabric. "I asked them to speak with you. To encourage you to show your affection for Mr Spigott more clearly, hoping he might then admit to his own for you. I felt you both needed encouragement." I placed my hand on my heart. "But I am sorry to have exposed you so."

"I know it was you, Papa." Mary's voice showed no sign of any anger.

"You are not cross with me?"

"Your actions were poorly thought out but taken with the best of intentions. To have you and Lizzy take such an interest in my welfare is a rare kindness. I am...grateful."

"You are most forgiving."

"We are taught to forgive."

"We are taught many things, but whether we practice them is uncertain." I leant forward and took Mary's hands in mine. "Perhaps it is time we talked directly. I thought Mr Spigott needed some incentive to overcome his selflessness. He does not think of himself, you see. I once found him walking to Meryton in the most atrocious conditions. He had promised to attend a Bible meeting at Mulcaster's. That is Mr Spigott. He worries that to give free rein to his affections would be selfish. I believe he loves you but does not wish to condemn you to a life lacking the luxury of your current situation."

"He told you all this?" A little light returned to Mary's eyes.

"Not in so many words. It is my opinion. And, yes, I have proven myself a poor judge at times." I held my daughter's hands tightly now. "Tell me, Mary, could you be a clergyman's wife? I should have asked this question before. The life is not always easy—you know how Lizzy speaks of Mrs Collins."

"I could, Papa, though you may not believe it." She must have sensed some distrust or disbelief in my manner. "I know my reputation. Stern. Moralising, even. It is a position forced on me by my sisters. I cannot be beautiful or intelligent or engaging. Instead, I am a voice of reason, one compelled to become ever more strident since no one ever listens to quiet little Mary. It makes me harsh and is not who I truly am."

"Shadows and light," I murmured. "I have let you down once more, Mary. The role you speak of—to teach my youngest daughters the meaning of right and wrong—should have been mine."

"But it was mine, and I have not played it well. Take me away from Longbourn, and I shall be the true Mary."

"Then I am all the more sorry to have made things with Mr Spigott more complicated."

Mary nodded and bit her lip. "I love him, Papa, but I do not know what to do."

"None of us do, Mary, none of us do. Let us sleep on it, and we will talk more tomorrow."

A Lady Speaks

Mary and I did not resume our conversation the following morning. Instead, I found myself galloping unexpectedly on horseback like a knight on some great quest. According to the stories told to children, my steed and I should have flown like the wind. Unfortunately, neither I nor my horse were young; at the bottom of the lane, we reached common agreement and slowed to a trot. This allowed me to read the letter again, written in Mary's neat, yet unremarkable, hand.

My dearest Papa,

If I am to leave the shadows, then it must be on my own terms. I have spent the last night seeking advice from Scripture. It is written "My little children, let us not love in word, neither in tongue; but in deed and in truth." And the Psalms urge us to "show forth thy loving kindness in the morning, and thy faithfulness every night." I have taken this as inspiration and shall make my declaration in deed and truth this morning. You may expect me for dinner, whatever the outcome.

Your loving daughter,
Mary

The hedges bordering the lane that wound its way into the village prevented me from seeing Mary until I had almost reached Mr Spigott's cottage. She stood a few yards shy of the curate's front gate. Thankfully, no villagers travelled the same road. I left the horse tied to a convenient branch and walked across to my daughter.

"Is he not at home?" I asked.

Mary did not react to my arrival with surprise. She seemed to reserve all her attention for her anointed task, her gaze fixed on Mr Spigott's home. "I do not know. I have yet to call."

My daughter's arm tensed at the touch of my hand. She had changed nothing of her appearance. Mary was as she always was—plain. But she was beautiful in her acceptance of it.

"What I think you propose to do is most improper, not to say foolish." I said.

"I know." Mary still stared toward the cottage.

"And somewhat out of character, if I may say so."

"Are you going to appeal to my sense of obedience and demand I return home?"

"No. What sort of a father would that make me?"

"Perhaps a wise one."

"You are sure of yourself? And you are certain that Mr Spigott will respond as you hope?"

"Of myself, I am sure." Now my daughter finally looked up at me. "As regards Mr Spigott, I am both confused and racked with doubt."

"Good. This marks you as a woman of intelligence, for life is all confusion and doubt."

"You are not helping, Papa."

"Listen to me, Mary. We all speak of morality and propriety, condemning the behaviour of others when they fail to meet the standards we demand. But then love comes along, and the lines between right and wrong, good and bad, well, they shimmer and fade. Love complicates everything. At such times, look to your faith and look to your heart. Do what you must do, and do it with courage."

"Thank you, Papa."

"Having said all that, we might at least give the appearance of propriety. It might be better if you were to call on Mr Spigott in the company of your dear father. Perhaps he wishes to see the curate about some of those delightful pamphlets. So shall we?"

Mary took my proffered arm, and we walked a little further before entering Mr Spigott's tiny front garden. The tumble of bright meadow flowers and shrubs offered a stark contrast to the order of the rear garden. Yet the curate kept the chaos on a strict leash, as if he managed these plants like a shepherd might guard his flock.

"You are ready?" I asked.

Mary nodded.

Mr Spigott answered the door himself. A broken leaf clung to one side of his old breeches. His eyes widened at the sight of myself and Mary.

"Mr Bennet, Miss Bennet, I…" After a moment, the curate found his voice again. "Well, come in. Yes, do come in."

The back room barely justified the name, yet it was cosy and clean enough. Mr Spigott directed Mary to the single armchair. A three-legged beechwood table next to it supported a few bound volumes, though I could not read their titles, and a small stack of pamphlets lay on the floor nearby. A wooden plate was lodged in the opening of the single window.

"I like to feed the squirrels." Mr Spigott must have noticed me glance at the gap. "One comes most days." His face coloured. "I named it Wills. Like my brother."

Mary sat without speaking, searching the room as if seeking clues, though she had a curious smile on her face.

"I have not much to offer you," said Mr Spigott.

"On the contrary," I said. "I would suggest quite the opposite."

"Perhaps a little tea?" The curate wiped hair from his eyes. "The bishop's wife is kind enough to send some over each month. My servant is not here, so I shall make it myself. If you will give me a moment." He moved off hurriedly.

Once he had gone, I caught my daughter's eye and raised an eyebrow.

"I should like to meet Wills," said Mary.

"The brother or the squirrel?"

"Both."

A little while later, Mr Spigott returned with a wooden tray on which sat three cups, one chipped, and a pot of what I assumed was tea. The leaf had gone from his breeches and his hair glistened as if he had run wet hands across it.

Mary watched the curate as he poured, her face a mixture of determination and admiration.

"Those aphids we once talked about," I said, as Mr Spigott made to hand me a cup. "Might I have a quick look? It will take but a moment."

"Let me accompany you." The curate started to leave the room.

"Stay here, Mr Spigott." I took out my spectacles to have something to wave at him. "Stay here and listen to what my daughter has to say. And if at any time you find this all quite improper, then I advise you to consider your Gospels. Jesus once expressed his distaste for the traditions of the elders. On this occasion, you might do the same."

I will not say I attempted to listen to the conversation that ensued, but neither did I attempt not to; the open window carried the exchange out into the garden.

"About the dinner at Longbourn..." said Mary.

"Do not mention it, Miss Bennet. I have no understanding of the intent behind your actions, but please allow me to say that it has by no means affected my respect for your person and that of your family."

"Mr Spigott, do you love me?"

Blushing for the curate, I edged nearer to the cottage, eager to know his answer. None came.

"I am not the person you saw a week ago," continued Mary. "I let others persuade me to act as I did. It was a mistake. I am who I am. Plain."

"Not to me, Miss Bennet."

"Pardon?" I could hear the surprise and confusion in Mary's voice.

"You are not plain to me," said Mr Spigott. "You are, in fact, quite lovely."

It was some time before Mary spoke again. "You know my true character. Better than anyone, I think. So, I would ask, again, whether you love me. I will not leave until you answer."

"Very well." The silence that followed drew me closer to the window. "Yes, Miss Bennet…Mary—I do."

"And I, you." Now the words poured forth from my daughter in an earnest rush. "I would make a good wife and be happy here with you. I do not ask for much. So, if you were to make an offer, it would be looked on favourably. By myself and my father."

I almost called out to confirm Mary's belief.

"I am not sure that love is enough." Mr Spigott spoke quietly.

"And how am I to understand that?" asked Mary.

"I do not wish to bring you low, to expose you to all this. I can offer so little compared to your life at Longbourn. And a clergyman's wife has such responsibilities. There are so many reasons why I should not make you an offer."

"But you love me, and that is enough. My reading of scripture tells me that love is everything. And I would suffer any privation if it meant I could be in this house. With you."

"Truly?"

"Truly."

"Well, then, in that case," said the curate.

I gave them a minute before shouting through the window. "That is settled, then. You will, perhaps, call on me tomorrow, Mr Spigott. And you, Mary, I had better get you home. We will surprise your mother after Mr Spigott calls, eh?"

Just for once, all seemed well in the world as I rode with my daughter wrapped in my arms. We did not speak, but we exchanged many smiles, and I entered Longbourn with a rare spring in my step, reassured that the next knock on my front door would be that of a future son-in-law.

Fate Visits Longbourn

The knock came just after midnight. Not the hesitant rap of a suitor, laced with hope and fear in equal measure, but the insistent hammering of a messenger. The family and servants had retired, but my books had kept me from bed and so I answered the door. As Colonel Forster's envoy handed me a letter, I paused briefly to listen for stirrings upstairs, but all was silent.

> *...Miss Lydia Bennet and Mr Wickham were both missed this morning; my wife has given me to understand that they departed to Scotland...*

Good tidings rarely arrive at such a late hour, when thieves begin to go about their business, and even the best of men allow doubt to seep into their thoughts and dreams. Another time, I might have felt more at the news. But my indifference to Lydia and the lack of immediate consequence for my family left me largely cold. After all, when people marry, few question the circumstances; a marriage certificate masks many an indiscretion. Part of me even felt relief, for Lydia would take up permanent residence in another household, sparing me the expense and no end of tiresome conversation.

"No answer is required, sir," said the young man. "The colonel says to expect him in person with more information."

"And you are to wait for him?"

"No, sir."

I took the young soldier around to the stables, fetched him bread, ale, and cheese, then advised him to be gone well before dawn. Despite my equanimity, I had no wish for the servants to begin speculating over news that arrives in the dark. The urgency in my voice and the reassuring weight of a few coins secured his promise of a swift departure.

~ ~ ~

"It may not be the most prudent match, Papa, but it is a match nonetheless." Jane stood next to me at the window, her arm in mine, offering the reassurance of an amiable character whose ramparts neither suspicion nor cynicism could ever breach.

Outside the study, a vine's delicate tendrils explored the window frame. A fat beetle plodded up a length of green, like a packhorse scaling a mountain path, all weary sedateness and strength of purpose.

"Very true, Jane." I looked back at the missive from Colonel Forster on my desk. "Let us both think well of them. I daresay that after they marry, we may consider the circumstances of little import. Though it is not truly the behaviour of a gentleman, nor of a gentleman's daughter. Your mother has not taken the news so well?"

"She will soon come round, Papa. After all, she will have one daughter married."

"Indeed. No doubt she simply mourns the lack of opportunity to witness the accomplishment or brag of its imminency with her friends."

"We may take encouragement from the hope that Mr Wickham acts with good intentions." Jane squeezed my arm. "Lydia has nothing to offer but her character and self. The match must be based on a genuine and mutual affection."

"A strange kind of truth, Jane. Mr Wickham is many things, but I did not take him for a profligate fool. He throws away his prospects of an advantageous marriage for the sake of a silly girl with no fortune to speak of. So, as you say, there must be true affection. It seems the currency of love is harder than pounds and guineas. I would not suspect it of them were it not the only possible explanation for their behaviour. We must forgive the impetuosity and rejoice that they have pursued the honourable course. I shall think no more of it until we receive Colonel Forster. He will surely not arrive for several days, by which time he should have a better understanding of the situation."

"I think we may expect him earlier, Papa." Jane pointed out of the window. "Is that not his horse approaching now?"

Outside, a man of familiar bearing rode up to the house.

"So soon?" My stomach tensed. "He must have left Brighton the same day as his envoy. But why?"

~ ~ ~

Colonel Forster used the final piece of bread to dab at every last drop and crumb on his plate, as if delaying the moment when his meal would end and the talking begin.

I held my wine glass with both hands, each sip forced through tight lips.

"I thank you for the meal, Mr Bennet."

The colonel dropped his napkin on the table, then stood, unbuttoned a pocket, and withdrew a folded note from within.

"As you know, my understanding was that your daughter and Mr Wickham were to go to Gretna with the intention of marrying. Such were the words used by Miss Bennet in a note to my wife. Please…"

I took the paper from his outstretched arm.

You will laugh when you know where I am gone, and I cannot help laughing myself at your surprise tomorrow morning, as soon as I am missed. I am going to Gretna Green, and if you cannot guess with who, I shall think you a simpleton, for there is but one man in the world I love, and he is an angel. I should never be happy without him, so think it no harm to be off. You need not send them word at Longbourn of my going, if you do not like it, for it will make the surprise the greater, when I write to them and sign my name "Lydia Wickham."

"Lydia's intent seems clear," I said. "And yet your presence suggests there is more to this tale. Let us hear it."

A knock at the study door prevented the colonel from responding.

At my urging, the door opened to reveal Jane, face almost as pale as on her return from London. "Mama is quite distressed, Papa, by the colonel's precipitous arrival. Might there be news I can give her?"

"If you would close the door, Jane." I motioned her to a chair and waited until she had settled. "It seems Lydia truly intended to marry in Gretna, but Colonel Forster is, I believe, about to cast doubt on that prospect."

Jane looked across sharply at the colonel.

"I am sure I do not wish to burden Miss Bennet with unpleasant news."

"Jane is my eldest," I said. "She has my highest regard, and it may help for us both to hear what you say directly, so we may compare our understanding later."

"Very well." The colonel stood to attention as if reporting news from the front. "Mr Wickham's swift departure from Brighton and the nature of his travelling companion led to talk among my officers. They informed me that Mr Denny was of the belief that Mr Wickham had…" The colonel swallowed hard. "Well, he had no intention of going to Gretna at all, nor of marrying your daughter."

Jane lifted a hand to her mouth but made no noise. I felt like a man exposed on the side of a mountain, feeling the scree begin to slip and slide beneath his feet.

"To what did Mr Denny owe this belief?" I steadied myself on a nearby table. "Was it mere supposition on his part?"

"Apparently, he claimed Mr Wickham said as such. Mr Denny proved less forthcoming when I spoke with him directly. I had scant opportunity to press him further, wishing to pursue the matter directly as a matter of urgency." The colonel bowed his head slightly. "I traced their route to Clapham, where they removed into a hackney-coach to continue on the London Road. Enquiries at all the likely turnpikes and inns proved fruitless. I say this with the deepest possible regret and sympathy for your family, but I must conclude that they have gone to London, not to Gretna. Their purpose for doing so, I cannot say. But it is almost certainly not to marry."

"Might they not wed in London?" said Jane. "It would save them a considerable journey, not to mention expense, yet achieve the same desirous end? I cannot believe that dear Lydia would accept any other situation than marriage. She is young but not so lost. I will not think it of her."

Colonel Forster shook his head. "I would earnestly wish it so for your sake, Miss Bennet. But I do not depend on it. In fact, I sincerely doubt it. Mr Wickham is not a man to be trusted. He left more than mere questions behind in Brighton. Rumours of debts circulate. Many debts."

Despite my strong grip, the glass trembled in my hand. Drops of wine tumbled slowly to a floor which slipped away below me, as if drawing me into the abyss. I would have fallen had the colonel not grabbed my arm.

"Such a fool," I muttered as Jane leapt to her feet, rushed over, and took my glass from me.

"Papa? You nearly fell. And your face. So pale. Shall I send for Mr Jones?"

"No, I am fine. Quite fine," I allowed my daughter to guide me to an armchair, where I sat for a good ten minutes without speaking further, letting the events and conversations of past weeks flood through my mind.

"My apologies," said Colonel Forster after I had recovered sufficiently. "I did not present my tale solicitously. You must forgive me."

"Forgive you? Ha. Forgiveness, yes, what we could all do with a little forgiveness." I ignored the churning in my stomach, the bile that threatened to rise and consume me, and sat up properly, closing my eyes until the dizziness passed. "No, Colonel Forster, it is not you who should seek forgiveness. On the contrary, I must thank you for your trouble and swift action in coming to Longbourn. Let no blame attach to you or your wife. You could not have known Mr Wickham's true character. It seems nobody did."

Jane blushed for a moment, perhaps embarrassed for the colonel. Then she knelt before my chair, her eyes searching my face earnestly.

"I am fine, child. If you would show the colonel to his room. The shock has passed, and I must begin to make my preparations. I shall leave for London tomorrow."

"London, Papa?" Jane shook her head. "No, you must rest a while."

"Rest? Good Lord, no. My very inactivity brought us to this point. Go now. Please."

"I will accompany you for a short time on your journey, Mr Bennet," said Colonel Forster. "I am expected in Brighton the following night."

"I thank you. Jane, give your mother and sisters the news. It will come better from you." My daughter held my gaze for a moment longer than normal before I shooed her away with our guest.

Once alone, I collapsed back into my armchair and remained there, numb to the shrieks that began to ebb and flow outside the door. Shame washed over me as I sat with my head clutched in shaking hands and contemplated my failure until long after the rest of the house grew quiet.

Why do you care so little?

Lizzy's words echoed in my head.

Men have a remarkable capacity for self-deception. We happily rewrite our own history, apportion blame to the innocent, and abandon all logic and reason to avoid a truth that declares us to be something less than we ought to be. I might have done so, too, were that truth not so clear and piercing. Like a snake pinned with a forked stick, no amount of twisting and turning could release me from understanding my own folly.

"Selfish, self-pitying fool." I knew what was now required of me.

"Papa?" Jane had entered the study without me noticing.

"I am well," I said, seeing her concern. "Tell me, how fares your mother?"

Jane hesitated. "I gave her one of Mr Jones's draughts to help her sleep. Hill watches over her."

"Good. And your sisters?"

"Kitty stays in her chamber, fearful of your wrath."

"Mary?"

"Mr Spigott called not ten minutes ago."

The bile began to rise again, a sickening feeling born of dread and guilt.

"Mary opened the door to him," continued Jane. "But I believe he left us without entering."

"Of course he did." I closed my eyes until the biliousness dissipated. "My poor Mary."

"I heard her rush upstairs and followed," said Jane. "She has locked her door and will not open it."

"And so it begins. It is my crime, yet others must suffer." The floor began to shift again, but I closed my eyes until the feeling passed. "Lizzy warned me, Jane. I might forgive myself were it a mere lapse in judgement on my part. But I knew, you see. I knew right from wrong and chose the latter. I risked bringing disgrace on the family out of indifference. For my own convenience. With a contempt for the fate of others born of my own disappointments."

"Papa, you are not yourself. I will fetch you a nerve tonic."

I caught Jane's arm briefly as she turned to go. "No tonic. There is no time, anyway. Please give my apologies to Colonel Forster. I must go to Meryton and the Society."

"Must you, Papa? Today of all days?" Jane placed her hands on my knees, as if to hold me in place in the chair.

"That is precisely *why* I must go." I lifted her hands off me. "Word of Lydia's dishonourable behaviour and our shame will soon reach the town. I would not have my friends hear it from others."

~ ~ ~

I did not bother with a carriage. Perhaps I thought the ride might offer respite, that it might drive away my chagrin and anger.

As the wind dropped, Mr Spigott must have heard my horse behind him on the lane, for he turned to face me. Then I knew that my own selfish brooding had truly begun to demand its price, measured out in the tears that ran down the curate's cheeks.

"You have heard the news from Brighton?" I dismounted carefully. My old bones could no longer leap to the ground safely, and the delay gave Mr Spigott time to collect himself.

"Miss Mary Bennet was kind enough to tell me. Mr Bennet, I…" The curate's voice trailed away, and he stood much as I recalled from the day he first brought pamphlets to Longbourn—shoulders hunched and bearing the heavy weight of knowledge.

"You did not wish to see me when you called?"

"I thought it best not to intrude and, besides, I must consider…the bishop, you know?" Mr Spigott looked at me like a penniless child at a baker, desperate for some scrap that would ease his situation. There was only one thing I could do for him.

"I have some unfortunate news for you. I cannot allow you to marry Mary, however much you may wish to. I believe circumstances unconducive to a union at this time. Do we understand each other?"

Mr Spigott nodded. To his credit, his features spoke of acceptance but not relief. I hoped he would sleep easier believing he held no responsibility for the breaking of a promise he could not keep.

"Perhaps it is for the best." The curate wiped at his cheek with his cuff. "Mary deserves more. And better."

"She deserves *you*, Mr Spigott." I gripped his shoulder. "And neither of you deserve what has come to pass today. I am in no position to offer advice at this moment, but do not abandon hope. Circumstances may change and my blessing with it. True love is loyal. Do not forget this. I did so once and live now with the consequences." The curate would not look me in the eye as I spoke, and I released him to take to my saddle once again.

"I will always speak well of you and your family, Mr Bennet. Be assured of that."

Mr Spigott's words sounded a death knell as I rode on toward Meryton.

The Meaning of Friendship

"That is all there is to say on the matter," I said. "Accept my good wishes for Dorking, gentlemen, for I cannot now join you on our excursion there. Who knows how long I shall be kept away in London? I do not expect your own good wishes in return, given my family's unfortunate situation. So, I will leave you to your own devices and save you the embarrassment of my company."

"You cannot leave now," said Jackson.

"We have barely touched the sponge cake, for one thing." Stanhope handed Fielding a knife.

"You know Mrs Tincton feels slighted if we do not send the plate back empty," said Elliston.

"But…" I struggled for words.

"But what?" Fielding began cutting the cake. "Should we abandon years of friendship simply because of the unfortunate actions of one of your daughters? If you believe us all capable of such behaviour, then you have misjudged us…and we you, my friend."

"I merely thought—"

"Nonsense." Jackson waved a hand as if pestered by a persistent wasp.

"The only people who will think worse of you are those whose opinions are of least interest to any of us." Fielding passed out plates laden with Mrs Tincton's latest creations. "Of far greater weight is how we might be of assistance in bringing this matter to a positive conclusion."

I sat down with a thump, eyes blinking, barely able to grasp the kindness and understanding extended by my friends. "Gentlemen, I hardly know what to say."

"You need not say anything," said Fielding. "We know you would do the same for us. In fact, I believe you may have forgotten one or two incidents in the past. Is that not so, Stanhope?"

"What?" Stanhope's forehead crinkled.

"The Frog and Flower? In Bristol?" Fielding raised his eyebrows at our friend. "You do not recall?"

"Ah yes, now you mention it." Stanhope shook a finger at us. "But she did not *behave* like a married woman."

"That was what you told her husband." Elliston gave a wry smile. "Which was when it all turned rather unpleasant."

"But my reputation...the reputation of my daughters," I said.

"Quite," said Fielding. "Obviously, you must track down this Wickham fellow and compel him to marry Miss Lydia. The disapproval of society will shrivel in the face of a wedding ring."

"Of that I need no convincing. Regrettably, the wish may be strong, the wherewithal to fulfil it somewhat weaker. We have no idea where they may be in London, if they are still there at all."

"Right." Fielding assumed leadership. "Then gather round, gentlemen." The others all pulled their chairs closer to the table and pushed plates and glasses to one side. "We have searched for outlaws in the woods of Virginia. We can search for an English officer in our own capital. Does he have relatives in town?"

I shook my head. "None that I am aware of."

"Has he ever mentioned friends or associates in London?" said Stanhope.

"No."

"Any favourite haunts? Hotels, inns, and such like?" said Elliston, hopefully.

"I fear his conversation did not mention London at all. We have nothing to go on."

"Then we shall have to take a different tack." Fielding pinched the bridge of his nose and closed his eyes for a moment. "Hmm...what are his habits?"

"He is an officer." I shrugged. "I know no more than that."

"So, drinking and gambling, then." Fielding turned to Jackson. "You know the London gambling dens? We shall need a list of those likely to attract the attention of our Mr Wickham. Does anyone have an acquaintance with the knowledge and discretion to help *in situ*?" Heads shook sadly around the table.

The efforts of my friends bore little fruit in providing much of likely use for my search in the capital, though it was enough to know they had tried. Men turn to many sources in search of reprieve from life's burdens. The arms of a lover, their faith, drink, or worse, but there is much to be said for the balm of true friendship.

I stayed with them only a few minutes longer, then took to the stairs with a lighter step than when I had ascended. At the bottom, an open expanse of chairs and tables greeted me, filled with the richness of Meryton society—Mr Weintraub's barrow boy, stealing a few minutes to enjoy a hot biscuit from Mrs

Tincton's ovens; tradesfolk discussing business and gossip in poorly lit corners; and gentlefolk taking a meal before continuing their travels to estates great and small. I wondered how many already knew of the Bennets' ignominy; rumour travels on powerful wings in such a town.

I turned at a touch to find Fielding at my elbow. "A word before you leave."

"More advice, Fielding?"

"Of sorts. There *is* one who might prove a useful ally in your undertaking."

"Who?"

Fielding simply pointed over to the crates of port and wine piled up behind the inn's counter, their wooden slats branded with the name of the merchant.

"No," I said. "Never. That would be impossible."

"Given her daughter's association with your family, she might be equally keen to see this matter resolved with as little impropriety as possible."

"That may all be true, but what do you expect me to do, Fielding? Should I march up to her London townhouse, announce myself, and say, 'Good day to you, Abigail. You may have described me as a coward and a fool, but could you see your way to giving me a hand with a matter of some delicacy? And at no inconsiderable risk to your own reputation.' I think not. The idea is preposterous."

"But she would not wish to see you fall," said Fielding. "And you have said yourself she is a powerful lady with many connections."

"I hardly think she would expose those connections to such a story. No. And that is my final word on the matter."

London

After parting with Colonel Forster and fruitless enquiries at Epsom and Clapham, I could no longer deny the call of London. The Bath Hotel on Piccadilly proved a dirty, noisy sort of place and, therefore, the perfect penance for my sins of neglect and selfishness. The same might have been said of the city itself.

Books and the Gardiners constituted the capital's only redeeming qualities. Unfortunately, I had too little time for the former and the latter were to be found with Lizzy in Derbyshire. Besides, neither the company of printed words nor my brother-in-law could have overcome my sense of disquiet, given the rather distasteful task ahead.

My wife feared violence, worried that Mr Wickham and I might duel and youth would prevail. I had no intention of challenging the man, but the prospect did not unduly concern me. Like many before her, my wife confused bravado with bravery and an officer's garb with courage. Mr Wickham, I suspected, would face a sword or pistol much like he faced his debts—by running from them. My courage had been tested at the hands of blade and musket. I would not shy from a confrontation, even though I did not care for one.

Having failed to find news of Mr Wickham at the list of gambling dens furnished by Jackson, I resolved to work my way through the capital's hotels in the hope the missing couple might have stayed in one prior to finding lodgings. The most expensive hotels I could ignore; Mr Wickham's purse would not tolerate the cost. Nor did I trouble myself with the cheapest alternatives; Lydia's pride would not tolerate the company.

The unceasing clamour of London accompanied me on my every journey, the cries of traders adding a discordant chorus to the constant refrain of horses, carriages, and roadside chatter. My search took me down Haymarket to Charing Cross, then up the Strand to Fleet Street, through Ludgate and Cheapside, up Bishopsgate Street, and back across. Each day saw me return to the Bath bearing nothing but dust and disappointment.

On one occasion, though, I found myself at a particular port of call that I knew Mr Wickham would never have visited. I entered Finsbury Square like a ship bullied by wind and wave but still stubbornly seeking its home harbour. The furore of the capital seemed to fall away at the sight of Brecknell's book merchants, my long-time haven and heaven in this blight of a city. Half-drawn blinds protected the modesty of the store's windows, offering no hint of the treasures within.

I did not enter immediately. Part of me felt guilty at the time lost to such an indulgence. Another part wished to prolong that moment of anticipation, just before the heady smell of paper enveloped the senses. And yet another part feared what might lie within—my previous visit had involved an unexpected encounter with Abigail. I reminded myself that such coincidences only occur in novels and turned the door handle.

Mr Brecknell looked over his spectacles and up from his desk, where lists and invoices lay scattered across the polished wood. "Ah, Mr Bennet."

I returned his greeting and waited.

"Hmm." Mr Brecknell eyed me up and down, as if I were a new acquisition waiting to be catalogued. "Normally I would recommend Direder's latest work on moths. The drawings are quite extraordinary. But not today. You do not enjoy poetry, do you, Mr Bennet?" He only included the question mark out of politeness. Mr Brecknell was never wrong about people and books. "And yet, I wonder..." He turned and lifted a slim volume from a small pile behind him, then thumbed through the book before handing it to me, his ink-stained finger pressed toward the fifth verse on the open page. The paper still carried the fresh scent of the printer's art, its words yet unsullied by human eyes.

> *Of all the truths I hear,*
> *How few delight my taste!*
> *I glean a berry here and there,*
> *But mourn the vintage past.*

"We can but mourn the past, Mr Bennet," said Mr Brecknell solemnly. "Those memories we hold dear may not be relived, those we would forget, we cannot. How fortunate that we have books to take us away from the pain of both. Will you be bringing gifts to your daughters?"

"My daughters? If truth be told, I have little time for books at this minute. I merely wished to pay my regards on passing. I must away. Pressing matters."

As I reached the door to leave, Mr Brecknell called out. "I shall add it to your bill."

I realised I was still gripping Cowper's volume of poetry. "Yes, very well. Yes."

The book became my hair shirt, carried with me everywhere, so I might suffer a verse or two while waiting for news that never came.

Tea and Memories

"Beg your pardon, sir, but a lady below asks if she might 'ave a moment of your time." The maid caught me on the hotel stairs as I set out for Westminster Bridge to extend my search to south of the river.

"A lady?" I dared not hope. "A Mrs Wickham, perhaps?"

"No, sir. A Mrs Hayter."

The name might once have left its mark, but what was one more blow to a spirit already crushed? I merely sighed and looked into the mirror mounted on the wall, where an old man stared back at me, rings beneath his lifeless eyes, hair dull and thinning, cravat slightly out of place. "Does fate ever tire of her games?" I asked, but the old man offered no reply.

The Bath's foyer held no false promises for potential guests, the furniture and fittings as drab as the rooms above it. The sofa and two chairs had adopted a dull brown colour that may once have been green. On the table, a fading rose hung over the side of a vase like an old drunk. Abigail perched on the edge of the sofa, dressed all in canary—a splash of brightness and colour.

"Mrs Hayter." I walked toward her with as much poise and

confidence as I could muster. "I did not…" My voice faltered, and I stopped.

"James." Abigail stood and advanced toward me, hand half reaching out.

"No doubt you heard the news," I said.

"Your daughter? Yes, I have friends in Brighton."

"The shame. The disgrace. The reward for my stupidity and lack of forethought. Do you come to gloat, Abigail? To see me reap the just rewards of my laxity? My lack of faith and understanding? My moral cowardice? My—"

"Stop, James. Please." Abigail took a step back.

My shoulders dropped as fatigue threatened to overwhelm me. "My apologies. I am a gentleman but seem to have forgotten what that means. If I ever knew." Rubbing my eyes did not dispel my tiredness or sombre mood.

"Perhaps a cup of tea?" said Abigail.

"Ah, tea? Yes. For what cares may not be solved with a cup of that fine beverage? Let Napoleon and other tyrants do as they will, for Albion will always prevail so long as ships sail from China."

"My dear James, you clearly need something stronger. But in its absence, we shall have to make do with tea. Come along." Abigail turned and moved toward the entrance, but I did not follow her. "I am not drinking tea here," she called behind her. "I could not be sure what is in it. We shall go next door."

We found seats in a corner, away from the few other customers. Inside Mrs Husket's Tea Emporium, London seemed somehow distant, as if the noise and commotion outside dared not disturb the ritual of the tea house for fear of vengeful gods riding porcelain carriages and armed with steel-tipped biscuits.

Abigail spoke quietly to a serving maid, who brought tea and two slices of sponge cake. I almost managed to smile.

"You remembered," I said.

"As I recall, we usually ate either sponge cake or those biscuits from Cottersham's. We are a long way from Bath now but may still enjoy sponge cake at least. Perhaps one day we might sit together again in Milsom Street and talk of happier times."

"Perhaps."

Abigail picked up the book I had put down on the table.

"Cowper, James? You were once fond of poetry, but of late I think you have a decidedly different opinion."

"Brecknell recommended it. Perhaps some of the words struck me as pertinent. I already regret the purchase."

"I have some fondness for Cowper, which my daughter does not share."

> *In vain he leaves me, I shall love him still;*
> *And, though I mourn, not murmur at his will;*
> *I have no cause—an object all divine,*
> *Might well grow weary of a soul like mine;*
> *Yet pity me, great God! forlorn, alone,*
> *Heartless and hopeless, life and love all gone.*

"You may quote Cowper, Scott, Wordsworth, and all the Greek classics to me, but I shall not rise to your challenge," I said. "I have no heart for the fight, and the time for games is past. More important matters concern me."

"Which is why I have sought you out." Abigail leaned

forward. "It is true—I know of your troubles with your youngest daughter."

"My 'troubles?' The word does not do it justice. But let me remind you of your own words in Gloucestershire. What were they? Ah, yes, 'let us never speak again. Not ever.' You had no wish to be reminded of my false pride and numerous other faults. Yet here you are, Abigail. Your nature is not vindictive, yet I can conceive of no other explanation for your presence given our parting at Rudford."

"My dear James." Abigail smiled sadly. "You understand nothing of women."

"A fact of which you, my wife, and my daughters constantly remind me."

"Why would I demand you declare your sentiments in Gloucestershire if I did not think—hope—they matched mine? I have never denied that I loved you once. Or denied that I still do."

Those words did not take hold as they once might have done. Though some part of me took them and stored them away carefully for later consideration.

"You recall the James Bennet you knew in Bath." I placed my elbows on the table, the better to hold my head in my hands. "Life has changed him, roughened his edges, and banished him to his books and butterflies. You cannot possibly love one such as me."

Abigail stretched out her hand and let her fingertips touch my elbow. "For an intelligent man, James, you can be remarkably ignorant. I love you, and you love me, even though you will not say it."

I reached for words to answer her claim but found none.

"Another time," I said, "and…well, I shall not speak of what might have been for I am mired in what is. Though I might note that you express your love strangely. You were most unkind to me in Gloucestershire."

"Love and anger often travel together. I am sorry for it." Abigail leant back in her chair and took a sip of tea, her hands clasped gently around the cup, her fingers slender and delicate. I imagined them intertwined with mine. Perhaps on a walk in Hyde Park in the shade of the oaks. We would talk of books and politics. I shook my head to dispel the thought.

"I have only one ambition," I said. "To find my daughter and that rogue, Mr Wickham, and see they marry. It is my task. It is my punishment. And my only chance at some kind of redemption for my mistakes."

"Such pride." Abigail put down her cup. "The affliction of so many men. No doubt you blame yourself, feel that somehow you alone are responsible for this unfortunate situation. Believe whatever you wish, James. It changes nothing. You asked why I am here. It is quite simple: you are in difficulty, and I would help."

"Help? Well, you have my gratitude for the wish." My bite of cake gave me no pleasure, though this was no fault of the baker.

"Listen to me, James," continued Abigail. "The wine trade made my late husband rich, but it is not always the trade of gentlemen. I have connections that are noble and others that are practical; it is how I found you so easily. Perhaps I may know of someone who can help find your Mr Wickham."

My first instinct was to refuse her assistance, but the

earnestness in her voice merited better.

"I do not deserve your help, but should you hear of anything…"

"And I may aid in other ways, too," said Abigail. "The gentleman in question likely has need of many things but money most of all. Will Longbourn provide for him and his wife, assuming it comes to that?"

A flare of umbrage briefly broke through my fatigue. "You presume much."

Abigail seemed untroubled by my accusation. "Our past entitles me to do so. We are not passing acquaintances observing the rituals of polite conversation."

"What can you know of my estate and finances?"

"And thus you have answered my question, James. I, however, am in a position to give Mr Wickham precisely what he needs should he require encouragement to do the right thing."

"That will not be necessary." I folded my arms. "You owe my family no debt, and I have enough pride to reject any such offer."

"You have the pride but not the circumstances. Come now, you say yourself the time for games is past. We speak as equals. You claim to be a man of logic."

"I *am* a man of logic. But I am also just a man."

Abigail's eyes grew moist and, in that moment, she seemed to age before me. "I wish it were so, James. How different our lives might have been if you *were* just a man, unbound by matters of family. Free of duty and much that you consider dear and good in a gentleman. We might have found happiness together."

"Perhaps." I felt like a tidal wall finally crumbling before the pounding of the waves. "Exhaustion takes me, Abigail. If you truly wish to help, then make all this disappear." The wave of my arm took in the teashop, the windows, the street beyond, the whole of London, Hertfordshire, everything. "Take me away from this wretched situation."

Abigail gave me a strange look that might have been pity. Carriages drove by outside, and I wondered if I had passed this way another time on a coach bound for Bath.

"There is one thing you might do for me," I said. "Give me the relief of understanding. I told you once how I dealt with my disappointment. How I sought solace in travel. In the army. But you have never talked of yourself. I wonder, did you love Mr Trott?"

I did not know what I sought with my question. Perhaps I simply wished to close our story by filling in the gaps. The answer held no fear for me. When all is lost, there is nothing more to lose.

"No, I did not love him. You believe me angry with you for your acceptance of my engagement, but much of my anger is toward myself. I played a game and lost. Gambled with your affections and lost. And I was too young, too much of a coward, to correct my mistake. Charles was a good man. A decent, honourable man. A man worthy of my respect but not my love."

"Who can say how love grows, Abigail?" I said. "Though I wonder that it does not fade."

"That is how we know it is love. It is an oak, not a rose."

Somehow our hands had come together on the table, and the warmth of her fingers did much to dispel my fatigue.

"And your second husband?"

"I lost Charles to a fever. We had not been married more than a year or two. I might have written to you, had I known where you were. Had I not given in to my shame at my earlier decision. Archibald Hayter had a kind and gracious nature, persistence, and wealth." Abigail pulled her hands away from mine. "The way you look at me now, James, as if I were some calculating woman of business. Would you condemn me for the same actions admired in a man? Is it not men who seek out young women, not for companionship or love, but for heirs and income? You wince, and well you might do so. Do I hold a mirror to you? It is how so many survive. Too few of us know the true value of a loving companion."

I thought of Fielding. And another man. "But John. And your daughter."

"Yes, Anne and John. They have the best of all worlds. But their joy is denied to me, James. And to you. We must live with our decisions, but we may rage against them now and then. So do not ever confuse my fury with hate. It is precisely because I still love that I am angry."

"I will always regret that day in the carriage." I pushed my hands across the table to rest over hers again. "God knows I have tried to forget or at least turn that regret to good use. It drove me to help John, you know."

"You were quite the Cupid, I understand."

The suggestion brought the first smile of the morning to my face. "I had help from my friends."

"So Anne said. I should like to meet them. They sound like entertaining company."

My eyes widened. "That I can never allow to happen. My friend Fielding already knows too much. It would be unbearable. Unforgiveable."

"Might we forgive each other, James?" Abigail clasped my hands tightly now. "Might we part as friends?"

"Friends?" I drew my hands away but squeezed hers first so she might know I was not cross. "A word to strike deep into the heart of a man. We can never be friends. But we may part on good terms. We may be friendly. And I shall try not to wilt like some Shakespearean fool when I see you. You cannot know the power you have over me."

"Not enough, though, it would seem," said Abigail. "Can you at least forgive me for any hurt I may have caused?"

"You had my forgiveness long ago, Abigail." Her smile at my words thrust its way past all fatigue and disappointment. I turned my head away for fear of what I might say.

"Good Lord." My mouth dropped open. "It cannot be."

Outside the window, a familiar face passed by.

Gracechurch Street

Ahead of me, almost at the Bath Hotel, Gardiner turned back at my call. On reaching him, I took his arm and attempted to lead him away from the teashop.

"Brother, how splendid to see you," I said.

"I came as soon as I could." Gardiner's portly frame proved a little harder to shift than I had hoped.

"Mr Bennet," came a voice from behind me.

We turned to see Abigail at the doorway to Mrs Husket's. "You left your poetry at our table." She held up my book. "Will you not come and fetch it?"

Both Gardiner and Abigail now looked at me, the former all politeness, the latter making a poor effort to avoid smirking.

"My poetry, yes. Mr Gardiner, may I introduce Mrs Hayter?"

"Will you not join us?" Abigail gestured toward the insides of the teashop.

"It would be my great pleasure," said my brother-in-law, almost causing me to revise my previous excellent opinion of him.

"I thought you in Derbyshire," I said, after we had reached our seats and ordered more tea.

"We were, but we returned to Longbourn earlier than expected once…" Gardiner's cough did not hide his discomfort. "Well, we felt it was time to return south."

"Mrs Hayter knows of our predicament. She is an old friend, so you may speak freely."

Gardiner nodded solemnly at Abigail. "Once the news reached Lizzy, we returned to Longbourn immediately. I have only just arrived from there and came straight to your hotel. Is there news?"

"Sadly, no," I shook my head.

Abigail sipped at her tea, apparently unconcerned by our conversation, though her eyes remained alert and sharp.

"As I feared." Gardiner frowned. "Well, I hope at least you will return with me to Gracechurch Street. Your choice of hotel can only be described as unfortunate. The Bath has quite a reputation."

"As I have discovered." I glanced down at the dust on my breeches, not all of which could be explained by the tread of hooves, feet, and wheels on August roads. "We may talk more at your home. But, tell me, how is Lizzy?"

"Somewhat distressed at first." Gardiner paused. "She has found her strength, now, though."

"That you should join me in this moment of need," I said. "You have my gratitude. I only hope you had some joy from your trip before it ended so precipitously?" I turned to Abigail. "Mr and Mrs Gardiner took Lizzy to the north. Derbyshire and the Peaks."

"How lovely." Abigail leaned back in her seat as if recalling a memory. "I am fond of Derbyshire."

"A most pleasant county, Mrs Hayter. Excellent fishing." Gardiner mimed the casting of a rod.

"I wonder you found time for angling," I said. "Lizzy would not wish to delay her explorations for long."

"If not for the kind offer from Mr Darcy, I would not have taken the time."

"Mr Darcy?" It seemed the day was to be full of surprises.

"Yes. As you know, Mrs Gardiner hails from the Lambton area and wished to visit old haunts. While there, we paid a visit to Mr Darcy's estate at Pemberley. Your daughter required quite some persuasion before she would support the idea." Gardiner grimaced, as if recollecting a difficult business negotiation. "It seems she did not wish to trouble the owner but largely withdrew her objections once we learnt he was not at home. As luck would have it, Mr Darcy returned earlier than expected and proved a most amiable and generous host. I fished in his pond. Such trout!"

"You astound me. Amiable and generous? And how did Lizzy enjoy Mr Darcy's attentions? Knowing her opinion of the man, I imagine very little."

"I am no judge of women, Bennet. She certainly had nothing good to say of him before Pemberley."

"Curious," I said. "We all know him to be a strange, unfriendly sort of fellow. Still, perhaps he mellows on home ground."

"I have found him to be a delightful host," said Abigail.

I blinked away another surprise. "You know Mr Darcy?"

"We dined three times at Pemberley. The Darcy ships carried some of Mr Hayter's wines. A somewhat proud gentleman, perhaps, but we may forgive a man a little pride." I wondered if those words were as much for me as for general conversation. "He always seemed uncomfortable when obliged to make meaningless chatter over dinner, though that speaks in his favour." Abigail finished her cup of tea with a flourish and placed her palms on the table. "Gentlemen, I have no wish to keep you from more pressing tasks. I shall take my leave. You will remember my offer, Mr Bennet, should you change your mind?"

I ignored the curious look from my brother-in-law.

~ ~ ~

Although the Gardiners possessed far fewer tomes than Longbourn, two bookcases framing a small fireplace sufficed to convey the title of library on the room we now sat in. My troubles seemed to lessen in the comfort of my brother's upholstery, though they did not retreat far.

"Now tell me," I said. "What news from Longbourn?"

My brother blew out a deep breath. "Your wife is in a most dreadful state, with trembling, fluttering, and spasms in her side. She has taken to her bed under Mr Jones's supervision. I am concerned for her."

"Do not be. She will not die until her daughters are married. The Lord would not dare take her beforehand, not if he wishes any peace in the Kingdom of Heaven."

Gardiner stood and moved to the mantelpiece where he picked up a miniature of his wife. "My sister says you are to keep from fighting."

"I shall endeavour to do as she wishes. Mrs Bennet need not worry. I hold out little hope of finding Mr Wickham, though I have not yet searched every hotel."

"Is such a task wise? We cannot know if they stayed in a hotel and, even if they had done so, whether you would receive notice of it."

"Yet what else can I do?" I held out empty hands to my brother. "I have no friends or connections here but you. And even if I did, I am not sure I would wish the matter to become such public knowledge."

"Ah." Gardiner put down the picture of his spouse. "It may be too late for that."

"Well, yes, you are likely right on that account." I sighed. "What need have we of the post and messengers when there is Mrs Philips? I must find Lydia. Then we might at least stem the loss of reputation before it is too late for my other daughters. How are they all?"

"Jane remains of good cheer, trusting to providence."

"No doubt she believes it all a misunderstanding that will soon be resolved. I would not have dear Jane any other way. And Kitty?"

"She is too young to understand the consequences of Lydia's actions."

"I fear the same may be said of Lydia herself. But what of Mary?" I found myself gripping the sides of my chair in anticipation of the answer.

"Much as always. She spent all the time I was in Longbourn with her books."

"What greater source of escape can there be?" I waved at one of the bookcases. "Nobody can blame her for doing so. How else would she find relief from her own disappointment? I thought to loosen the chains that bind her to books and have achieved quite the opposite."

"Her own disappointment?" Gardiner cocked his head to one side.

"Nothing worthy of your attention." I lifted myself from my seat. "I shall take to my bed. My searches continue tomorrow."

"And I shall begin my own enquiries. I will write to Colonel Forster in the hope he might supply us with the names of Mr Wickham's relations or connections in town."

"A fine idea, and one I should have thought of myself."

"Perhaps fortune will favour us," said my brother.

"I fear fortune has long since abandoned the Bennets, but perhaps it has not abandoned the Gardiners."

A Decision

The next days passed much like the previous ones. After three or four nights at Gracechurch Street, the weather finally offered me its sympathy, skies darkening as the day progressed, the promise of summer rain encouraging those with no purpose to stay indoors and the rest to hurry from one address to another. Each hotel added a new disappointment to my collection. At Longbourn, I valued my solitude. In London, it seemed to close in on me and remind me of my vulnerability and insignificance in the vastness of our capital city.

My final address had a huge awning out front where its guests waited for their vehicles. It brought me shelter but no more luck than the previous hotels. Once outside, my upturned palm caught the first spots of rain. The clouds lacked menace, though, casting out their drops reluctantly, as if saving their energies for a more propitious moment.

I chose to walk all the way back to the Gardiners' home, perhaps in some fevered hope that the rain might worsen and wash away my thoughts. But the rain faded, and the tumult of London seemed to grow at my every step. A post coach thundered along so close that the rush of air sent me scampering to one side. Chattering sailors bullied their way across my path, their voices loud and raw, their skins darkened by the sun or their African heritage. Maids brushed past, their hurried apologies dying away in the cacophony of a small marketplace.

Each stall announced itself with signs and smells. The rancid air of the sea at a fishmonger whose products had spent too long out of water. A sharp tang from a stall manned by a bespectacled gentleman whose wares apparently cured all manner of complaints, though, sadly, none of mine appeared on his sign. The musty scent of cloth fresh from storage; above the draper's booth, floral letters spelled out the words *Weintraub's Haberdashery*.

"Are you by any chance related to Mr Weintraub of Meryton?" I asked.

"Meryton? Never heard of the place, sir. Might your lady like some fresh linen, sir? None finer in all of London. Fit for a royal table, sir."

A hint of cinnamon and fresh bread drew my eyes to a nearby bakery where the pastries put me in mind of the Flighted Duck and my friends. I imagined Jackson standing in torment at the choice. Fielding would wait patiently and smile at Jackson's gruff indecision. Stanhope might add extra cake to his order to take home to his wife, provoking Elliston into doing the same, albeit reluctantly. The yearning to return to Longbourn grew strong. Lizzy enjoyed cinnamon buns. My hand reached toward my cheek, to where she might lay a gentle kiss if I brought her a baked surprise. Then a burst of thunder tore me back to London and sent me hurriedly on my way. The clouds had finally chosen their moment.

~ ~ ~

"The market off Lombard Street? You were fortunate to escape with your purse intact from that haven for thieves." Gardiner sat with me as I ate.

"I believe they run the stalls there. The fish was almost as high as the prices."

"We are fortunate that Mr Trollope offers better wares."

"And I am fortunate that your cook always remembers my love of fish soup. She has my undying gratitude."

"You will find sponge cake in the library, too." Gardiner smiled as if offering a gift to a favourite child.

"With raspberry jam?"

"Of course. And a glass of port to wash it down with. We may not ease your mind, brother, but we may, perhaps, ease your body."

I closed my eyes and breathed deeply. "I do not deserve such relatives."

Gardiner waited until I had scraped the last of the soup from my bowl before pressing me with questions and hearing my report of another day of disappointment.

"Do not be harsh on yourself, Bennet. As for myself, I still await word from the colonel. May I suggest you return to Longbourn until I have news? There is little you can do here, now, but wait."

"I am disinclined to leave until my task is complete. I owe that to my family."

"If I may speak plainly?"

"Of course." I gave Gardiner an approving nod.

"Your family would benefit most from your presence. With Mrs Bennet bound to her bedchamber, it falls to Jane and Lizzy to manage affairs. They need their father."

"Perhaps they do," I said. "Though they have done without one for so long, a few days more will make no difference. But I will think on your words."

"Then do so over cake. I shall not disturb you in the library. Perhaps we may ease your mind after all by allowing you time with one of my books."

~ ~ ~

I lowered myself into the large armchair that sat near the fireplace and within an arm's length of a bookcase. A small table held an empty glass and a bottle of fine port. Of sponge cake, there was no sign. "Are even such simple pleasures to be denied me?" I murmured. "Though if that is the worst of my punishments, then I may be grateful."

A gentleman may express opinions designed solely to influence those of others. He may pursue interests to build connections, rather than address his true desires. Even his clothes may project the man he wishes to be, rather than the man he is. But a gentleman's library offers true insight into his soul. Judge a man by the books he possesses but also by the books he *reads*. Cracked spines and worn edges speak of a sincere love of the words within. Gardiner's library suited that of a well-read gentleman of reasonable means, but his books told of a mind for trade, business, geography, and little else, excepting one small volume, its cover spotted and faded, the sheen long gone from its golden lettering, the paper well-thumbed. In my hands, it fell open at one page.

O, never say that I was false of heart,
Though absence seemed my flame to qualify.
As easy might I from my self depart
As from my soul which in thy breast doth lie.
That is my home of love; if I have ranged,
Like him that travels I return again,
Just to the time, not with the time exchanged,
So that myself bring water for my stain.
Never believe though in my nature reigned
All frailties that besiege all kinds of blood,
That it could so preposterously be stained
To leave for nothing all thy sum of good;
For nothing this wide universe I call
Save thou, my rose, in it thou art my all.

I returned Shakespeare's sonnets to stand among discourses on the northern counties, trade with India, and shipping routes.

"Good evening, Uncle."

A familiar face appeared in the doorway, carrying an equally familiar item.

"My dear Julia, how pleasant to see you again."

"You look tired," said my niece with a child's honesty. "Old. And sad."

Julia walked to me, holding the plate with both hands, seemingly determined that nothing should fall off. "I have brought you this that we might share." She placed the plate next to my glass, lifted off the top piece of cake, laid it to one side, and then handed me the jam-covered bottom half.

"Oh, my dear child," I said. "Such kindness. And to one so undeserving."

"Do not cry." Julia reached up to wipe away my tears.

"You have made a poor day better. Your parents can be proud of you."

"Papa says just as light follows dark, so a good day may follow a bad one. Tomorrow you may be happy again, Uncle."

"You have a wise father. And a good mother. Let us eat up our cake, and I shall tell you a story." Julia climbed up on my knee, just as she had at Longbourn.

"Are there rabbits in the story?" she asked.

"There could be."

"And does it have a happy ending?"

"Perhaps. We shall have to see."

"They are the very best kind of stories."

My niece proved an adoring and willing audience, but she reminded me too much of Jane and Lizzy when they were young. I left for Longbourn the following day.

Longbourn

A home should bring comfort. But I returned to mine having achieved nothing; I had merely passed on the task of finding Lydia and Mr Wickham to my brother. To have erred is one thing, to be obliged to leave rectification of that error to someone else is a further twist of fate's sharp knife. The prospect of redemption slipped further away.

On reaching Longbourn, I marched straight to my study to evade the questions I knew would come. But my shame followed me even there in the form of a letter, recently arrived from Mr Collins.

In expressing his sympathies, Mr Collins succeeded only in losing the few I had for him. He condemned Lydia's nature and my nurturing of it, suggested her death would have been preferable to her disgrace, then ended with praise for his own good fortune in Lizzy's refusal of his proposal. When faced by indecision, some clergymen suggest we ask ourselves what our Lord Jesus Christ would do in such a situation. I determined to always consider what Mr Collins would do and then undertake quite the opposite.

The walls of Longbourn echoed with the misgivings of my wife. The news from Brighton had bestowed numerous afflictions on her, though, remarkably, none that affected her voice or throat. United in our grief, we all retreated to old ways as we awaited news from London.

Mary spoke little at all and never to me, but her presence reminded me of my broken promise. Kitty, too, kept out of my way, wary of offending and conscious of the impact her sister's behaviour would have on her own liberties. Jane's ghostlike pallor belied her constant words of reassurance. And Lizzy withdrew further into herself, almost as if she felt responsible for the tragedy that had befallen us. Yet the blame lay with me alone.

The release from suspense and introspection came two days after my return through an express from Mr Gardiner. Remarkably, he had succeeded where I had failed, found Lydia and Mr Wickham, and even gone so far as to arrange for them to be wed, contingent on my agreeing to two minor conditions:

> *...to assure to your daughter, by settlement, her equal share of the five thousand pounds secured among your children after the decease of yourself and my sister; and, moreover, to enter into an engagement of allowing her, during your life, one hundred pounds per annum.*

Such requirements constituted a small price to pay for restoring some form of honour to the family. And while the news brought a kind of relief, it could not bring contentment, especially knowing someone must have paid off Mr Wickham. While I let Lizzy and Jane believe that person to be their uncle,

I could not help but wonder if Abigail had somehow made good on her offer. Nevertheless, released from the immediate torment of one consequence of my mistakes, I could now begin to address another. As soon as word arrived from Gardiner that arrangements concerning Mr Wickham had been finalised, I took myself off to Mr Spigott's cottage. Perhaps there I might find the redemption I sought.

~ ~ ~

With advancing age, we should enjoy the boon of summer, not knowing how many are left to us. Yet the malaise of recent events and my own role in them still clung to me, despite the satisfactory conclusion to Lydia's adventures. The August sun brought little warmth to my cheeks, the drone of bees, bugs, and beetles failed to reach my ears, and the scent of the meadowsweet seemed tame and ephemeral.

My knock at Mr Spigott's door received no response, but I found him—as expected—in his garden. He was kneeling in a pile of clippings, hair bedraggled by sweat.

"You will pardon my rudeness in coming to you directly, Mr Spigott. I knocked but was not heard."

The curate got to his feet to dip his head in greeting. "My servant is hard of hearing, even if she is in the house. Shall I fetch tea?"

"No," I said. "No tea, please. I do not wish to take up more of your time than necessary. You have heard the news from Longbourn?"

Mr Spigott nodded. "I believe you are to be congratulated on the marriage of Miss Lydia Bennet to Mr Wickham. It is a good thing."

"It is the *right* thing. Whether it is a *good* thing only time will tell. The news should please your bishop."

The curate's cheeks turned the colour of his roses. "I wish it were so. The bishop has clear views on the value of marriage. But also on how it comes about."

"Am I to understand, then, that he would still object to any interest you might have in Mary?" I already knew the answer and hardened my heart to the disappointment it would bring.

"Yes."

Mr Spigott's face had assumed the same stoic expression that had frustrated me in the past, though his stance gave the lie to his apparent equanimity. If nature infused his character on that day, it was the touch of winter when all is still and brooding.

I withdrew a hip flask from my pocket, removed the lid, took a long draught of brandy, then waved the vessel at Mr Spigott, who shook his head.

"Sit down, young man," I said.

"Let me find a bench for you, Mr Bennet. Your clothes…"

"Forget my clothes and sit down with me on the grass. The last few days and weeks have been particularly trying, and I am in no mood for any demands of society that are not entirely practical and reasonable. So, sit."

Mr Spigott took a position opposite me, wiping the hair from his brow and squinting up at the sun.

"I have listened to your parables and sermons in the church," I said. "You will do me the honour of listening to one of mine. Now, what defines your relationship with your God, Mr Spigott?"

"His love for us."

"Precisely. And do you think the Lord would find something improper in true love between two people, whatever their circumstances?"

"I do not. But the church, the bishop…I am a clergyman, after all."

"Ah, yes. That you are. Let me speak plainly, then. Your clerical superiors have no moral authority over you or me—only God does." The words tumbled out of me. Perhaps it was the drink, perhaps the heat of the day, or perhaps regret fighting its way once again to the surface, like a drowning man who makes one final effort before the light dies within him.

"Consider your exalted bishop. A man who warns of the seven deadly sins but represents the very epitome of at least four." I counted off gluttony, pride, envy, and sloth on my fingers. "On the very rare occasion he visits our part of his diocese, it is only to display his love of pomp and puddings."

I took another slug of brandy, relishing the familiar sting in my throat.

"You are a clergyman, Mr Spigott, a man who preaches the teachings of our Lord. Remind me, how goes the Gospel according to Matthew? 'Blessed are the merciful: for they shall obtain mercy.' And, of course, 'For if ye forgive men their trespasses, your heavenly Father will also forgive you: But if ye forgive not men their trespasses, neither will your Father forgive your trespasses.' Oh, and let us not forget, 'Judge not, that ye be not judged.' Shall I continue?"

"But I am bound by duty." Mr Spigott did not look at me as he spoke.

"Duty? Oh, yes, duty is a fine thing. But ask yourself to

whom you owe it. You have two paths before you now. If you choose your duty toward the church, you cannot remain here, surrounded by reminders of what you lost. You will move away, eventually, to find solace in work elsewhere. To no avail, believe me. It may be a phrase in one of your pamphlets, a scent, a piece of music, but something will remind you of the love you abandoned in the cause of duty.

"However, if you choose love, then you will find true happiness. Your bishop may disapprove, but can love be a sin in the eyes of the Lord? Has Mary sinned in loving you? Should she be punished for the acts of others? Should you?

"Now, you may think I speak to you out of selfishness, as a father who merely wishes to see a daughter married. But you must believe me when I say I speak to you as a man. No more and no less. One who has loved and who lost his way in honour and duty. You only need to ask yourself one question: do you love Mary? If the answer is yes, then do not fail yourself. And do not fail your God, for whom love is all."

Mr Spigott did not reply or even look at me, and I knew then that he was lost to us. I had this one task that I alone might have fulfilled for my family, and even that was to be denied me. My penance would continue.

The Use of a Sword

My acknowledgement of my failures together with the wish to make up for them did not, it seemed, suffice to appease fate. Longbourn remained her stage, and she appeared determined to ensure I would ever exit my bedchamber pursued by a bear. After Mr Spigott, the next ursine challenge arrived in an officer's uniform.

In the army, I spent a week in a frozen farmhouse with nothing to drink but melted snow and nothing to eat but a rind of cheese, stale bread, and apples whose better days lay far in the past. I had no idea why they obliged us to billet in that building. Perhaps it was out of principle; farmhouses in distant lands exist to be occupied. But the discomfort of the cold, the gnawing hunger, and the soul-destroying pointlessness of our task was like heaven compared to the inexecrable agony of sharing a house with Mr and Mrs Wickham. They arrived shortly after their wedding in London and against my better judgement.

We may distinguish ourselves from animals in our ability to learn quickly from our experiences. Evidently this quality had yet to manifest in either of our guests. Lydia seemed to believe she offered some kind of example for her sisters to follow. Mr Wickham remained Mr Wickham—all charm on the surface, with little substance beneath it.

The newlyweds received a mixed reception at Longbourn. One small part of the family sought to celebrate, the other larger part to grieve, with Jane mediating between the two.

The letters M, R, and S in front of Lydia's name trumped all concerns and criticisms in the eyes of Mrs Bennet and led to a recovery of health worthy of Lazarus. She took her daughter's marriage as reward for all her worrying and scheming, even if the circumstances were not as she might have wished.

Kitty seemed torn between jealousy and joy, but her curiosity got the better of the former, and her willingness to listen to Lydia's tales of Brighton and London soon returned both of them to each other's affections.

Jane was all grace and politeness, revealing nothing of her beliefs concerning the propriety of Lydia's actions. Had a horde of marauding Huns rampaged through Longbourn, Jane would have greeted them kindly and asked how they preferred their eggs.

Mary spoke to neither of the Wickhams. Not a word, not even a look. Used to her silence and disapproval, none of the family passed comment on her recalcitrance, but I felt its intensity in the hardness of her shoulders at dinner, the tightness of her lips, and her swift removal from a room should the topic of love or—God forbid—clergymen arise in conversation. Mr Spigott did not visit during their stay, a fact that confirmed he had made his choice.

Lizzy addressed Lydia with restraint, knowing the futility of moral lectures and inhibited by the vestiges of sisterly affection. Mr Wickham, though, she treated with outright disdain, as if the affront to the family was hers to feel alone.

As for myself, I felt my duty fulfilled by allowing that reprobate into my home. My governess used to tell me stories on stormy nights, when the fire seemed to shrink in fear of the thunder, leaving us to cower beneath blankets and find some relief in tales of heroism. Good and evil would always reap the rewards of their behaviours. But life is not a story. To see Mr Wickham drinking my port, eating my food, and smiling at his good fortune proved hard to bear. My chief consolation was the prospect of their moving to Newcastle, a part of the country I would never likely visit, not even in error. Mr Wickham had acquired an ensigncy in a regiment quartered in the North.

I found no reason to converse with either Lydia or her husband away from the breakfast or dinner table. To his credit, Mr Wickham did not seek me out either, so it was to my surprise that I saw him on the threshold of my study a full five days after his arrival at Longbourn.

"All the times I had dinner here, I never did see your collection, sir." Mr Wickham leant against the door post as I fumbled with the catch on a display cabinet.

"No, you did not."

"Perhaps I might do so now?"

"If you wish." I lifted the glass top that protected nature's jewels from the dust and light.

"So many butterflies." Mr Wickham peered into the cabinet. "I wonder you do not put them on the walls. They deserve to be seen."

I looked across at the bright rectangles above and between the shelves and bookcases, where frames had once hung. "Perhaps, but I am not so proud of my collection as I once was. A friend reminded me that butterflies might be best observed in the wild, allowed to roam free and do as they will."

"I might almost be jealous of such a life." Mr Wickham smiled. I did not.

"Fluttering here and there without so much as a by-your-leave only leads to trouble," I let my eye roam over the coloured delights in their trays. "A butterfly leaves no mark on the flowers he visits. But a man usually does and not always a good one."

"I should like to make *my* mark in Newcastle. The regulars suit a man of action like myself. I hope to bring honour to my name and that of my wife's family."

"Honour?" It was all I could do not to laugh. "I wish you luck with that."

Mr Wickham smiled again. "As I recall from dinner conversation, you were an army man yourself, sir. Did you see action?"

"I did."

"How fortunate to have had the opportunity to earn the gratitude of your King and country."

"If either were grateful, they have been remiss in communicating the fact," I said. "And my good fortune was not in finding action but surviving it."

"That would be your sword." Mr Wickham pointed at a blade mounted on the wall.

"Given your powers of observation, Mr Wickham, perhaps you should join military intelligence."

I retrieved the sword from its wooden hooks.

"Heavier than I remember," I said. "I wonder if I can still wield it."

The air seemed to shimmer as the blade passed through it, the movement calling forth echoes of shouts across muddied fields, distant drumbeats, and the cries of the wounded.

"It has been a few years, but I can feel the blood rise again. *En garde*, Mr Wickham. One swift blow is all it takes to cut a man, to spill his blood."

The tip of the sword hung a few inches from my son-in-law's throat. He swallowed as the point edged closer to his Adam's apple.

"You must remain in command of your emotions," I said. "An angry man is quick to fight but quicker to lose."

Mr Wickham nodded, though his usual confidence seemed to be reconsidering its position.

"Some say a sword fight resembles a dance," I continued. "The way a man dances says much about his character. But the heat of battle reveals all of it."

The point of the sword now wavered a mere inch from Mr Wickham's skin. The smile still clung to his face, likely out of habit, but a bead of sweat had formed on his forehead. "Well, enough of that." I let the sword drop. "I hope you may have a chance to prove yourself. You face a simple choice should you enter battle: death or honour. Let us hope for the latter, eh?"

"I should see if my dear wife needs me." Mr Wickham bowed as he manoeuvred toward the door.

"There is always the option of an honourable death. Would that suit you?" I said to his retreating back. "It would certainly suit me," I muttered.

I returned the sword to its cradle and was almost content for a moment. But only for a moment. Mr Wickham did not seek me out again.

The Return of Friends

Mary's pain and the loss of Mr Spigott continued to gnaw at me as September began to caress the hedgerows and woodlands, bringing forth a rush of nuts and berries but tainting the chestnut trees with uncaring splashes of russet and gold.

Life without some kind of delusion is no life at all, so I clung to the forlorn hope that time, love, and longing would eventually melt away the curate's concerns. And though I was resolved to pay more attention to the futures of my children, the opportunity rarely presented itself in the weeks that followed. The Bennet ladies avoided social engagements, perhaps fearing the poisonous touch of tongues still wagging over events in London. My daughters all still carried some unspoken sadness about them, as if they mourned for something lost—an innocence, a sister, a love. Lizzy lost herself in the classics and peppered me with questions about the character of men, despite my protest that the only reliable way to understand a man's character was to assume he did not have one.

"I feel like I have become the Oracle at Delphi, Fielding, but without the divine inspiration."

My friend and I stood in his study, slowly sorting through some of the insects he had brought back from the Society's Dorking excursion.

"And what is to blame for the lack of spirit among the ladies of Longbourn?" asked Fielding.

"Better ask who. When ladies fall into despondency, the fault lies mostly with men. Mrs Bennet and Kitty blame Mr Wickham for taking Lydia away to the north, and I suspect Jane still rues the loss of Mr Bingley. Though I understand he has returned to Netherfield, so she may now enjoy the pain of both loss *and* hope. As for Lizzy, well, her expectations of people can never be met, for she stands above all men in character. We are doomed to ever disappoint her."

"But Mrs Bennet must be pleased at a daughter wed?" Fielding squinted at a cloth on his desk covered in bugs and beetles.

"She is, but she has also discovered the price of victory. Lydia is married but gone from home, and the circumstances of her wedding make it less likely that any of our other daughters will find husbands. As you know, the affair has already frightened away Mr Spigott."

"Poor Miss Mary. Though you cannot blame the curate for his decision."

"I suppose not, though he will come to regret it. Mary is quite equitable in her apportioning of blame. Only Lizzy and Jane escape her censure." I held up a pill beetle, its legs tucked into the grooves below its body.

"Hard to find, those," said Fielding. "Quite inconspicuous unless you get up close."

"Much like Mary." I cast my mind back to the one meaningful conversation we had had since the arrival of Colonel Forster's express.

"I am sorry, Mary."

"For what, Papa?" Mary did not look up from her book.

"For Mr Spigott."

"Just for him?"

"For all that has passed. I know I bear some blame for—"

"For ruining perhaps my only chance at happiness?" Now Mary looked up, cheeks flushed, eyes ablaze. "But I should thank you, Papa. You have shown me my foolishness. I should never have listened to you. Never have trusted you. I shall put my trust in scripture again, become the old Mary. Perhaps then I shall avoid future disappointment."

"Do not do this to yourself, Mary."

My daughter shied away from my outstretched hand. "Oh, I have not done this to myself, Papa. You have. You. And Mama. And Lydia. And Mr Wickham. And, yes, Mr Spigott. All of you."

"Do not despair," said Fielding. "The glass may be half full after all. Your two eldest daughters possess a beauty and character that may cause admirers to overlook any consideration of Miss Lydia's fate. Pass me the tweezers, would you?"

I handed my friend the tool but did not let go immediately. "Tell me, Fielding, what is it like to go through life with your boundless optimism? Are you not condemned to disappointment?"

"If the cynic is correct, then the satisfaction of being so offers no compensation for the troubles so accurately predicted." My friend took the tweezers and began picking out small beetles from the cloth. "Should I be misplaced in my optimism, then I always have the prospect of another day, a turnaround, a hope for the future to keep me in good spirits. Talking of which, how are those regrets of yours?"

"They have lessened somewhat. I met Abigail in London."

Fielding paused, one of nature's shimmering jewels held in mid-air, its colours undimmed in death. "And?"

"We understand each other better. It seems she has forgiven me. Now we need only forgive ourselves, and we may face the future with élan and panache."

"I am happy for you, my friend. You can now have no excuse for your cynicism."

"Apart from a lifetime of experience and observation of my fellow man? The poets write of unrequited love, Fielding, but unfulfilled love seems of less interest to them. Where are all our stories and poems?"

"You forget *Romeo and Juliet*."

~ ~ ~

On my return from Fielding's estate, I found Lizzy sitting on the steps outside our front entrance, book in hand, oblivious to the wind that did unspeakable things to her hair as she read.

"Your mother has cast you out, Lizzy? Perhaps Mr Collins will take you in, all the better to remind you of what you forsook by refusing him."

"Mama is quite content, Papa. Which is why I wished to catch you before you get home. There is news."

"After all the news of late, I am unsure if I can bear more. Do not say the Wickhams are coming to stay again. There are only so many days a week I can visit Mr Fielding."

Lizzy stood and rested a hand on my arm. "Mr Bingley called."

"Mr Bingley? Good gracious."

"And not alone. Mr Darcy accompanied him." The short pause between Lizzy's sentences led me to wonder, once again, what she had not told me about her encounters with the latter gentleman. "They stayed for a few minutes and then left."

"I know full well what your mama will say," I said. "But what are we to make of this?"

"I have no answer, Papa. Though if obliged to guess at Mr Bingley's purpose, I would say he wishes to re-establish a prior acquaintance with a certain sister of mine." She smiled.

"Really? Perhaps Fielding has a point."

"Papa?"

"Nothing. That would be good news indeed. But what of Mr Darcy? What could bring him to these parts?"

Lizzy raised her hands. "I have no more idea than you, Papa. They are close friends, so perhaps where Mr Bingley goes, Mr Darcy follows."

I paused with my hand on the door latch. "And you really think Mr Bingley might still wish an understanding with Jane, after all our troubles?"

My daughter nodded. "And I believe Jane would not find the prospect disagreeable."

"Not disagreeable? That is practically a declaration of undying love when it comes to Jane."

The revelation brought a familiar mix of hope and resentment. Hope of a secure future for Jane, resentment that only the actions of others would bring it about. Atonement would still elude me.

"Can we expect Mr Bingley again?" I said.

"I very much think so." Lizzy pushed the door open for me, revealing distant murmurings of excitement within. "Mama told Mr Bingley you would save the best of the covies for when he has killed all his own birds. He and Mr Darcy are to come to dinner next Tuesday. Along with the Gouldings, Mrs Long, her nieces, and others."

"Mrs Long and her nieces? My cup of joy doth overflow. Still, let us not count any chickens until they have begun laying golden eggs. That lesson I have learnt many times. I suppose I better let your mother tell me the good news. Has she begun choosing wedding gowns yet?"

~ ~ ~

Mr Bingley did indeed return for dinner, along with his taciturn companion. Mrs Bennet worked her magic once again with the seating arrangements, placing Jane opposite her intended and, in an act of remarkable sacrifice, putting Mr Darcy next to herself. The master of Pemberley redeemed himself somewhat in her eyes by complimenting the partridge.

Though I spoke little with our neighbour from Netherfield, those times I did I found him entirely as amiable as I recalled from his previous stay in Hertfordshire. Like Mr Collins, Mr

Bingley sought to please people with his conversation. Unlike Mr Collins, he succeeded. And, in contrast to our Hunsford rector, Mr Bingley's wish to please derived from his respect for others rather than a desire to seek their approval.

Hardly a day or two had passed before Mr Bingley called again, this time alone. And again, the next day. That he was very much in love with Jane could not be doubted, but it seemed the long list of Mr Bingley's qualities did not include decisiveness.

"I do not understand, husband," said my wife. "He is so attentive to Jane, yet he will not make an offer. Will you not talk to him tomorrow when you shoot with him?"

Asked several months ago, such a question would have met with scorn and refusal. I now welcomed the prospect. Perhaps Mr Bingley might offer some atonement after all.

~ ~ ~

The noise of the dogs and guns offered little chance of conversation the following morning. After a few hours, though, my birds wisely decided to abandon flight for the day, and I sent the men on ahead to bring our feathered booty to the kitchens. Mr Bingley and I walked slowly back to Longbourn along the old quarry lane. The weight of wagons carrying stone to Meryton and beyond had left its mark, the lane now a deep trench in the landscape, like a furrow on the brow of an old farmhand. Raised hedges on either side offered added protection from prying eyes and curious ears.

In the few minutes we walked together, my wish to intervene grew stronger, far more than any lingering sense of shame at my earlier ignorance of my daughters' needs might have caused. I cannot truly say why. Perhaps Mr Bingley's situation reminded me a little of my own all those years ago—a man in love but unwilling to declare it. Perhaps I thought of Mr Wickham. If a man wholly undeserving of a wife should have the joy of one, then it seemed only right that a deserving man should reap his reward, too. Or perhaps I simply needed to regain my faith in the truth of stories.

"Now then, Mr Bingley," I said. "You know when you were last in Hertfordshire, I found myself almost liking you. And I do not say that about many gentlemen."

"How kind, sir!"

"You are a fine young man, but your rushing off to London did not sit well with Mrs Bennet. She was obliging enough to share her displeasure with the rest of the family."

"Yes, sir, I am sure that was never my intention. My sisters, you see…" Mr Bingley began criss-crossing the lane like a fledgling stalking up and down a branch. Then he stopped, turned to me, and opened his mouth as if to speak. No words came out.

"Mr Bingley?"

"I…that is to say…what an admirable lane. Rather excellent for walking along!"

I eyed him closely. "You have returned to Netherfield without your sisters, is that correct?"

"It is! They both chose to remain in London."

"Perhaps they know your intentions for returning to Netherfield?"

"I could not say, sir!"

"I am a man of books and logic, Mr Bingley. Or at least I try to be." I picked up a small branch from the ground, torn from its timbered home by some storm. "Would you indulge me in a little reasoned speculation?"

Even Mr Bingley's nod of acquiescence seemed to have its own exclamation mark at the end.

I began to swing the branch before me, the swish of the wood adding emphasis to my words. "Let us assume you have returned to us in order to renew a particular acquaintance with a young lady. Let us also assume you wish to reach an understanding with this lady, whom you have, shall we say, 'disappointed' in the past. Perhaps you even seek to make an offer of marriage to her."

Our Netherfield neighbour stood entirely still now, a hint of a blush on his cheeks.

"The lady in question has remained patient and devoted to your memory for some months," I continued. "But such patience, like all things on this earth, cannot last forever."

"Ah," said Mr Bingley.

"Take this advice from one who knows—if you are sure, then declare now. Do not give fate a chance to write another story for you. Talk with Jane. You would have my blessing, of course. My goodness, you are an estimable fellow, Mr Bingley. With a wonderful library, even if you do not use it. I shall be happy to see more of it once we are related."

Mr Bingley placed his hands behind his back and began walking again, untroubled by the raucous call of a pheasant and passing through a cloud of midges without pause or notice. "But what if Miss Bennet should refuse?" he called back.

I tucked the branch under my arm and followed him down the lane. "Ignorant I may be of the ways of young ladies, but I do believe you can expect a positive response to such an offer.

However, Jane cannot accept one that is never made. Besides, should she refuse, you will have the pleasure of my company at Netherfield—life at Longbourn would be quite unbearable."

"I understand. I shall speak with her soon!"

"You will not speak with her *soon*, Mr Bingley." I pulled out the branch and poked it at him. "You will speak with her *today*. Return to my house, take dinner with us, and seek out Jane. Then approach me for my blessing. Now off you run. I shall take a more leisurely pace."

The young man's smile seemed to banish the shadows that had slowly grown across the lane. At first, he left me at a brisk walk, perhaps torn between the desire to appear gentlemanly and a wish to reach Longbourn as fast as possible. Love, however, got the better of propriety, and I watched Mr Bingley as he fair sprinted around the far bend.

For the first time in a while, I felt a moment of true contentment. Then I recalled what happened the last time I expected to hear the knock of a suitor.

A Lady Calls

Fortunately, fate proved kinder to Jane that she did to Mary, and the understanding between my eldest daughter and Mr Bingley helped restore something like peace to Longbourn. Though it was an uncertain one, like a ceasefire brokered between two sides long at war.

"He will make you happy," I told Jane. "And many others, too. I might even say it brings me some contentment and that is not a feeling I am much accustomed to of late."

Jane's security, and by implication those of her sisters and mother, had its price, though. I took to rising early and walking to avoid the chatter on wedding gowns and arrangements.

Drifting through the shrubs and trees a few days after Mr Bingley's proposal, one part of me saw firewood for the house, heard the call of pigeons destined for our kitchen, and caught the sharp odour of freshly cut timber intended for the sawmill over at Hatfield. Another part chose instead to see the dark greens of summer fall to the touch of autumn, hear starlings cry their last goodbyes before departing on their winter journeys, and smile at the wild garlic, its scent still drifting on the October wind. It seemed my malaise had begun to lift, though the church spire in the distance provided a constant reminder that not every problem had found its resolution; Jane's engagement to a gentleman of Bingley's status and connections had not led to a renewal of Mr Spigott's attentions. Mary continued to keep to herself, refusing to allow another to share her burden. Perhaps her anger had yet to burn out, fuelled by righteous disappointment in a world that seemed intent on rewarding others for their inconstancy.

"Oh, Mr Bennet," said my wife on my return. "You have missed such excitement. Lady Catherine called on Lizzy but not a few minutes ago. Such a shame you missed her."

I gave little thought to the great lady's visit, assuming it a mere courtesy call to a former Rosings guest. The following day, though, a letter arrived from Mr Collins that threw an entirely different light on the event.

Your daughter Elizabeth, it is presumed, will not long bear the name of Bennet, after her elder sister has resigned it, and the chosen partner of her fate may be reasonably looked up to as one of the most illustrious personages in this land. This young gentleman is blessed, in a peculiar way, with every thing the heart of mortal can most desire,—splendid property, noble kindred, and extensive patronage.

Yet in spite of all these temptations, let me warn my cousin Elizabeth, and yourself, of what evils you may incur by a precipitate closure with this gentleman's proposals, which, of course, you will be inclined to take immediate advantage of. My motive for cautioning you is as follows. We have reason to imagine that his aunt, Lady Catherine de Bourgh, does not look on the match with a friendly eye.

"What a preposterous notion." I waved the letter at Lizzy in the library. "That Mr Darcy—Mr Darcy!—should be inclined to propose to you. Mr Collins has clearly taken leave of his senses. Imagine! But it seems he is not alone in giving credence to this misunderstanding. Did Lady Catherine call to refuse her blessing?"

"She laboured under the impression that Mr Darcy and I had an understanding. That we were to be engaged." Lizzy stood primly, no hint of humour in her demeanour.

"Oh, I am much amused by the thought. I might almost laugh, had I not lost the habit of doing so. No doubt she made her opinion on the matter clear with all the sensitivity of one who believes herself vastly superior to the Bennets?"

Lizzy nodded.

"Stupidity and incivility plague every part of society. Why, she should be glad of a connection with one such as you, Lizzy. You are better than any Darcy or de Bourgh."

"I am sorry, Papa."

"*You* are sorry? I am sure you have nothing to be sorry for. Though I do sense there is more to this story than you let on. You must credit your father with some degree of intelligence. Lady Catherine would not find it worth her time to travel to Longbourn if she did not have good cause. Why would she think that you might be engaged to Mr Darcy?"

"I cannot say, Papa." Lizzy twisted her hands as if wishing to trace the outline of every one of her fingers.

"Good Lord," I said. "*Has* Mr Darcy made an offer to you?"

"I am not engaged to that man." My daughter ceased her fiddling and folded her arms. "There is no such understanding between us."

"That, my girl, does not answer my question."

"Please, Papa, I do not wish to talk of such matters."

I dropped Mr Collins's letter on a table, where it joined one from John that expressed his conviction that matters with Mr Spigott might be resolved to Mary's benefit; one missive a bearer of false claims, the other a bearer of false hopes.

"Though I have not been the best of fathers, I have always looked out for your interests, Lizzy. I would not have you unhappy or wronged by some arrogant gentleman who does not recognise your qualities. You told me before that Mr Darcy had simply caused you to reflect on your own beliefs, but there is more to it than that. And if you will not tell me of your troubles—do not deny their existence—then there is nothing I can do for you. I believed us able to talk of most anything. Did I perhaps do you some injury? Is that why you are changed toward me?"

"No, Papa." Lizzy's eyes grew moist. "I blame myself for Lydia. That is all."

"You are not being truthful." I turned away from my daughter.

Lizzy moved around to face me once again. "We are neither of us being truthful, then. If I have been reticent in revealing my troubles, I have merely followed your lead."

"Nonsense."

"You have not told the full truth about Gloucestershire." Lizzy wiped her eyes and placed her hands on her hips. "I know there is more to your relationship with Mrs Hayter than an old acquaintance."

"Heavens, child, you have read too many of those novels. Quite what do you imagine, Lizzy? Do you believe me guilty of some kind of dishonourable behaviour? Some midnight tryst, a reunion of old lovers wantonly abandoning the strictures of society? Look at me, Lizzy. I am long past such adventures, even if I had the inclination. Which I do not. There is nothing to speak of regarding Mrs Hayter. No more than you have anything to say about Hunsford or Pemberley."

"So, this is how it is to be between us now, Papa?" My daughter's stance burst with defiance and intelligence.

After a short period of mutual glaring, I dropped my eyes and let out a sigh of surrender.

"No," I said. "I would not lose you to a misunderstanding, Lizzy. Sit yourself down. Goodness, it seems barely a day passes when I must not conduct a serious conversation with a young gentleman or lady." I waited until Lizzy had settled into an armchair, her face now calm, though her chest still rose and fell faster than normal.

"You may have guessed at much of this. Or been told by Mrs Barton," I said. "When I lived in Bath, before I met your mother, I was close to Mrs Hayter. No, let us speak plainly. I *loved* Mrs Hayter. But I failed to declare myself in a timely manner, and she married another. I have never ceased to love her."

Lizzy's mouth formed a soundless "oh," and she even had the grace to blush.

"It is like an illness," I continued, speaking as much to myself as to my daughter. "The kind where the doctor prescribes complete abstinence from alcohol. You hardly notice it until someone places a glass of port in front of you. When I see Mrs Hayter, I am confronted by memory, regret, and the torment of being so very close to precisely that which I may not have. Society does not permit it. *I* do not permit it. You asked if something passed in Gloucestershire? She and I spoke of these things and did not part well, though we are reconciled now. At least, I believe we are. My disappointment and anger clouded my judgement, and I indulged in selfish behaviour. I need not remind you of the unfortunate consequences for Lydia and us all."

"I did not realise…I mean to say, I knew there was something," said Lizzy. "Anne hinted as much, and Mrs Hayter always seemed peculiarly interested in your welfare."

"Now you know why." I noted with relief that my hands did not shake. Perhaps I had truly found some peace with Abigail. "But, there, you have my truth. And now you must tell me yours."

Lizzy paused for a moment, as if reflecting on her choice of words. Or perhaps she needed time to consider my own admission.

"Mr Darcy spoke clumsily to me in Hunsford."

"Good Lord!" I almost laughed at the ridiculousness of the complaint. "Well, Lizzy, he is a man and one of few words, so you might forgive him the odd poorly chosen expression."

"That is not what I meant, Papa. He insulted my pride." A little colour appeared in Lizzy's cheeks once more. "More than just my pride. I am not at liberty to reveal all that passed, for much of it I have no right to tell, but I would say only this: Mr Darcy at Pemberley bore little resemblance to the arrogant gentleman at Netherfield and Hunsford. When we cannot seem to know even our own feelings, how are we to judge those of others?" She took my hands and held them tightly. "I was so certain in my understanding of people. And now? If I have changed since Hunsford, it is merely through confusion and uncertainty. Oh, Papa, what a pair we make!"

"Perhaps, my dear girl, you now understand why I lock myself away in my study and library so often. And yet the circumstances of recent months have drawn me out more times than I care to remember. John. Mary. Lydia. Jane. And I fear my days of action are not yet over. I will not relinquish Mary's happiness without one last attempt."

"But I thought Mr Spigott quite decided? The church..."

"He is determined to stay loyal to that confounded institution. But, if nothing else, someone needs to remind him of the suffering he causes. Mary lives each day like a bitter hermit. He may be willing to pay the price of his sense of duty, but will he let Mary pay it, too?"

An Unexpected Visitor

The bees weaved their way through Mr Spigott's front garden, jostling for space on the Michaelmas daisies, eager for a final harvest before the cold descended and closed the doors of the hive. I followed the flight of one smaller bee that pursued nectar with a singleness of purpose that made me quite envious.

"You have no regrets, little friend? Or do you still recall flowers of yesteryear and wish for their return? No. You see only the flower before you."

"Mr Bennet?" The voice came from behind me.

Given Mr Spigott's propensity for walking and gardening, his sallow complexion suggested placing duty before love did not sit well with his constitution. It gave me hope.

"Since you are already out," I said, "perhaps we might take a short walk and enjoy the autumn colours?"

We walked together and apart, bound by distance and separated by our differences. Neither of us spoke until we reached where the honeysuckle spilled out of the hedgerow, its fragrance now only a memory, the lane flecked in smears marking where feet and hooves had crushed the plant's red fruits.

"You will know, of course, that Mr Bingley is engaged to my Jane. It seems he, at least, does not share your bishop's misgivings."

Mr Spigott seemed to sag at my words, but then he ruffled his hair and drew himself up to his full height. "I know what you wish to say to me, Mr Bennet. Let me save you the time and effort. My opinion has not changed."

"You are still determined to ignore your feelings towards Mary? Surely you cannot harbour concerns, now, Mr Spigott? If Mr Bingley has none, why should you?"

"Mr Bingley is no clergyman." The curate adjusted his hat as if readying himself for church. "Have you no more argument for me than this new connection to your family?"

"Have *you* no thought for Mary and how she suffers? You abandon her with so little concern or emotion?" Only years of trained English restraint prevented me from grabbing the curate by his lapels. "I have seen you in your garden, Mr Spigott. You are not some calculating man of commerce. You are a kind curate who would give cherries to the poor and walk four miles in the rain just to keep a promise where none need be kept. I will not believe it of you. Or am I so very wrong in my assessment of your character?"

Mr Spigott dropped his head before answering. When he met my eyes, his face showed no sign of anger, guilt, or even shame. "If you have any respect for me, Mr Bennet, then I ask only this of you: do not speak to me on this subject again."

The curate began to walk away from me and back toward his cottage. After a few steps, he bent down to retrieve some stray insect and place it on a nearby bush.

"What of Mary?" I called out. "She pays a hard price. Will you not think of her?"

Mr Spigott stopped and turned to face me. "I think of her every day. Every hour. If I appear lacking in contrition or emotion, it is because that is how I survive without hope."

I almost wished he had said—or done—anything to change my good opinion of him. But perhaps his very goodness and integrity prevented him from disappointing his church. I cursed his moral purity as he walked from me, and I railed against a society that punished the pure of heart and rewarded the wicked. All I wished for now was to return to Longbourn and bury myself in cake and port—away from suitors, daughters, ladies of great reputation, and clergymen.

But fate does not grant wishes.

~ ~ ~

Back at Longbourn, the peace of my library lasted only a few minutes; long enough to allow me to pour myself a glass of port, not long enough for the arrival of the much-desired cake.

The knock at the door began authoritatively enough, then faded. I was all ready to rebuff whichever daughter had chosen to disturb me in my melancholy, but the door opened to reveal a rather unexpected visitor.

"Mr Darcy?" I said.

The master of Pemberley stood in the doorway, twisting his hat in his hands. He lacked the bearing one might expect of an estate owner with ten thousand pounds. On the contrary, he looked instead like a young nephew come in search of a loan, his face dark with unease but underpinned with a tinge of embarrassed hope.

We confronted each other in silence. Then Mr Darcy seemed to remember himself, opened his mouth as if to speak, but fell silent again.

"Mr Darcy?" I repeated.

"My apologies, Mr Bennet. I am not good with words."

"So I have heard. Perhaps a glass of port might help?"

"Port. Yes. Thank you, sir."

"Come in, then, and sit yourself down." I waved at a chair, then proceeded to pour my guest a glass with a nonchalance I did not feel. "This particular bottle comes on the recommendation of my friend, Mr Fielding. I doubt you have met."

"I have not had the pleasure." Mr Darcy neither perched nor relaxed in the armchair, seemingly unsure whether to ready himself for a long conversation or a rapid exit. He projected a unique combination of pride and humility, as if some experience had taught him there is always a better version of oneself that one might aspire to, if not always reach.

"Whatever else the Portuguese might do in this world, we will always be grateful to them for their port. To your health, Mr Darcy!"

"And to yours, Mr Bennet."

The ringing as our glasses met soon faded away to be replaced by renewed silence. The house seemed unusually still, like the land before the storm.

"Now, I have had enough excitement recently," I said at last. "So I hope you do not bring more."

"Ah." Mr Darcy took a sip of port. And then another. "Mr Bennet."

"Yes?"

"I am here to ask for…" Mr Darcy lifted his chin slightly, then placed his glass on a nearby table. "I am here to ask for the hand of Miss Elizabeth Bennet."

When a blade strikes you in battle, there comes a moment of shock before the body and mind react, as if both are unable to comprehend quite what has happened. If you are quick and trained for that moment, you may take action to remain of sound thought. I emptied my glass of port and let the shock pass through me like a ghost might…cold, clammy, and gone. Then I refilled the glass up to the very brim.

"You wish to marry my daughter? Elizabeth? My second daughter?"

"Yes, Elizabeth. I mean, Miss Bennet…Miss Elizabeth Bennet," said Mr Darcy.

"But she—I mean to say, is Lizzy aware of your interest?"

"She is. And she has kindly accepted my proposal—conditional, of course, on your approval, sir."

In that moment, a man of great worth stood before me asking for Lizzy's hand—a man she had recently praised, albeit indirectly, and already accepted. Whatever misgivings I might have had, there could be only one answer to his request.

"Well, you do Elizabeth a great honour, Mr Darcy. If she has consented to your proposal, I would find it hard to deny her. You have my blessing, of course."

At my words, Mr Darcy's face assumed an expression I had never seen there before—a smile.

"Thank you, sir. I am much indebted to you." The smile remained in place, seemingly reluctant to part from its new home.

"Well, good Lord." I finished my port, refilled my glass, and drank the contents down in one draught. "I am quite undone."

The contrast in our affairs to just a few weeks previously seemed almost farcical. Then I thought of Mary.

"Would you do me the favour of satisfying my curiosity, Mr Darcy?"

"Of course, sir.

"Do you love my daughter?"

"I do."

"She speaks her mind, you know."

Mr Darcy grimaced at my words, and I wondered at the nature of the conversations that had taken place between him and my daughter. His reaction reminded me again of my poor judgement; I had never thought to consider his perspective, hearing and believing only Lizzy's.

"Her willingness to speak her mind is one of the reasons I love her."

"Then I wish you a long and happy marriage." I leant over and patted him on the knee, an act which seemed to startle, then please, him. "I understand this can be no marriage of convenience for you. Quite the opposite, in fact. You gain only Lizzy through a connection with our family, not wealth or position. So I must believe you when you say you love my daughter. That is a fine thing, Mr Darcy. A wonderful thing. Now, go to Lizzy. Perhaps you might ask her to come and see me in my study for I would talk with her."

Mr Darcy made no move, and the hint of uncertainty in his posture returned once more.

"Mr Bennet, there is something I would say to you first." He twisted the port in his hands, then swiftly downed his drink. "I must offer you an apology."

"An apology? Whatever for?"

"In the past, with your daughter, I made some remarks about your family that were...poorly chosen. They reflected badly on my character."

I gave Mr Darcy a stern look normally reserved for any daughter that took the last breakfast egg before I had eaten. "Did you perhaps mention our want of connections? Perhaps some impropriety in our behaviour?"

A blush crept across my future son-in-law's cheeks, and he seemed to stiffen, as if readying himself for the lash. My finger made a satisfying tapping noise on the end of the arm of my chair.

"Well, I cannot fault a man for telling the truth, can I?" I patted poor Mr Darcy on the knee again. "Though I suspect you have come to realise there are more important matters in life."

Mr Darcy's expression suggested he had, and that he very much wished he had done so much earlier.

"I should warn you that the impropriety is likely to continue," I said. "Welcome to the family. Do not be too hard on my wife and never mention scripture to Mary. Now, off with you to Lizzy before she tears down the door herself."

~ ~ ~

"My dear Lizzy, have you taken complete leave of your senses?" My daughter stood before my chair, arms folded, deep brown eyes looking at me from the side.

"Papa?"

"Mr Darcy? *The* Mr Darcy. A man who you, despite your revised opinions, once described in worse terms than you have Mr Collins or any number of unfortunate fellows? You would accept him?"

"I would." Lizzy shifted her feet, eyes narrowing, perhaps expecting some argument from me.

"Very well." I began to read a note on my desk from Mr Criswick, proposing another of his interminable talks to the society on his Jamaican voyage. Silence and disinterest were the best encouragement for a daughter with Lizzy's refusal to be ignored.

"I misjudged him, Papa. We have all misjudged him. I have come to know his true character, which is not as we—I—imagined. I am not at liberty to offer any details, but you must believe me when I say he has proved himself kind, loyal, and more than generous. All without hope of personal gain or satisfaction. I do not enter this understanding unwillingly."

"Not unwillingly?" I said. "What an endorsement. You shall not lack for fine clothes and carriages, but will they make you content? Will *he* make you happy? In other words, my dear child, I must ask if you love him? For love will forgive a multitude of sins and allow happiness where none may otherwise be found."

"I do love him, Papa." Lizzy looked away as if picturing her intended. "He is proud, but only in those parts of his character that give him just cause for pride. And those parts that do not, he recognises as such and works to improve. And he has shown that his wish to do so is born entirely of understanding and not in hope of reward. In short, Papa, Mr Darcy is a good man."

The love expressed so clearly in her eyes almost brought tears to mine. I tapped my knee, but my daughter did not understand the gesture.

"Let me hold you once more, Lizzy, as I used to. Before you leave us to become Mrs Darcy. Allow a father to say goodbye to his child."

As Lizzy settled on my lap, she wrapped her arms round my neck and placed a gentle kiss on my cheek.

"I concede my impression of Mr Darcy from our conversation did not reflect what I previously knew of him," I said. "He was quite amiable. A little formal but not unpleasant at all. He even smiled."

"It was not love at first meeting. But on greater acquaintance with Mr Darcy, on beginning to understand his true character, which so few have truly seen, each of his words and actions stole a single piece of my heart until it was all his."

"A marriage based on love, eh? Perhaps there is hope for you both. But I could not see you enter into any such understanding with anyone of inferior character or intelligence. You may love him, but can you respect Mr Darcy, too?"

"There is none I respect more."

"Not even your own father?"

"Not even my own father." Lizzy tapped my nose with her finger.

"Then it is settled. I have given him my consent. He is the kind of man, indeed, to whom I should never dare refuse anything. I now give it to you wholeheartedly. I will part with you, shall we say, not unwillingly? Though any parting from you, Lizzy, is not easy for your papa. But I daresay I will survive it."

In that moment, the events of recent months faded, and we

were, once again, simply father and daughter, united in shared affection.

"I am sure that with greater acquaintance, Papa, you will come to respect Mr Darcy as much as I do. His generosity and goodwill extend far beyond his attentions to me."

Some earnestness in my daughter's voice caused me to lean forward, obliging her to slip from my lap and stand up. I took her hands in mine. "What do you imply, Lizzy? The truth now."

"It was Mr Darcy who found Lydia and Mr Wickham. It was he who ensured they married. Mr Darcy did all of it. He even arranged the commission in Newcastle. And he did all this without hope of receiving my gratitude. He did it because he felt it was right and because he loves me."

"But your uncle?" I said.

"He was sworn to secrecy. Do not think ill of him, Papa. Mr Darcy would not allow news of his actions to reach us, but, even so, I believe my uncle took some persuading before he gave his oath."

"Then how did you come to know of it?"

"Lydia let slip Mr Darcy's name when she and Mr Wickham stayed at Longbourn, and I obliged my aunt to reveal everything."

"This is quite a story." I sat back in my chair. "Do we deserve such an ending? We shall see if Mr Darcy truly loves you, for if he does, he will refuse any offer to pay him back with such determination that I shall be forced to concede. I quite look forward to it."

"Papa!"

"If he wishes to take my Lizzy away, then I shall have some

fun at his expense. Now, off you go and send him back to me. He no doubt awaits news of our conversation. Mrs Darcy! And you had better tell your mother, though you might wait until I am in Meryton. I could not bear all the excitement."

Lizzy paused at the door. "You think Mama will be happy? She does not like Mr Darcy."

"Believe you me, Lizzy, if she would have accepted Mr Collins, she will accept Mr Darcy. I suspect ten thousand a year will improve her opinion rather quickly."

A minute or two later, and my future son-in-law stood before me once again.

"Now, Mr Darcy," I said. "You will excuse dear Lizzy for confiding in her father, but she has told me of all that you did for us concerning Mr Wickham."

The poor man froze, some mixture of umbrage and embarrassment coursing across his face.

"If I am any judge of character," I continued, "then you will not wish me to speak of these matters or thank you. But I will do so just the once. You have my gratitude. For finding the pair of them, for arranging the marriage, for the costs, and for finding the commission for Mr Wickham. How may I repay you?"

"You cannot, sir. You may insist on repayment, but I will not hear of it."

"Excellent. I thought as much."

Mr Darcy looked for a moment as if he felt I should at least try to change his mind for the sake of propriety.

"Come now, Mr Darcy. If we are to be family then we should be honest with one another. You are too stubborn to change your mind, and I too poor to want you to do so. My everlasting gratitude must suffice. And that of Mrs Bennet, which she will not tire of giving. You may regret ever having helped."

Mr Darcy shifted his feet slightly, seemingly uncomfortable with the praise.

"There is no shame in good deeds," I said. "Your embarrassment does you credit, but you must simply accept my thanks and shake on it. My admiration and respect are yours. You also have the love of my daughter, which is worth so much more."

Mr Darcy ignored my outstretched hand, and the stiff pose I remembered from his first visit to Hertfordshire returned.

"You will not shake?"

"I cannot. I am unable to claim credit for all that you thank me for."

"Oh? Someone else, then? But not my brother, surely? Am I to thank Mr Bingley, perhaps?"

"No." Mr Darcy stared straight ahead, his discomfort palpable.

"Well, speak up, dear fellow. The truth must out. Or shall I set Lizzy on you? You will soon learn she is not to be trifled with. Ask Lady Catherine." I frowned. "Ask anyone."

"I am already familiar with Elizabeth's temper."

For a moment, Mr Darcy looked almost haggard, and I wondered again just what conversations the two might have shared.

"Well, you may keep your secret, then, Mr Darcy. And there shall ever be a taint on our relationship. For I owe a man a debt yet know not who he is or how I may repay him. You do me an injustice."

My words seemed to pain him. "You are mistaken, sir."

"You consider your silence honourable?" I said.

"No, I meant you are mistaken in your assumption. It is no man to whom you owe your thanks. All I will say is that it was a lady who arranged Mr Wickham's commission. And paid for it."

"Good Lord. Who?" I already knew the answer to my question.

"I could not possibly say."

"I think you could. And since I expect that you cannot lie, you must tell me the truth. Was it Mrs Hayter? You could have no reluctance to tell me if it was not?"

"Ah." Mr Darcy bore the look of a child with his hand trapped in the biscuit jar and his mother's footsteps approaching.

"It seems I am correct in my assumption." I stood silent for a moment. "But why?"

"Your daughter will tell you I am a poor judge of character, Mr Bennet, but I would say that the lady in question has a personal interest in the welfare of your family. In your welfare in particular."

"I see."

"Well." Mr Darcy coughed. "I confess I am unaccustomed to such conversations. I do not possess a talent for them."

"A little peace and quiet would do me the world of good, too," I said. "It has been quite a day. Quite a few weeks now that I think about it. It will all take some mulling over."

I walked over to a shelf, reached behind a stack of paper, and pulled out a bottle.

"For emergencies." I waved the port at Mr Darcy. "Will you join me?"

"An excellent proposal, Mr Bennet." Mr Darcy smiled for the

second time in my company. And so we began work on a proper understanding between a father and a son-in-law by avoiding all talk of wives and daughters. Instead, we discussed our estates, tenants, and plans for our gardens and wine cellars. I even found myself sharing my disappointment over Mr Spigott with him. And I learnt, once again, never to judge a man before sharing a drink with him.

The Meaning of Contentment

Despite the grand nature of the bridegrooms, the wedding party was a relatively small affair. We all fitted quite snugly in the Longbourn church, where Mr Toke did the honours.

Relatives and friends attended, of course, including the Gardiners, to whom we owed so much, and John and Mrs Barton, who argued over the wording of the vows and thus reassured me that all was well in their own marriage. Charlotte Collins smiled throughout the service; the joining of her good friend to such a man as Mr Darcy appealed to her sense of both economy and romance. Lizzy and Jane, knowing my discomfort at such occasions, even insisted on inviting two of my friends from the Society. Jackson spent much of the service retrieving edible items from his pockets. Whenever I chanced a glance at Fielding, he was watching Mrs Hayter.

As for those happiest of all individuals, Mr Darcy and Mr Bingley claimed the sartorial elegance of their positions. Jane looked no more or less beautiful than she always did. Lizzy revelled in the love and affection that surrounded her and was content, no doubt, to have found someone her equal in character and intelligence—or as near to both as any man could hope to get.

Mrs Bennet glided through the church like a sailing boat in a gentle breeze, full of serene joy, though utterly unable to decide where she should weigh anchor when she had two new sons to praise to more than one guest. Kitty was almost well-behaved, leading me to suspect her silliness derived from spending too much time with Lydia rather than any inherent character flaw. Lizzy had predicted that my youngest daughter and her husband would not attend and so it proved. I imagined they were put off by the cost of travel, though Lizzy's smiled response to that suggestion hinted at other reasons. Perhaps I was to be a grandfather.

Yet, as the guests poured out into the churchyard after the service, a sadness crept over me, like a lone cloud shading the sun on a summer day. Mary sat at the back of the church, seemingly lost in thought and oblivious to her isolation. She would want for nothing now, given the new position of her two elder sisters. She would want for nothing but the love of a good man. One who, undoubtedly, loved her still but remained out of reach, the two separated by his integrity and the hypocrisy of the church.

"Mr Bennet?"

I turned to find the source of Mary's disappointment standing behind me, his face still a masterpiece of stoicism. Not so much a young stork as a statue of one.

"Mr Spigott." I did not know quite what to say.

"A fine day for your family."

"For most of them. And one I have no desire to spoil, so if you will excuse me."

"A peace offering of sorts, Mr Bennet." Mr Spigott held out

a small pot with some shrub in it. Since I made no effort to take the container, he simply placed it on the pew next to me. "Keep the buddleia warm over winter, and it will flower next May."

"Well, if that is all." I turned again to leave.

"I spoke with Mr Darcy," said Mr Spigott. "He had much to say on the importance of allowing love to overcome any reluctance one might have about the propriety of, well, a particular connection."

The curate's words lit a brief flame of hope.

"And did he convince you?"

"He did not. As I once told you, Mr Bennet, I believe a clergyman is bound to duty and service. My opinion on this matter remains firm. My respect for you and your family knows no bounds, yet I cannot in good conscience ask for Miss Mary Bennet's hand in marriage, knowing that to do so would incur the anger of my bishop and cast a shadow on my position. My duty to the church and my allegiance to my vows prevent me from doing what my heart wishes me to do."

"So you keep telling me, Mr Spigott." Any good humour I may have had melted away. "Do you have anything more to say to me? If not, I have guests to attend to."

The curate straightened, then pushed back his hair. "Mr Bennet, I would like to ask for the hand of your daughter, Miss Mary Bennet, in marriage."

I stared at the man before me, hearing his words but failing to understand them.

"It has been a long year, Mr Spigott. So perhaps I misheard you. You ask for Mary's hand yet have made it clear that a man in your position cannot do so."

"That is correct."

"You set me a riddle, but I am at a loss."

A smile broke out on the curate's face. "A man in my position cannot marry Miss Mary Bennet. So I have chosen to leave that position. I submitted my letter of resignation this morning. Since I owe no further duty or service to the church, my heart is free to choose of its own accord. And, with your permission, I choose Mary."

I nodded, sat down, and picked up the plant pot. "Buddleia, you say? Which colour?"

"Lilac. But Mr Bennet—are you well? Did you understand me?"

"Quite well. Very well indeed." The tears started slowly, pushing their way past years of disappointment and frustration to fall in unreserved delight. "So very, very well, but I do not think I can bear so much joy in one day. It does not sit well with me. I do not deserve it. So much good has come to pass with so little effort on my part."

"If I may be permitted an observation." Mr Spigott sat down next to me. "Without your intervention, I do not know if I would have ever admitted my love to Mary. All our actions—good or bad—have brought us to this place, Mr Bennet. All of them."

"Well, that is a strange kind of consolation. But consolation nonetheless." I accepted Mr Spigott's proffered handkerchief. "You are a wiser fellow than I gave you credit for. You have my hearty blessing. Though, much as I approve of the match, you might tell me your plans. What will you do?"

"Mr Darcy has found me alternative employment."

"Mr Darcy?"

"It seems he learnt of my situation from your conversation with him. He wishes to remodel part of his estate and invited me to help him and his steward. Mary and I may stay at Pemberley, and if the work goes well, he will recommend me to other estates in need of a similar service. I may perhaps earn a living through it."

"Well, I never." I shook my head in disbelief. "Mr Darcy comes to our aid once more. Who would have thought it? So, no more pamphlets?"

"No, sir. To be truthful, I never felt comfortable preaching. But it was my duty."

"Ah," I said. "That word again. Still, the day gets better and better. Does Mary know?"

"No." For a moment, uncertainty passed across Mr Spigott's face. "I wished your approval first and hoped you might know if she would forgive me."

I glanced over to Mary, who sat with her head bowed, seemingly unaware of us or our conversation.

"Forgive you? Most certainly not, dear boy. Not for many a year. But that will not stop her from accepting you. Such is the nature of love. You had best give her the good news. But do not let her come to me should she say yes. I have had quite enough diversion of late. She may express her gratitude and love appropriately in the morning."

I watched as Mr Spigott approached Mary and spoke to her. He gave a long speech interspersed with excessive gestures, which Mary listened to quietly, giving no sign of any emotion. Then I saw him offer another handkerchief. Afterwards, as they clasped hands, my daughter looked over to where I stood, and she smiled. A smile of unconditional joy and love. Later that day, she danced. And sang at the piano, though only for one song, giving up her seat without prompting, though we might have listened happily to her for hours.

Two daughters wed and one betrothed in a single day might be considered hubris. Divine retribution arrived in the form of a familiar voice outside the church, where the wine and ale flowed in celebration of a day that autumn blessed with bright sunshine.

"Mr Bennet! Mr Bennet!"

Married life clearly suited Mr Collins. He had gained in weight, though not, I suspected, in wisdom. "May I congratulate you on such a felicitous occasion?" said my heir.

"You may."

"I flatter myself that if it were not for my good self, Mr and Mrs Darcy would never have reached such an understanding."

"Really? And what was the nature of your decisive role?"

Mr Collins leant sideways and turned his head slightly, a strange stance he adopted whenever explaining some nugget of wisdom to those in need of clerical enlightenment. "If I had not married my dear Charlotte, then Miss Elizabeth Bennet would not have visited Hunsford. I believe it was there that the true beginnings of mutual affection began." He may have winked at this point, but clearly lacked practice at such a gesture.

"Let us hope Lady Catherine does not share your belief," I said. "She would be most put out."

Mr Collins's eyes widened. "Well, of course, I would not wish to claim *all* the credit for myself. Indeed, on reflection, I wonder if the seeds of affection were not first sown in Hertfordshire."

"Nonsense." I slapped Mr Collins on the back. "Your humility is to be expected from a man in your profession, but do not allow natural modesty to disguise your part in this happy event. The Lord works in mysterious ways, does he not? And he chose you, Mr Collins, as his Cupid. I am sure Lady Catherine, once her anger has lessened somewhat, will overlook the offence to her sensibilities. After all, is she not the most condescending and generous of patrons? I wonder, though, at your presence today. Does Lady Catherine approve?"

Mr Collins looked about him, as if expecting the grand lady to make an appearance from behind the shrubs that lined the church wall. "We are spending some time visiting with Mrs Collins's family. On our return, it would be remiss of me to burden Lady Catherine with all the details of our happy stay in Hertfordshire."

"Most wise, Mr Collins, most wise. Oh, is that Mrs Hayter? You will excuse me. I must speak with her."

~ ~ ~

"Abigail! You cannot know how glad I am to see you." She sat apart from the others in the shade of an apple tree in the meadow that adjoined the church. I sat down next to her, sharing the straw-covered ground as if we were children at a country fayre.

"You are glad, James? That is an unexpected pleasure."

"I meant what I said in London, that we may be friendly. I have spoken to Mr Darcy, you know. He told me of what you did for us. For Lydia and Mr Wickham."

"He did?" Abigail arched a trim eyebrow. "I expected better of him. At the very least that he might maintain a confidence. Perhaps I have misjudged Mr Darcy."

"On the contrary, Abigail. You cannot blame him for his indiscretion. I put him in an impossible position: to take credit for something he did not do or betray your confidence. Once I guessed at his dilemma, he had no choice but to speak of what happened."

"Very well, then I shall retain my good opinion of him."

"My family owes you a debt." I waved my hand toward the ongoing celebrations. "None of this may have been possible otherwise. Or even if it had been, you risked your own reputation to protect ours. It was more than generous of you. I shall repay you, obviously, for the expenses you incu—."

The touch of Abigail's finger on my lips silenced me in an instant. She held it there for a short while, long enough for the scent of lavender to grow ever more intense. "There is nothing to repay," she said. "If you could do so, then I would not have needed to intervene. Do not protest! We are past any deception."

"Then you leave my family grateful and in your debt."

"Your family owe me nothing, James. I thought only of you. As, I believe, Mr Darcy thought only of Elizabeth."

"And yet we shall be denied their happy fate."

The straw scratched at my hand, but something soft touched it, too. Abigail's own hand. A soft, secret touch. I risked a look into her eyes. There is a moment in a day, not long after rain, when the rays of the sun first break through the cloud. The air seems to sparkle and fill with promise, and all seems possible. In another story, we might have kissed, talked of the children we had, and gloried in love and life. But not in this one.

"Husband! Husband!" My wife called from beyond the meadow gate. "Whatever are you doing? Come along, we are all having so much fun. What a year, Mrs Hayter, what a year! Three girls married. And another newly engaged."

"Bennet!" cried Fielding, just behind my wife. "Jackson here has dug out a rather decent bottle of port from goodness knows where, but we will not drink it without you. He has brought biscuits from Egham."

"Papa!" Lizzy leant on the wall a little further along from the gate. "My husband has no idea what butterflies haunt the woodlands of Pemberley. You must visit and catalogue them for him. Will you promise?"

"I will," I said, then shouted toward my wife and Fielding, "I shall be along in a moment."

Abigail smiled. "It seems you have much to be content about—friends, family, and butterflies. A man in your position might almost forget a love that causes him to wonder what might have been."

"He might." I stood, pulling something from a pocket. "But he will not. Not for all the contentment of friends, family, and a thousand butterflies. Perhaps, though, he can learn to look on that love with fondness, rather than regret."

I took Abigail's hand and closed her fingers around the silver swan brooch. "Keep it close. Always." I lingered over the touch of her skin, let her hand fall away, and turned back toward the church.

"Now then, Fielding," I shouted. "About that port…"

THE END

Author's note

Thank you for reading Port & Proposals. If you enjoyed the tale, then Mr Bennet would be delighted if you might consider writing a review at Amazon, Goodreads or elsewhere. He will save you his best port as thanks.

Acknowledgements

It takes more than one person's words to create a novel. In particular, I owe a huge debt of gratitude to the following…

My editor, Sarah, who has an extraordinary eye for both detail and the big picture. Edwin, whose feedback and encouragement has made me a much better writer. Aimee for the wonderful cover design. Everyone at the Albermarle Writers Retreat: thank you Tom, Cheryl, Zac, and Hazel. Alex for sharing creative journeys. All those whose enthusiasm and generosity of spirit enabled me to remain focused and creative during 2020, particularly the online Jane Austen community of writers, readers, and academics.

Renate, Michael, and Patrick for their support, inspiration, chiding, coffees, and love. You are my everything.

About the Author

Mark Brownlow is a British-born writer, journalist, and lecturer living in Vienna, Austria.

Follow Mark on:
Twitter: @markbrownlow
Facebook: facebook.com/lostopinions/
Web: LostOpinions.com

Made in the USA
Columbia, SC
15 February 2021